Books by Anina Collins

THE WITCHING HOUR

ANINA COLLINS

2017 Eight Feathers Press, LLC

Published in the United States

ISBN: 978-0-9982084-2-8

Book Cover design by Natasha Snow Designs
www.natashasnowdesigns.com

The Witching Hour

Poppy and Alex are back in this sixth book in the Poppy McGuire series!

In the middle of a late summertime heatwave, a woman Poppy interviewed for an article on paganism is found with a dagger buried in her chest in the woods out near Alex's house. Initially, Stephen and Craig are given the case, but when Derek determines that this murder shouldn't be their first big case together, Alex and Poppy are brought in to help.

But Stephen has never liked Poppy, and tensions quickly begin to run high between the two sets of partners. The Sunset Ridge police force can't afford to have infighting if they want to solve this case before a fear of witches takes hold in town.

It doesn't take long before everyone reaches their breaking point and Alex wonders if he will be a Sunset Ridge police officer for much longer. Life is about to change for him and Poppy, but will that change mean the end of his time in town?

Chapter One

FIREFLIES DOTTED THE darkness around Alex and me as we sat at the old wooden picnic table in my backyard enjoying a romantic candlelight dinner. He'd worked late on the day shift, so we grabbed some take-out from Diamanti's and set up our meal under the stars on a beautiful September night. Not a cloud marred the sky, and the temperatures of the day had subsided enough that even though Sunset Ridge was in the middle of a scorching heat wave, after the sun set it was comfortable enough to sit outside without melting into the seat.

The candle in the center of the table flickered, making a shadow dance across Alex's face as he finished the last bite of his maple glazed pork chop. Although I'd watched him eat hundreds of times, something about how he looked tonight as he relished that final bit of his meal made me smile. He could be so cute when he relaxed and let himself enjoy his time off.

Wiping his mouth with a paper napkin, he tossed it onto the Styrofoam take-out plate and let out a contented sigh. "Diamanti's never disappoints. How was your baked chicken and asparagus? It looked good when I took it out of the box."

"It tasted great, as always. Did you have enough to eat? I thought maybe we should have gotten some dessert, but I don't think I could have another bite."

Alex shook his head and blew the air out of his lungs. "Me neither. I like their desserts, but the dinners are usually more than enough for me."

"This is nice out here. We should do this more often," I said, trying to direct the conversation away from how delicious Diamanti's food was to the topic of us.

For months, we'd been dating and had gotten as close as two people could be. It was rare that we didn't spend the night together. The past few weeks had seen him at my house more than at his own. I'd thought we were moving toward something more in our relationship, but even though all the signs were there, he hadn't said anything about moving in together.

Or even more, taking that next huge step and planning a wedding.

But so far, nothing.

Not that I knew for sure that I was ready for that. The moving in I could do. We practically lived together already, so the change wouldn't be much. Giving up a drawer here or part of a closet there wouldn't be so different than what we were doing now.

Marriage, on the other hand, seemed very different. I didn't know how or why, but it did.

The one thing I knew for certain was I loved Alex. That I had no doubt about. But marriage? That felt like something I had nothing but doubts about.

"You look lost in thought, Poppy. What's on your mind?"

I looked into his dark brown eyes and thought about

telling him the truth of what I'd been mulling over, but then I decided against it. Maybe I had been reading the signs all wrong. Maybe there hadn't been signs. We were happy just like we were. No need to jump the gun and rush things along.

"Just enjoying the beautiful night."

For a moment, he said nothing and simply stared at me in that knowing way he did when he was sure the person in front of him wasn't telling the truth. I'd seen that look time and again as we spoke to suspects and knew at that very moment he was deliberating about what I could possibly be thinking about that I didn't want to tell him.

If he figured it out and broached the subject, then I'd happily discuss it, but if not, then I'd stay silent about my thoughts.

"It is a beautiful night. Almost the kind of night perfectly made for two people to—"

As I waited for him to say the words I secretly wished to hear, the police radio he'd forgotten to leave at the station interrupted him and Craig's trembling voice came through loud and clear.

"Woman f-f-found in the woods off Miller Road. Sta-stab-stabbing victim," he said in a shaky voice.

Alex and I looked at each other across the picnic table, and I wondered if we'd be leaving for the murder scene any moment. "Time for us to roll?"

He shook his head and shrugged. "I don't think so. It's time for Craig to work a real case. Stephen's on tonight anyway, so it's not like he's alone. He's already nervous about everything, so better we don't hover."

"True, but murder cases can be difficult, and by the sound of his voice, I think he might be more than a little nervous."

Craig's voice came through the radio once again, this time even shakier. "We need...re...re...requesting backup immediately."

Alex's eyebrows shot up in worry more than surprise. "Maybe we should take a drive over and see how things are going."

The tone of his voice worried me more than what I expected to find out at the scene with Craig and Stephen. As he began to stack up our take-out plates, I asked, "What's wrong? You sounded strange there."

He stopped and forced a smile I knew was meant to make me feel better about this. "I just know those woods out near my house are dense this time of year, so maybe having a few extra people there to help them might be a good idea after all. Nothing strange. Just preemptive cautionary measures."

"Okay. I'm always up for a trip to a crime scene," I said with a smile, handing him my empty cup of iced tea.

Looking up at me, he chuckled. "That's one of the things I love best about you, Poppy. You're always up for an adventure."

I stood up from the picnic table and grabbed the forks and knives. "This is Sunset Ridge, Alex. I don't know if I'd call anything that happens here an adventure."

As we headed inside, he said, "You live one of the most exciting lives in town. You write for the local newspaper and solve crimes with me on the side. In my humble opinion, that's pretty damn exciting for a small town."

Maybe he was right, but some part of me yearned for more than just tracking down suspects and doing Howard's bidding at *The Eagle*.

THE DISPATCHER GAVE Alex directions to the crime scene as we headed down Barn Street, and as we turned off Miller Road a few minutes later, his Mustang was acting more like an SUV climbing the rocky dirt road. Craig waited for us as we pulled up to take us to where the body lay. One glance at his expression and I thought he looked like the dictionary definition of worried.

"Thanks for coming out, you guys," he said as he hurried over to the car to greet us. "Stephen and the Chief are waiting for us, so follow me."

Alex and I walked behind him over the barely worn path through the trees, and in a minute, we reached the spot in a clearing. Derek smiled over at us as Alex joked, "This looks like we're having a shift meeting."

Chuckling, the Chief of the Sunset Ridge Police rolled his eyes. "Yeah. This one shows how committed you are since it's definitely what I'd call off the beaten path."

On the ground, surrounded by what looked like nine pieces of coal of varying shapes and four white candles, lay a woman I recognized from a story I wrote on paganism for the paper right after I started. She wore a long white peasant dress with red and blue embroidered flowers around the neck. Her long blond hair lay spread out around her head, giving her an angelic look, but a deep red bloodstain around the dagger in her chest showed what had happened to her was pure evil.

Amy Perkins had been sweet to interview, so willing to share her beliefs openly with me, and when I had to break the bad news to her that my editor refused to run the story because it might upset the paper's readers, she had been completely understanding. I'd never forgotten that. To see her lying there dead made me sad because she had been so full of life and genuinely kind.

Stephen crouched near the body writing in a small notebook and looked up at the three of us, one eyebrow arched. "I'm sure Donny will disagree, but I'm guessing she's dead at least two hours."

As Alex and I exchanged glances at his assumption since my partner would never jump to that conclusion, and even I might hesitate to venture into the coroner's area of expertise, Craig turned toward a bush behind him and began to retch.

Derek quickly challenged Stephen's assertion. "I'll bite. What makes you think you can pinpoint the time of death?"

Standing, Stephen waved his pen around the body. "Those candles look like they've burned for at least a couple hours. Hence, she's been dead that long. I'm betting some kind of witchcraft ritual."

I wanted to jump in and ask how he knew the candles surrounding the victim's body had been new when they were placed around her and then lit, but I kept my mouth shut for the time being in an attempt to foster a sort of peace with Stephen. I also wanted to say I knew Amy wasn't a witch and ask how he knew they'd been lit after she'd been killed. But I silently thought that at any rate, he sounded ridiculous and wished one of the other detectives standing beside me would let him know.

As if he read my mind, Alex said in a low voice, "That's possible, but we have no proof that these candles were new when the murderer placed them around her, assuming he or she even did that."

Derek added, "And we have no idea if she lit them herself before the murderer came into the picture. I don't think we can jump to any conclusions, other than this woman is dead."

Stephen drew in his eyebrows and mumbled under his breath, "Not even that she died from being stabbed in the heart?"

Derek looked down at the body and sighed. "Well, I'll give you that one. Feel free to run with that conclusion."

"Do we have anything else to go with?" Alex asked as he began to walk around the body. "Like who this poor woman is?"

The other three men looked at one another and shook their heads. Stephen immediately spoke up and said, "There was no identification on her. I checked."

They all looked at him and then at the body as I spoke up and explained who our victim was. "Her name is Amy Perkins. I interviewed her for a story a while back. She was very nice and kept to herself, for the most part," I said sadly.

Alex moved around the body to stand next to me as Derek made a sound that said he recognized Amy. "Huh. I should have noticed who she was, but she looks different than the last time I saw her."

The sound of Craig retching in the bushes again punctuated Derek's comments on our victim, and Alex quietly asked, "Was she someone you knew, Chief?"

I understood exactly what he meant by the word *knew*. Derek had dated virtually every woman of Amy's age in town, so it wasn't an outrageous question. She hadn't exactly been his type since he didn't usually prefer to date the spiritual kind of female, but Amy was pretty with long blond hair and dark blue eyes that gave the impression she knew more than she'd experienced in our small town. For that alone, Derek may have given her a second look.

The Chief shook his head and frowned. "No. I helped her once when her car broke down on Main Street. When the tow truck took her car to Jerry's, I gave her a ride home. She seemed like a nice lady. She had darker hair then, though. That's why I didn't know who she was at first."

I knew Amy wore a brunette wig when she read cards, so his description made sense. She'd told me she felt people didn't take her tarot readings as seriously when she did them with blond hair. When she began to wear a darker wig, she felt she got more respect, so by the time I interviewed her, she regularly read the cards as a brunette.

Craig stopped throwing up long enough to rejoin us, and as he stood on the edge of the group looking pale, he asked, "Shouldn't we be doing something else other than talking about her?"

Derek grimaced at the unintentional reproach from his most junior officer and walked over to stand next to him. "I know you're eager, rookie, but this is the way it works. Until Donny gets here, we need to protect the body and investigate the scene. Did you find any clues in the bushes while you were doubled over in front of them?"

Not usually so sly with his insults, Derek nonetheless made his point to poor Craig, who looked like he was going to start throwing up again. Blowing the air out of his lungs with a frustrated whoosh, he shook his head.

"No, I didn't see a thing."

"Well, let's see what we can find over there away from that pile of puke," the Chief said as he guided Craig toward the other side of the crime scene.

Alex turned to me and smiled. "Poor kid. I remember seeing my first dead body. I felt like I wanted to lose my lunch too."

"Yeah," I quietly answered, not really interested in discussing the urge to throw up at that moment as poor Amy lay dead in front of me.

He touched my arm softly and turned us away from Stephen so he couldn't hear what he had to say. "Hey, you okay? You look a little like Craig there, but that's not your style. What's wrong?"

Hanging my head, I quietly answered, "I knew Amy. Or maybe it would be better to say I had worked with her. I interviewed her once about a story I was writing about paganism in the area. I had heard she read tarot cards and asked her if I could speak to her about her beliefs. She was really nice. I came away from that interview with respect for her and her beliefs."

"She was a witch?" he asked.

"No. She called herself a Druid. She said there were distinct differences, but we didn't focus on them for the interview, so I'm not sure what they are."

"Did she get any blowback after the article ran?" Alex asked from his unique perspective as technically a Sunset Ridge outsider, even now after years of living in town.

I remembered Howard killing the story before I even got a chance to really pitch it to him. It had been so easy for his narrow mind to not be interested.

"It never ran. Howard said it was too controversial and *The Eagle*'s readers wouldn't want to read that kind of thing in the local paper. He thought they'd be offended. God forbid anyone in town got a different perspective other than the perfectly engineered one he thought should be forced on them daily."

Turning my head, I glanced down at Amy's dead body. "I bet he'd like it well enough now. He'd probably run it next to the headline about her death. Or worse yet, next to her obituary."

From behind us, Derek asked, "Anything you two would like to share with the class?"

Too angry to answer, I said nothing and assumed Alex would clue his Chief in on what he'd just learned about our victim. But he didn't.

Instead, Alex turned around and said, "Sorry, Chief. Didn't mean to act so inappropriately."

I hid my surprise at his concealing the information about Amy's religious beliefs and turned around to rejoin the conversation. Alex pointed at the rocks arranged around her.

"What do we think is the significance of those and why they were placed in exactly that way?"

Derek brushed off the black rocks possessing any importance, though. "Looks like someone might have had a party. I suspect we'll find some beer cans and other party garbage nearby too."

Stephen nodded his agreement and added, "I still say it's witches. These aren't just rocks found in the woods here. They look like the kind of things witches would use."

I opened my mouth to correct Stephen's incorrect assumption about Amy and her beliefs, but Alex stopped me by speaking first. "Well, it looks like you guys have this all under control, so I think Poppy and I will return to our evening. Have a good one!"

Out of the corner of my eye, I saw Donny walking into the clearing. I wanted to protest our leaving simply because I wanted to ensure this case didn't devolve into some nonsense about witches like Stephen seemed intent on believing, but before I could say anything, Craig began retching again.

Derek turned to look at us and groaned. "I want you to help Stephen with the case since Craig might not be ready yet." He then looked at me and said, "Looks like you and your partner have a new case."

Seemingly satisfied, even as his junior officer remained throwing up in the bushes, Derek began to walk back toward the road, patting Alex on the shoulder. "Good luck. Those two are going to be a handful. Just remember if she tries to kill him, I'll have no choice but to end this arrangement between you two. And I want this case solved quickly. If this has even the hint of witches being involved, this could get out of hand. Let's avoid that, okay?"

Slightly offended that he thought I might do something so unprofessional, I said nothing. I had no intention of doing anything to jeopardize my working with Alex. My dislike for Stephen aside, I wouldn't let my feelings about him ruin something so important to us.

Stephen frowned at us and said in his usual nasty way, "I've got this under control. We can pick this all up in the morning when we'll at least have Donny's preliminary report."

"Thanks! Sounds good!" Alex said as he quickly began to usher me back through the woods toward the car.

I spun out of his hold and headed back toward the scene to take a closer look at Amy's body and that dagger before Donny and his guys hauled her away. As he crouched next to her, I examined the weapon protruding from her chest. No ordinary knife, the silver dagger had a pentacle carved into the handle surrounded by what I believed was a Celtic knot design. As much as I knew Amy hadn't considered herself a witch, the weapon that had killed her made Stephen's claim that witches were involved all the more likely.

Alex leaned in close and whispered in my ear, "You ready?"

I wanted to look at those black rocks surrounding her body a bit more since I doubted they were ordinary stones that belonged in the woods, but his words carried a tone of impatience, so I put off my examination of them until the morning and left with him.

WE STARTED BACK toward my house, and he said in a hopeful voice, "That was nice of him."

Confused, I looked over at Alex. "Who?"

"Stephen. It was nice of him to let us get back to our night."

I held onto the door handle as the Mustang bounced over the rocky road and thought about Stephen's gesture. I suspected being nice wasn't his intention. He disliked my being involved in cases, so creating an excuse to get me away from the scene was likely his real motive.

But I was more interested in why Alex had withheld information from his fellow police officers.

"Why didn't you tell them about what I knew about Amy?" I asked as we got back onto the paved road.

Alex looked over at me and shook his head. "The last thing Sunset Ridge needs is some modern day witch hunt. The investigation will be a mess before it even begins, and we'll get nothing done if people get wind of this being anything tied to witches."

"Druids. Amy was a Druid, Alex."

He turned back to look at the road and pressed his foot on the gas. "Witches. Druids. It doesn't matter. Sunset Ridge is a small town, Poppy. Anything out of the norm could cause this case to be a mess."

As we raced past the trees in the darkness, the headlights the only light showing us the way back to town, I warned, "At some point, it's going to come out. What then?"

"Why should it? Would it come out if she practiced any mainstream religion? So she was a Druid. So what?"

I knew he was just being hopeful, but I knew what would happen. "You just said it. This is a small town. Anything out of the mainstream will be important. It's just the way it is."

Alex sighed and nodded his agreement, resigned to the reality of what life in our small town was like. "I know. I just want to put it off until we can't anymore. I like cases to be as uncontroversial as possible."

Reaching over, I squeezed his forearm in sympathy. "I know, but this is life in Sunset Ridge."

I knew all too well truer words had never left my lips. But I also knew Alex was right. If we weren't careful, this case would turn into a circus once the news got out that Amy was a Druid.

"That knife was no ordinary weapon, Alex. Did you see the pentacle etched into the handle?"

He nodded and bit the inside of his mouth. "Yeah. And those rocks and candles weren't ordinary either. Whatever Amy was, she was involved in something in that clearing that killed her. I just hope we can get this case solved before the gossips begin to talk about witchcraft."

Chapter Two

THE CLOCK SAID it wasn't even eight o'clock in the morning yet, but a quick step outside onto my back porch told me it was going to be another stifling hot day. The heat wave had definitely settled in to Sunset Ridge. My pale blue sundress practically stuck to my skin after just a few seconds, and I barely got a full breath of humid air into my lungs before turning around and heading back into the air conditioned splendor of the house. I loved sun and summertime as much as anyone, but air that felt like it hung off you like velvet draperies wasn't really my favorite thing.

The delicious smell of coffee brewing brought a smile to my face as I hurried to close the door to leave the humidity outside, where it belonged. Hopefully, wherever the case of Amy Perkins' murder led us today, it would be inside where sensible people would have their air conditioning blasting.

"Poppy? Is that you?" Alex yelled down the stairs, his voice full of worry.

"Yeah. I just went out to see how hot it is today. Word to the wise: shorts and a t-shirt is the optimal outfit for the day."

A few seconds later, he appeared in front of me

wearing his dark blue police officer uniform, complete with long sleeves and pants. He certainly wore it well, but just seeing him standing there with so much clothing on made me sweat.

"Or you could wear the usual and die of heat exhaustion," I joked as he leaned against the doorway buttoning the second button on his shirt and smiled at me, ever so slightly amused by my teasing.

"You know I don't really have a choice, right? I don't think the people of Sunset Ridge would think much of seeing their police force answering calls dressed like surfers. Doesn't exactly inspire the level of confidence we're going for."

"I think you look great in shorts and a tank top, but there are a few on the force I could definitely go without seeing so much of. A few come to mind immediately," I said, grimacing at the thought of Craig with his chicken legs out for all to see.

It was bad enough I'd had to see them a few times when we ran across each other on his days off and he dressed in his regular street clothes. Craig wasn't a bad looking guy, but the poor soul had the skinniest legs I'd ever seen on a man. I doubted those pasty sticks could hold him if he ever had to run, bless his heart.

Alex, on the other hand, had great legs. The man worked out every day, getting up before the sun to head out on a run or to go lift at the gym, so his legs, like every other part of him, were toned and muscular. I wouldn't have minded seeing him in any state of less dress, even though I could see as much as I wanted of him on any given night.

"Coffee ready?" he asked, tearing me out of my fantasy of him wearing shorts and a t-shirt like I'd suggested.

"Of course. You're at the house of Poppy McGuire, and we worship at the altar of the almighty bean here, sir," I said as walked across the room toward the counter to pour us some morning go-go juice.

But he stopped me before I even reached the coffee maker by positioning himself between me and the counter. "I got it. Why don't you take a seat at the table and I'll bring it to you?"

"Okay. Thanks!"

I wasn't going to say no to being waited on by a gorgeous man in a uniform, so I sat down at my tiny kitchen table and watched him carefully make both our cups of coffee. He preferred his black these days, so that wasn't much of an effort, but he took time to make sure mine was exactly as I liked my first cup of the day and before I knew it, he'd set the cup down in front of me.

He took his seat across from me and smiled, so I joked, "Well, service with a smile. A girl can get used to this."

"Good, but it's nothing. Just a cup of coffee."

I lifted the cup to my lips and enjoyed my first sip of my favorite drink as it hit my tongue, loving the sweet yet tangy taste as much as I did the first time I drank coffee back in college. Until then, I'd been a tea drinker, but finals week in freshman year had required something more caffeinated than chamomile tea, and at that moment sitting in my dorm room the night before my Psych 101 final, a coffee lover was born.

"You make one hell of a cup of coffee," I said, lifting my mug to toast his ability.

"It never ceases to amaze me how much you love this stuff. I don't think I've ever met another person, man or woman, who loves coffee as much as you do. And you never seem to get jittery, even though I've seen you put away five or six cups of coffee in a day."

"It's the nectar of the gods," I joked. "The gods on Olympics are said to have loved ambrosia, but I think it was coffee. I know I'd need coffee if I had to rule an entire world."

Alex gave me a tiny smirk, much less than the smile I'd expected from my joking, and then it faded quickly and he returned to looking serious, like usual. I had a sense something might be on his mind, so I waited a few minutes for him to bring it up, reveling in my first coffee of the day.

When he didn't say anything, I finally broached the topic. "I know I'm no comedian, but you usually give me more than a tiny, forced smile when I tell you something sort of funny. Have we reached the point in our relationship where you don't feel like you have to pretend to think I'm amusing anymore?"

In usual Alex fashion, he shook his head and looked at me like he couldn't believe I'd ever think that. "No, and I hope we never get to that place. I'm sorry I didn't laugh. I have something on my mind."

As I had yesterday while we ate dinner out at the picnic table, I wondered if the something on his mind was us taking our relationship to the next level. He had mentioned how much time he spent at my house a few times, so maybe he was having a hard time coming up with a way to say he wanted to move in. I wanted to tell him there was no reason to be diplomatic. All he had to do was say the word and I'd be happy to say we were living together.

But so far, I hadn't heard that word or any others

that told me he wanted to live with me, no matter how much we were basically living together already.

"Anything I can help with?" I asked quietly against the lip of my coffee mug before taking a drink to steel my nerves for what he might want to discuss.

"It actually involves you, so I think it's definitely something you can help with," he answered with a smile I had a sense was an attempt to hide how uncomfortable he was about what he had to say.

I set my coffee down on the table in front of me and leaned forward a little, hoping my body language told him he had the green light to tell me anything. "Well, I just want you to know whatever it is, Alex, if it involves me, the answer is probably yes. I mean, I can't imagine anything you have to tell me being something I wouldn't like."

Rambling aside, I hoped he understood he had a willing audience in me for whatever he had to say.

Slowly, he lifted his cup to his lips and tilted it so the last of his coffee spilled into his mouth before he abruptly stood up and walked over to the sink. His sudden change of location surprised me, and I turned around to look at him as he stood with his back toward me.

"Is something wrong? You don't seem okay, all of a sudden."

He said nothing while he washed his cup and then set it upside down in the dish drainer, but then he turned around to face me and nodded. What could be wrong?

"I didn't want to mention this last night, but I can't stop thinking about how I have to tell Stephen the truth of what I know about Amy. I regret not telling him last night."

I hated seeing Alex unhappy, and at that moment,

the frown on his face told me he was truly troubled, like not telling Stephen the tiny bit of information I'd given him less than twelve hours earlier was some major infraction of the police officers' code or something. My feelings for him made me want to change that.

Standing, I walked over toward the sink and set my cup on the counter as I slid my arms around his waist. I looked up into those dark eyes so serious and smiled. "You said last night that mentioning what Amy believed could cause this case to become a mess. Isn't that why you didn't mention anything to him last night?"

His expression twisted into one of almost pain, and he shook his head. "Not really. I didn't tell him because I don't trust him like I should trust a fellow officer."

"Why?"

Alex sighed. "Because of how he's been toward you. I don't like that because that means I'm letting my personal opinions color my professional ones. That's not good."

Tilting my head, I kissed him softly on the cheek for being such a good man. "Thank you for showing me chivalry isn't dead."

He gave me a tiny smile but said nothing, so I continued. "That doesn't make you any less a great cop, though, Alex. I hope you know that."

Nodding, he said, "I just want to be honest with him. He's as much my partner on this as you are, and you wouldn't expect any less than complete honesty."

As much as I was loathe to admit it concerning Stephen, he was right. On this case, he was his partner just like I was and holding back information that may help us solve the case did no good. I just hoped Stephen reacted the way I would when he found out what Alex had to tell him. In that way, I had a sinking feeling he was nothing like me.

And the fact that he seemed to dislike me intensely didn't help matters, in my mind. True, he hadn't been outright rude to us last night, but had that been more about doing a favor for Alex as opposed to doing something to be nice to the two of us?

Unable to hold back anymore, I looked up at Alex and quietly asked, "Do you know why he doesn't like me? Have I done something wrong that I should apologize for? I would, you know. I would because I don't want you feeling like this case is going to be harder because we don't get along. Even if it was something that I was completely innocent in, I'd still swallow my pride because I don't want this to make your life difficult. This is your job, and I respect that."

Now it was his turn to smile, and this time it was nothing less than genuine, warming up his brown eyes in that way I knew meant I'd made him happy.

He brought my hand to his lips and gently kissed my knuckles before looking up at me in that way that never failed to make my stomach do somersaults. "You haven't done anything, Poppy. I don't know why he doesn't like you, and to be honest, I don't care. I like you, so that's all that matters to me."

"Just like me?" I asked playfully, knowing the answer and loving it.

Alex winked at me and grinned wickedly. "I think last night was proof that I'm way beyond like. I might be way beyond love, if I'm being honest."

"What's way beyond love?"

He looked up toward the ceiling, as if he was actually thinking of what the answer to my question could be, and then lowered his head to kiss me. "Completely and utterly devoted to you?"

Oh, my. When he said things like that, I wanted to tear that crisply pressed uniform off his body and show him right there in my kitchen how completely crazy I was about him. I didn't even care if my neighbors saw us through the windows either.

"You know, I think you say these things to me at times like this because you know it drives me nuts that we can't do anything since we have to go to work. I think you're a tease, Alex Montero. A tease, I say."

That wicked grin returned, and he chuckled. "Me? A tease? No way. I always deliver on my promises. I offer last night as evidence of that, Miss McGuire."

As memories of our time together flashed through my mind, I had to admit he was telling the truth. He did deliver. There was no arguing with that.

"You're lucky I have a healthy respect for the fact that you just spent all that time ironing your uniform or you'd see how I deliver," I teased, playing with the buttons down the front of his shirt.

He brushed his lips against mine and whispered, "Tonight. I promise. We'll come back right after my shift is done, and I promise to deliver whatever you want."

I loved that idea, but his suggestion made me wonder if he'd ever bring up the topic of us moving in together, so I decided to gently bring it up now. "You want to come back here again? You've been here a lot in the past couple weeks. I'm not sure I can remember when you were last at your house."

He nodded and hummed for a second. "True. I don't think I've been home for more than a few minutes since last month. Are you saying you want me to spend more time there? I have sort of just moved in here without even mentioning it to you. I'd understand if you felt like you needed some space."

Clearly this was going all wrong. Now I had him talking about giving me space, which I didn't want, and spending less time at my house, which I didn't want either.

"No, no. That's not what I meant at all. I just noticed you were staying here most nights is all. I don't want you to think I don't like that, though, because I do."

He studied my face for a moment, likely wondering what the hell I was talking about since I'd been the one who brought up this whole conversation in the first place, and then shrugged. "Okay. I like staying here, if I'm being honest, so that's good that you like having me here."

"Good. Please know that you're welcome to stay here as often as you like."

Pressing a kiss to the top of my head, he said, "That makes me happy because a lot of nights it's just easier to fall asleep here after you and I have dinner and hang out. In the winter, it was like torture dragging myself out of a warm house to drive to my house, freezing all the way since the heat in my car would never get really hot before I reached home."

I looked up at him and had to smile at how utterly practical he could be. "That's true. It's also nice that we get to wake up next to one another each morning. That's a good thing too, right?"

"Definitely. And what happens before we fall asleep is absolutely a good thing."

"Exactly. So stay over whenever you like and as often as you like," I said as I straightened his collar.

"And you know what else it helps with? I'm not nearly as far away from the station if I get a call as I am out at my house. Ready to start this case?"

With that he walked up the stairs, leaving me standing in my kitchen with the Alex practicality that I knew was just him being logical, but it made me want to smack him sometimes. Sleeping at my house was good because it meant he was closer to his job? Not exactly what a girl wanted to hear as a reason why a man stayed with her each night.

I'd learned with Alex through trial and error, though, that making something like this into a much bigger discussion was a waste of both our time. If I said anything more after that, he'd grow quiet and that would make me feel pressured to fill in the silence with more words.

That never worked out in my favor, unfortunately, and more often than not, I had to apologize for something I said in the heat of the moment when I cooled down. It also meant that a fight was injected into what should have been a calm discussion.

No, I didn't want that to happen this time. Taking our relationship to the next level, whether it be moving in together or the much bigger step of becoming engaged, shouldn't have an argument attached to it.

So for the time being, I could choose to drop more subtle and not-so-subtle hints into our conversations about where he spent his nights or I could drop the entire subject and wait for him to bring it up. I'd never been very good at waiting for much of anything, so hints was how I'd go.

Now I just needed to think of a way to drop those hints so he'd understand just what I was talking about.

Alex returned to the kitchen as all of this played out in my mind, so I quickly washed my coffee mug and hurried into the downstairs bathroom to brush my teeth before leaving to begin our investigation on Amy Perkins' murder.

"I haven't gotten any text about Donny having his preliminary report yet, so I hope it's just a matter of him forgetting to message me," he said loudly as I rinsed out the toothpaste from my toothbrush.

Ready for the day, I headed back out into the kitchen and found Alex waiting for me at the door. "You're pretty eager today. Maybe Donny doesn't have it because he didn't get the body until late last night. He's good, but maybe he's not that good."

Alex rolled his eyes. "He's a legend in his own mind. I want to get started on this case and see if Stephen, Craig, you, and I can set some parameters. I don't want us stepping all over one another, and that's likely going to happen with four people on a single case if we're not careful."

"What kind of parameters?" I asked, suddenly worried about what he meant.

Opening the door, he ushered me out into the oppressive heat. "I just don't want the four of us chasing the same leads. We're going to have to come to some agreement as to who is looking into what."

We walked toward his car parked behind mine in the driveway, and I noticed he was frowning again. Hoping to make him feel better about what I suspected might be a difficult case, I said, "Don't worry. I'll follow your lead."

He opened the driver's side door and looked over the roof at me, arching one brow. "It's not you I'm worried about. I've never been a big fan of working with other people on cases. I'm sort of a lone wolf."

His claim made me laugh, and I shook my head at how silly it sounded on its face as I stood there ready to go to work with him on this case. "You work fine with me, so I don't know what you mean."

"That's not the same thing. You're not a cop. Police officers can get very territorial about their cases, and this one is technically Stephen's. I just want to make sure this doesn't turn into an issue."

I leaned on the doorframe and smiled over at him. "You won't let it, so I'm not worried. Maybe if he and Craig take her personal life we can investigate her professional life. Or vice versa."

He thought about it for a moment and nodded, smiling again. "That's a good idea, Poppy. For that, you get air conditioning all the way to the station."

"Oooooh, five whole minutes of cool air. Time to pay up, Officer Montero, before your partner melts into the driveway."

I got into the car and felt the cool air blowing out of the vents, happy for the prospect of this case being nothing but a normal case for us. I just hoped Stephen didn't let his dislike for me ruin that possibility.

Chapter Three

I N THE FEW precious minutes it took to reach the police station, I enjoyed the refreshing air the car offered, but it ended all too soon and Alex parked the Mustang on the street in front of the building. I didn't know if it was because I hated going back out into the heat or if the idea of dealing with Stephen bothered me, but a feeling of dread suddenly overcame me as Alex turned the car off.

"Ready?" he asked in a chipper voice as he moved to open his door.

I grabbed his arm to stop him before he could reach the handle, and he turned his head to look at me with a concerned expression. "What's up?"

"Nothing. I'm just not looking forward to going back out into the stifling heat. That's all."

He stared at me for a long moment like he was studying my face to see if that was really why I was dragging my feet on going into the police station, but then he just smiled. "It's not that far a walk to my office. I'm betting you won't even break into a sweat in that time. Come on. Let's go. We have work to do."

I couldn't put my finger on why, but I had a sense that if I mentioned that one of the reasons why I might not be eager to go inside was because of Stephen, Alex might be annoyed. He always supported me, and I knew he'd tell his fellow officer off in a second if he stepped over the line with me in any disrespectful way. Of that, I had no doubt.

But I had a niggling fear that all of this drama between Stephen and me had begun to get on my partner's nerves. I hated that. It was like everything bad about the town we lived in boiled down to a tit for tat juvenile behavior issue, and that's what he saw this thing between the two of us as.

A typical Sunset Ridge spat.

I couldn't even disagree with that since I truly had no idea why Stephen had taken a disliking to me. Until that night in front of Bethany's apartment when he was working her murder case, I had never even noticed him much. He was just another police officer on the force but nothing more. That he seemed particularly disgusted by me baffled me then and still baffled me to that moment.

Alex flashed me a smile and turned to get out of the car, so I did the same and followed him into the station. As we passed the new receptionist, the fifth this year, I wished her a good morning and wondered how long she'd be in that job. From what I heard listening to the other cops talk, they had a bet that she'd be gone before Halloween. Why so many receptionists seemed to hate the job I had no idea. It didn't seem like a difficult job to do, but on the other hand, since the town had combined that job with the dispatcher job a little over a year ago, it ceased to be just a nine-to-five business and often included overnight shifts.

As Alex and I headed down the hall toward his office, I whispered to him, "What's your bet for the new receptionist leaving? Do you think she'll make it through the fall?"

He turned around and looked over my head back at her as she sat at the desk filing her nails and pursed his lips before answering. "I'm going with late September."

I thought about his assessment and wondered if he'd be right, but then he added, "Of course, if Derek and his girlfriend break up, all bets are off since from what I understand, there's never been a receptionist before these last few that he didn't date."

We walked into his office, and he sat down behind his desk while I took my usual position in the chair in front of his desk. "I thought he and Solange were chugging along just fine. Did I miss some gossip?"

Alex shrugged and shook his head. "No, but Derek is Derek, so I'm not putting any bets on that relationship."

His words bothered me because I wanted to believe Derek had finally found someone that he could have a happily ever after with. After dating through nearly the entire single female population of Sunset Ridge, it seemed that the past few months had seen a real change in him. Alex's dismissal of his actually being a different person because of his feelings for Solange made me hope that he wasn't right. I wanted to believe in true love and its ability to turn a man around.

"I guess, but I'm putting my money on those two. They've been stuck together like glue since they made their romance public. I saw them at the Food King a few weeks ago, and they looked like newlyweds."

Before I could bring up that I thought they'd be moving in together soon, Alex stood from his desk and pointed toward the hallway. "I'm going to go find Stephen so we can get this investigation going. I'll be back in a minute."

He left me sitting there wondering if Derek and Solange would begin living together before Alex and I did, which only made me wonder if there was something wrong in our relationship. We'd been together much longer than they had, so why were they moving toward something more permanent while we seemed to be stuck in a holding pattern?

As my mind whirled with possible reasons why, his office phone rang, startling me. Jumping up, I quickly picked up the receiver, forgetting in my confusion that I probably shouldn't be answering it.

"Hello, Alex Montero's office," I said, sounding like the receptionist down the hallway.

"Alex? You wearing your pants too tight or something?" Donny, the coroner, asked with a throaty chuckle.

Amused by his joke, I relaxed from my momentary scare and sat down behind Alex's desk. "Donny, it's me, Poppy. Alex is off talking with Stephen. Is there anything I can do for you?"

"I just wanted to let him know I have the preliminary report for you guys to take a look at. Will he be back soon? I want to drop it off with him and I have time now."

"Oh yeah. He just went to confer with Stephen and then he'll be right back."

"Good. I'm heading there now. Oh, and Poppy, make sure to tell him about the joke I made about him wearing his pants too tight and sounding like a member of the Vienna Boys Choir. He'll like that," Donny said with a full laugh before hanging up.

I put the receiver back down on the phone and

wondered if the coroner and I knew the same man because I was pretty sure Alex wouldn't find his joke amusing in the slightest. I could imagine Alex's usually stoic face cracking with a forced smile after hearing it and then immediately returning to its regular seriousness with possibly an eye roll to top the whole response off.

"You look pretty comfortable there in my chair," he said as he walked back into his office.

Quickly, I stood up and offered it to him before I returned to my usual seat. "Just keeping it warm for you, boss."

Alex rolled his eyes, just as I knew he would for Donny's sad attempt at humor. "Enough boss talk. We need to get working on this case. Any chance that call for me had anything to do with it?"

"Donny said he's on his way. He should be here in a minute or two. He's got the preliminary report."

Taking his seat, Alex nodded. "Good. Hopefully, that gives us a solid place to begin. I'm not in the mood for another case full of false starts."

"What did Stephen say when you told him what you knew about Amy?" I asked, curious about how their conversation went and if Stephen had been upset about Alex not telling him until today.

Alex shook his head. "I couldn't find him. He seems to be MIA this morning."

Instantly, the thought crossed my mind that Stephen was avoiding Alex because of me. Because I'd be working the case with him. Why did he dislike me so much? I honestly had no idea. I'd gone through every possible time we could have met, and I still came up with nothing. I hadn't been introduced to him before Bethany's case, and from that moment, he'd shown a complete disdain for me.

Maybe we'd met sometime before he became a police officer? I knew little about Stephen, but I believed he had been born and raised in Sunset Ridge. Perhaps we'd had a run in before and I didn't remember.

Or maybe it was because of the town gossips and what they used to say about me. I'd become so used to their snide talk that it hadn't bothered me much in years, but if he'd heard all that about me and then heard I was helping Alex on his cases, maybe he'd thought badly of me because of it.

Or it could be something entirely unrelated. I had no idea. All I knew was his dislike for me made working with Alex uncomfortable, even though he didn't seem fazed by his fellow officer's opinion on this or anything else.

As if he read my mind, Alex said, "Whatever you're thinking, don't. This whole thing with Stephen is a non-issue to me, and I hope you'll see it like that too. Not everyone has to get along, Poppy."

His resistance to the very realities of the small town we lived in both amused and confused me. "You clearly aren't from here. Not getting along with people in a small town is a huge problem. People in this town talk, Alex. If you have a problem with someone, it's an issue."

Alex's gaze moved from my face to behind me, and a knock on the door stopped our conversation entirely. Twisting in my seat, I saw Donny standing in the hallway just outside the office. A quick glance at him told me he looked different, but I couldn't place why. Had he gotten a haircut or worn a different shirt from the usual five or six blue, white, and yellow short-sleeved dress shirts he seemed to wear in rotation from April to

November?

Nope. His hair seemed the same as the last time I'd seen him the week before, and he wore a white shirt like he often did in the warmer weather. While I tried to figure it out, Alex said, "Saved by the coroner. Please come in."

He walked in and sat down next to me as he handed Alex a sheet of paper. "Another day, another murder, huh?" he said like it pleased him as he got comfortable in his chair.

Anyone who knew Donny understood this was just the coroner's way of saying hello. I couldn't help but smile at his method of being friendly in the face of yet another death. It was very much a Sunset Ridge thing. Alex mentioned one time that this was the first place he'd heard of where the coroner brought reports to cops and not the other way around. I had explained to him that Donny might come off as a curmudgeon, but in many ways, his style was pure small town. It was also indicative of how much he liked to present his findings in his own particularly theatrical way.

"Never a dull moment in our little town," I said back to him as Alex perused the report Donny had given him.

"So what I'm reading here is that Amy Perkins didn't die from a knife being plunged into her chest?" Alex asked incredulously.

I turned to look at him in amazement at what he'd just said. I saw the dagger buried in her heart with my own eyes. How had that not killed her?

Next to me, Donny shook his head as his grin spread from ear to ear. "Nope. That certainly didn't help, mind you, but she was going to die even before whoever killed her stabbed her in the heart."

I sat there listening to all of this, stunned by Donny's news. "Why would anyone stab her if she was dead already?"

The coroner turned in his seat and wagged his finger at me. "Oh, I didn't say she was dead when the murderer stabbed her. She wasn't. But the stabbing wasn't necessary. She was going to die anyway. I guess you'd call that overkill."

"Then what killed her?" I asked.

"She was smothered," he answered flatly.

I turned to look at Alex, whose eyebrows were raised in surprise. "Any idea by what? Hand? Cloth in the mouth? Pillow? What are we talking about here?" he asked.

Pillow? I thought back to how the murder scene looked the night before and tried to remember if I saw anything like bedding or pillows. I couldn't recall seeing any.

Donny shrugged. "Not sure yet. Don't know if we'll ever be. Smothering is hard to detect, and it's even harder to determine what may have been used to smother a person. I didn't see any whitening around the nose and mouth, so I'm leaning less toward a pillow as the murder weapon since that's usually a key clue that something like that has been pressed against the face to smother someone."

Reading the report, Alex said quietly, "No signs of sexual assault. What's this about the back of her head?"

"I found a contusion on the back of the victim's head, deep enough that it looks like she could have been pushed backward after being stabbed. Or maybe the killer pushed her down hard enough to hit her head after trying to smother her and then stuck the knife in her chest. I'll be able to tell better after a few more test results come in."

Alex took a deep breath and dropped the paper onto his desk. "So she was asphyxiated and the stabbing was just for show?"

"That I don't know. If the murderer is someone who knows very little about how the human body works, maybe they didn't think they did the job well enough to kill her so they grabbed a knife, thinking they needed to finish her off, and then pushed her away. I'll leave it up to you guys to figure all that out."

I wondered what that meant. "Why would they think they didn't kill her the first time?"

Donny turned to face me and began to flail his hands, as if he couldn't believe I didn't know the answer. "Because death by asphyxiation takes a few minutes. Maybe they got scared. Maybe they got angry. I have no idea. All I can tell you is that the dagger sticking out of her chest didn't kill her."

Still unsure of why anyone would do such a thing, I looked over at Alex as if to say, "Who knew?" and he smiled. "Well, thanks, Donny. Let me know when you find anything else, okay?"

"Will do. Good luck."

The coroner left us sitting in the office, and I wondered aloud, "Who wanted to make it seem like Amy's murder had to do with her religious beliefs when it didn't?"

Alex raised his hand to stop me before I continued with my train of thought. "We don't know she wasn't smothered for that same reason, so we can't say this doesn't have anything to do with her being a pagan."

"But for someone to specifically use a weapon that

looks like something a pagan or witch might use when they didn't have to since they had already smothered her sounds suspicious, don't you think?"

"Everything is suspicious in a murder case. You know how I work," he said with a sly smile.

"I'm just saying it feels like someone wanted the police to believe she was killed with something related to paganism."

He didn't respond but simply hummed and pursed his lips, as if he was thinking about what I'd said. Alex may not have been the type to come up with ideas immediately at the beginning of a case, but he tolerated my tendency to do so.

Just then, Stephen showed up in the doorway. "I saw Donny on his way out. I guess the idea that we at least knew what killed her just flew out the window."

"Well, we know now, but we'll just have to keep in mind that whoever our murderer is they wanted to throw us off their trail. Why they chose that weapon is what we need to find out."

"Seems like a lame attempt, though," I said and was happy to see Stephen nod in response.

Alex stood to leave, so I moved to join him, but he waved me off. "I'll be right back, Poppy."

He walked out to speak to Stephen alone, leaving me wondering why he didn't ask me to join them. Then again, the reality was that even though he and I worked on cases together, I wasn't officially part of the police force. I'd just grown used to being included on every part of our cases.

It seemed that I better get used to a different reality on this one.

When he returned a few minutes later, Stephen was

nowhere to be found. I waited for Alex to say something about what they'd discussed, and when he didn't, I asked.

"Was it something I said?" I joked half-heartedly.

Alex's expression grew serious, and the corners of his mouth turned down ever-so-slightly. "Stephen is the lead on this case, so I offered our help in investigating Amy's private life. He said he preferred to do that, so you and I are off to find out what the local pagan community may know about who would want our victim dead. Then we'll look into her job while he focuses on her family and friends."

I couldn't help but think that Stephen wasn't the cop who should be the lead on this case. Alex was a much better officer and a better detective, but I didn't want to rock the boat and cause problems by commenting on it since he'd made it clear the whole Stephen thing was a non-issue to him.

"Sounds good. Do we have any details on those stones and candles found around her?"

"Yeah. Craig found out that the stones are hematite and one found nearby is malachite. That one is green. The candles appear to be standard unscented white pillar candles. He's working on where they can be purchased locally, but I doubt that detail is going to be integral in finding our killer. Any chance the research you did on paganism can help us figure out where to find people in that community to talk to?"

I thought back to my talks with Amy and knew just where to start. "We have one or two places in town I can think of that might help us with that. I'm thinking the Third Eye Mind and Body Center should be our first stop, don't you think?"

Eager to get started, I stood to leave but saw confusion in Alex's eyes. "What's wrong? Did you have some other place in mind?"

"I'm just wondering exactly what the Third Eye Mind and Body Center is and where they've been hiding it in this town," he said with a smile, clearly amused by the idea of Sunset Ridge having such a place.

Now it was my turn to tease him.

"I'm surprised you don't know about the place, Officer Montero. It's located out near your house, and I imagine you've driven by the place nearly every day since you moved here."

His eyebrows shot up into his forehead to show his shock at missing such a detail of the local area. "Really? How is it I have never noticed it? It must be back off the road a bit."

"Nice excuse for not being observant," I joked as I headed toward the door to walk out to the car. "It's not far enough off the road to not be seen. I just think you're amazed our town has a place dedicated to paganism."

I looked back at him and saw him nod. "Of course I'm surprised. Maybe I was wrong about the whole pagan angle being a problem in this case. I mean, if the people in town don't mind about this Third Eye place being around, maybe they wouldn't care what religion Amy practiced."

"Oh no, you weren't wrong on that. They'd care. As to why the town doesn't seem to have an issue with the Third Eye place, as you call it, being around, it's mainly because it's not smack dab on Main Street. It's an out of sight, out of mind kind of thing."

His smile spread into a genuine grin at knowing he'd been right in the first place. "Ah. There's that small town mentality I'll never understand. Well, let's get going to the Third Eye Mind and Body Center and see if anyone there can tell us anything that might explain why someone would want Amy Perkins dead."

Chapter Four

A LEX SLOWLY PULLED into the parking lot in front of the Third Eye Mind and Body Center and shut the car off. Staring out the front window, he said, "I thought this place was a storage center every time I drove by it."

"That's because you never thought in a million years that a town like Sunset Ridge would have a place like this," I said with a hint of satisfaction in my voice at how he'd missed the center, even though he had to drive past it each day on his way into town.

Smiling, he turned to look at me. "You're enjoying this, aren't you?"

I didn't even try to stifle my smile in return. "I am. It's not every day that I notice something and you don't. Let me have my moment of glory."

He looked back at the building, which did look very much like one of those self-storage facilities, except for the glass front door and sign on it that said Third Eye Mind and Body Center. "I imagine there was a huge issue when this place let the town council know it wanted to open up shop. How bad did it get? Was there yelling and screaming at the monthly meeting? I can only imagine."

I thought back to when the center applied for its

business permit and didn't remember much of a hubbub about it. Then one memory did remind me that it hadn't been entirely smooth sailing.

"The town council didn't have a huge problem with it, but I do recall Mrs. Girard having something to say. Mayor Sanders' wife Christine stood up in defense of the place and shut down the former mayor's wife pretty quickly too."

A look of surprise came over Alex's face. "Really? I've met Christine Sanders a few times and thought she was very nice, but I had no idea she was so open-minded. I like her more already."

Unlike the former mayor's wife, Christine Sanders kept to herself, for the most part, and didn't treat her position as anything more than decorative usually. Educated and well-mannered, she was the complete opposite of Mayor Girard's wife, and I'd always sensed that she worked hard to make sure of that.

"Well, this was before she became First Lady, but once she gave her stamp of approval, nothing Mrs. Girard could say would sway the council and the center got its permit. They've been out here ever since. I want to say they've been open for at least four years."

That last bit of information wasn't particularly helpful to our case, but it allowed me the opportunity to tweak Alex's ego about not noticing a place that had been around for as long as he'd lived in town. My subtle teasing didn't go unnoticed, if the smirk he gave me right before he got out of the car was any indication.

We walked to the front door and saw a sign that said the center didn't open until ten. Looking down at his watch, Alex said, "It's a quarter to ten now. Let's take a walk around the building. Maybe we'll find something that might help us with the case."

"Hoping to find a dagger that matches the one we found buried in poor Amy's chest?" I joked somewhat macabrely.

He looked at me and shook his head as he headed off toward the left side of the building. "You're dark sometimes, Poppy. Very dark."

I followed him around the corner and immediately saw an herb garden toward the back of the building. Thrilled to check out another garden similar to my own at home, I passed him and hurried to where the area was marked off with a tiny wire fence. Cute signs about a foot high with drawings of each herb and their names marked where each herb was planted.

"Look how cute those are!" I said as I pointed at the one for basil. "I would love to have those in my garden. I'm going to have to ask the person we talk to where they got them. They are adorable!"

I crouched down and inhaled deeply, smelling the sweet scent of basil and the rosemary planted next to it. Alex stood behind me and chuckled at how much enjoyment this herb garden was giving me.

"You know, I hadn't pegged you for the gardening type, but your green thumb has impressed me this summer. You're full of surprises, Poppy McGuire."

Turning my head, I looked back and saw him smiling down at me. If I was so full of surprises, then why had we stalled out in our relationship? I never wanted surprises out of Alex, so his calm and steady way made me as happy as I could ever ask for, but maybe he wanted surprises. Maybe I wasn't surprising enough. Being able to grow some plants in a garden in my backyard didn't exactly make me exciting.

Or maybe the surprises he'd seen so far were too much for him? He was a pretty serious kind of guy. Was it because I was surprising and not reliable that he didn't know if he could count on me for the long haul? The thought sounded ridiculous, but I couldn't shake the feeling that we'd been together for a while and we seemed to have stagnated.

A noise inside the building interrupted my growing paranoia about my relationship with Alex, and he tapped me on the shoulder. "Let's go see what we can find out about Amy."

We walked back to the front door and knocked on it. A woman with bright red hair that fell far past her shoulders and very pale skin appeared before us. She wore a long white flowing dress similar to the kind Amy had been wearing when she was murdered, a number of colorful, cheap-looking bracelets on each wrist, and numerous rings on nearly every one of her ten fingers.

"The center doesn't open until ten," she said loudly through the glass.

Alex pressed his badge to the window and said, "We need to speak to you now, ma'am."

For a moment, the woman looked unhappy and grimaced, but then she began to unlock the door. Alex turned to me and quietly said, "I think this is exactly what Mother Nature must look like."

As the door opened, I whispered, "Well, I think you've angered Mother Nature, so I expect something awful to happen any minute. Fire and brimstone awful. Watch out for lightning bolts."

The woman held the door for us to walk in, throwing us nasty looks as we passed by, and then she locked it again as I scanned the room we walked into.

The store at the Third Eye Mind and Body Center had a variety of items, some I recognized like candles and gemstones, but others I'd never seen before like the shelf of what looked like ornate pendants.

For some reason, I'd expected to see a Spartan, minimalistic décor inside the center, probably because everything I knew of other religions seemed to reveal that clutter of any sort muddled the person. My friend in college practiced non-traditional religions, and I remembered her saying all the time that the mess of my dorm room inhibited my happiness and productivity because it stifled my chi. I had no idea if she was right or not, but I did get more work done after each time I gave the room a good cleaning. But the room I stood in at the moment felt very cluttered, and I wasn't sure about my chi, but I didn't feel wonderful being there.

The woman who'd answered the door walked behind the counter on the far side of the room and lit a stick of incense I recognized as patchouli scented. It stunk up the entire room almost instantly, making me dislike this place even more than when it just felt like a messy collection of tchotchke.

"So what can I do for the Sunset Ridge police today?" she asked with a forced smile, and I immediately noticed her teeth looked very dingy and desperately in need of some whitening strips.

Alex took out his notebook and pen from his shirt pocket and began his interview with her by politely saying, "My name is Alex Montero and this is Poppy McGuire. What is your name, ma'am?"

With a flourish of her hand near her face, she answered his question quite dramatically. "Tamara Ridgeway."

The way she said her name as Ta-MAH-ra and not TA-ma-ra like I'd always heard the name pronounced seemed entirely affected. I also felt quite sure this woman would freak out if anyone dared to call her Tammy.

"Thank you, Miss Ridgeway. What can you tell me, if anything, about how you know Amy Perkins?"

Immediately, she became on edge and began waving her hands around in excitement, her brown eyes flashing her unhappiness at his question. "Why? Did she call the police on me because of what I said at the meeting? For Goddess's sake! It's gotten to the point that two people can't even have a simple religious disagreement anymore. I swear this place is becoming like Communist Russia!"

Alex let her finish her ranting and calmly replied, "No, ma'am. She didn't call the police on you. We're simply investigating a case involving her and need to know the nature of your relationship with her."

Tamara set her hands on her hips and frowned. "She's a witch and refuses to admit it. That's our relationship. It's that simple."

He wrote down her answer and then looked up at her. "Are you a witch, Miss Ridgeway? Do you have a problem with her being a witch?"

"No! I'm very proud to be a witch, but Amy Perkins refuses to admit she is too, as if there's some reason to be ashamed of being one. She insists on calling herself a Druid. Ridiculous! She's a witch, and that's it!"

Every word became shriller than the last until Tamara Ridgeway was practically screeching at us. I didn't know if she'd murdered Amy, but she certainly didn't like her much.

"Uh-huh," he said as he jotted down the words VERY

EMOTIONAL ABOUT THE WITCH THING in his case notes.

As Alex readied his next question, I took the opportunity to ask one of my own. "What does it mean to be a witch, Miss Ridgeway? Is there something you do to qualify as one? For example, are you in a coven that Amy Perkins didn't join that makes you a witch and might make her think she wasn't?"

Clearly exasperated by this question, Tamara huffed her disgust at my seemingly ridiculous notion of witches. Pointing at me, she snapped, "This! This is the reason people still think we should be burned at the stake. The ignorance of your partner is astounding!"

Alex looked up from his notes and smiled. "Calm down, Miss Ridgeway. My partner was asking a perfectly innocent, and if I do say so myself, useful question that I would be interested in knowing the answer to. Perhaps if more people knew about witches and what they do, they wouldn't want to burn anyone."

For a moment, Tamara said nothing, but then she spun on her heels and walked into the back room for a moment before returning with a pamphlet she thrust into my face. "This will tell you everything you need to know. I hope you read it and educate yourself."

I took her pamphlet on witches and wondered why this woman had to be so abrasive. If she wanted to get people to be more understanding about her beliefs, she may have wanted to at least try to be pleasant. I would have even taken enthusiastic evangelism rather than her continued nastiness.

"So other than your disagreement about what Amy is, how would you categorize your relationship?"

Tamara twisted her face into a scowl. "We don't have a relationship, Officer Montero. What are you insinuating?"

Alex looked over at me, and we exchanged looks that told me he was as baffled about Tamara's rudeness as I was.

"Does Miss Perkins frequent the Third Eye Center often?"

"Not anymore. She used to, but not recently."

"How not recently?"

"She used to come in every Tuesday for the witches' circle meeting we have in the back room every Tuesday night at eight o'clock, but she hasn't been in for over a month."

"I'm going to need the names of every person who has attended those meetings in the past six months, Miss Ridgeway."

She opened her mouth to argue with him about his demand, but he continued asking his questions. "Do you know why she stopped attending the weekly meeting?"

"Because I challenged her to admit what she was or not join us in hypocrisy. She hasn't been back since."

"And when was that?"

Tamara spun around on her heels again to look at the calendar and flipped two pages down to July. "July 18th was the last meeting she attended."

"And was that the last time you saw her?"

For once, her answer didn't come out of her mouth like she was spitting out rancid food. "Yes. I haven't seen her since."

Tamara began to write down the names of the members of the witches' circle meeting group, and Alex wrote the information down she'd given while I scanned the room. Drawn to the shelf of gemstones, I scanned the various colored stones before asking, "Miss

Ridgeway, can you tell me about hematite and malachite?"

She lifted her head and glared up at me. "Why? What do you know of those stones?"

"Nothing. I just remember reading somewhere that gems had symbolic meanings and I saw your shelf of them over on the wall."

After a moment, she said, "Hematite is worn for protection, and malachite lets a person know about impending danger."

Alex jotted down her answer as I continued to look around the room and suddenly came upon a shelf full of daggers and knives on the bottom of one of the displays. Nudging Alex with my elbow, I pointed at them. Alex walked over to the shelf and looked at them, careful to not touch even one.

I asked, "What role do knives and daggers play in the world of witches?"

"They're called athames, and we use them in our spellcasting. They're used to cut herbs, carve symbols into candles, cast circles, and call quarters. If you're thinking we use them to harm chickens or anything ignorant like that, you're totally off the mark. They are ritual aids only."

Alex turned back toward me and motioned it was time to leave. Taking the list of people who attended the witches' circle meetings off the counter, he said, "Thank you for your help today, Miss Ridgeway. My partner and I will be leaving now, but if we have any more questions, we'll be back."

"What is this all about anyway? Is this the Sunset Ridge police department cracking down on our right to practice religion freely and respectfully again? Because if it is, I'm going to call the ACLU this time," Tamara said in her outraged tone.

As I joined him at the door, Alex calmly explained to her, "No. Amy Perkins was found murdered last night, stabbed in the heart with a knife in a circle of stones and candles. Good day, Miss Ridgeway."

We left as Tamara's jaw hit the floor, and when we got to the car, I couldn't help but laugh at what he just did. Looking over the roof of the car, I said, "I wasn't sure anything would be able to shut off that constant stream of nastiness, but you found it. From the rest of the world and the bottom of my heart, thank you."

As he opened his car door, he looked over at me, clearly concerned. "You forgot to ask her about the herb garden markers. Do you want to run back in?"

The mere thought of having to spend even another minute with Tamara Ridgeway made me cringe, even if I could find out about those garden markers, so I waved off his concern. "No big deal. She probably would have given me a lecture on how I was undeserving of growing herbs being a non-witch and all. I'll just look online for some."

Alex chuckled and we got into the car, neither of us unhappy about having to leave the Third Eye Mind and Body Center. As we drove down the road away from our first interview in the Amy Perkins case, I had to admit that Tamara Ridgeway had certainly done very little to make us think she couldn't be the murderer.

"So what did you think of her?" I asked as Alex turned the corner toward town.

He gave me a sideways glance and grimaced. "I think she's not the best ambassador the pagan community could have. That's what I think."

As usual, his dry way of describing someone perfectly made me chuckle. "I can't disagree with that. She seems more likely to turn someone away from being a witch than toward it. No wonder Amy didn't want to call herself one. I wouldn't want anyone associating me with that woman either. But what do you think of her regarding our case? Do you think we can consider her a suspect?"

"I don't know. She claims that she hasn't seen our victim in weeks since mid-July. Hard to kill someone if you aren't anywhere nearby them. And she certainly looked surprised when I told her about Amy's death."

"So you believe her when she says she hasn't seen her in weeks?" I asked, unsure if I did.

He remained silent for a moment, staring at the road ahead of us, until he answered, "I don't know."

The part of me that loved jumping to conclusions found this part of Alex quite frustrating. I knew his way was the better way for an investigator to be, but it still drove me nuts at times like this.

"Well, she definitely wasn't Amy Perkins' biggest fan. I think we can both agree on that, right?"

"That I'm willing to agree with," he said with a grin. "Amy certainly upset her religious apple cart by refusing to say she was a witch. Seems to be six of one, half dozen of another to me."

"I don't think so. That's like saying all Christians are the same. There are definitely differences between someone who's Catholic and someone who's Baptist. It obviously meant something to Amy that she called herself a Druid instead of a witch."

As he brought the car to slow stop and turned onto Main Street toward the station, he looked over at me and nodded. "I stand corrected. You're right. I wasn't seeing it that way, but you're right."

"So I'm curious, why did we leave so quickly? I thought those daggers looked a little like the one Amy was stabbed with. I was surprised you didn't want to take them to check them out."

He parked the car in front of the police station and turned to face me. "Whether or not they looked like what was in her chest, I didn't have a warrant and no valid reason to take them as evidence."

"Aren't you worried she's going to do something with them?"

Shaking his head, he shrugged. "No. She's more consumed with the news we gave her right before we left, so I doubt she's even thinking about what we were looking at. She's either worried about us suspecting her or stunned by what I just told her. Once I get a look at the report on the weapon, we might want to go back there with a warrant for them, though."

The mere idea that I might have to spend any more time around Tamara Ridgeway made my chi feel like someone had it in a vice grip. That was one witch I preferred never to see again.

"Maybe next time I'll stay behind at the office and answer the phone. That sounds more enjoyable than another visit with her."

Chapter Five

"I HAVE A few questions for Stephen before we head out to talk to that list of people Tamara gave us. Do you want to make a coffee run while I do that?" Alex asked as a sheepish look crossed his face.

Was he intentionally keeping Stephen and me apart?

"I guess. I'll be at The Grounds if you want me," I said, not meaning to sulk but definitely sulking.

Spinning away from him, I headed toward the coffee shop, ignoring what he was saying behind me. I knew he wasn't doing anything wrong, but this whole Stephen thing had me feeling defensive and my confidence all up-ended. I wanted to fix whatever was wrong, but I couldn't, and the mystery as to why Stephen disliked me so much had already gotten under my skin.

Maybe a good cup of coffee would help me get a grip on things. I hoped it would because if not, I had a feeling Alex and I were heading toward a doozy of a fight about Stephen, and I definitely didn't want that.

The owner of The Grounds, Pam Branch, stood behind the counter as I walked through the front door and smiled at me as I approached her. "Poppy McGuire! I was wondering if I'd see you today. How is your Friday going?"

"Pretty good, I guess. You know how it is," I answered noncommittally, careful not to let how I really felt out for her to see.

She prepared my coffee and set the Styrofoam cup down in front of me. "Just you, or are you ordering for your partner today too?"

I'd stormed away in a huff without asking Alex if it was a black day or a coffee with cream day, so I didn't know what to order for him. Waving her question off, I smiled. "You know how he is. I thought I'd let him get his own for a change."

None of those words made any real sense, and I had a feeling that the confused look on Pam's face meant she knew it, but she didn't press the issue and I paid for my coffee. She handed me my change as she asked, "Are you and Alex investigating that girl's murder in the woods from last night?"

I nodded my answer, and she continued. "Such a shame. I hate to see that happen to anyone, but for such a young woman to be taken like that makes me so sad. I swear I don't know what the world is coming to, Poppy."

"I know. I feel the same way. It's hard when it's someone who has their whole life in front of them."

"Do you know what happened? I heard some gossip this morning that she was part of some demonic cult. I thought that was ridiculous. Who here in Sunset Ridge would be involved in that?"

Pushing down my first instinct to defend Amy and set the record straight about her beliefs, I waved off what she said again and shook my head. "You know how gossip is here in town. People say the most bizarre things that have no basis in fact whatsoever. I don't believe much of anything I hear these days."

She nodded her agreement and let the whole thing drop, even though she likely hoped I'd give her something to go on about the case. "I agree, but the more incredible stuff makes me wonder sometimes."

I sighed like I knew exactly how she felt and quickly made my escape to the table the farthest away from the counter to put some distance between us. It wasn't that I didn't want to talk to Pam, but much more talk about demonic worship and I'd have to set her straight about Amy's being a Druid.

Alex showed up a few minutes later, and looked back toward our usual table for me. I saw disappointment cloud over his expression when he didn't see me there, so I waved my hand and said loudly, "Alex, I'm over here!"

He turned his head toward the sound of my voice and smiled. Walking toward me, he said with a chuckle, "I thought maybe you decided to head to the office instead of going out and investigating with me today."

Joking, I said, "I wouldn't do that without at least messaging you about it."

That we were talking about me actually choosing my work at *The Eagle* over investigating any case, even the most banal one, meant I wasn't the only one who thought there was a problem between us.

"Howard texted me this morning and gave his full-throated approval of my working with you on this case. I didn't ask, but I suspect that article I wrote has suddenly become far more acceptable for his newspaper."

"So I get you all to myself today?" he asked with a sexy grin as he sat down opposite me.

"I guess, unless we're being joined by Stephen and Craig," I said, floating that suggestion out in the most sincere hope that the answer would be no.

Alex shook his head and looked down at my lone coffee cup before looking up at me. "No. It's just us, but I guess only one of us is going to be caffeinated."

Embarrassed by my hasty departure a few minutes earlier, I hung my head. "I didn't know how you wanted it. I guess I would have if I had asked, though."

"Is something wrong, Poppy? Why did you storm away like that?"

I so didn't want to have yet another conversation about Stephen, and when I lifted my head and looked into Alex's dark eyes, I saw he didn't either, unless it had to do with this case. So I let my worry go for the moment.

"Just the need for coffee. I can get you one now. Black or with cream today?"

He stood up from the table and shook his head. "I got it. But I'm getting it to go because I want to get through that list of people today."

Thankful we didn't end up in a fight, I drank the last of my coffee and headed toward the door as he paid Pam for his. She waved goodbye to me, and I smiled back at her, happy I had avoided any more discussion about the case with her.

As Alex and I crossed Main Street to walk toward the car, he handed me a bag from the coffee shop. Surprised by his gift, I opened it and instantly smelled the delicious scent of an orange cranberry muffin.

"What's this for?" I asked before taking another deep breath of sweet orange.

"I thought you might like it," he explained and then winked. "Think of it like candy that goes nicely with your morning coffee."

Looking up at him, I couldn't help but love how adorable he could be at times. When he shed the very serious way he usually preferred to be, Alex had the ability to be so thoughtful. I knew he'd understood why I walked away so quickly, and I also knew that he appreciated that I hadn't chosen to rehash the whole topic again in The Grounds. So the muffin was his way of thanking me.

"Well, thank you. It's even better than candy, you know, because I can justify a muffin in my mind as something more than pure sugar, even though that's probably what it really is."

I wished I could stop and kiss him, but since we were in the middle of the street, it seemed like the wrong time. When we reached the curb, I wanted to at least tell him how much I loved him, but out of the corner of my eye, I saw a poster tacked to a telephone pole that caught my attention.

A bright yellow image of a sun sat in the middle of the poster with the words "Third Annual Tarot Readers Convention, Jacob's Hall, Caston, MD" in big black letters underneath it. At the bottom it said, "Come and find out the secrets of your future!"

"Look! We could go there to do some investigating too!" I said excitedly as I pointed at the poster.

Alex walked over to the pole and stopped to read the information. He turned to look at me with suspicion in his eyes. "A tarot reader convention?" he asked in a tone full of skepticism.

"Yeah. We might get some good leads. What else do we have to do for this case? Stephen is busy investigating our victim's personal life, so we have time to check out her social and professional life. She did read tarot cards for people."

He pulled out the list Tamara had given us and waved it in front of me. "We have to track down all these people and interview them. That's what we have to do."

Discouraged for a moment that we wouldn't get to go to the tarot reader convention, I perked up as a good reason to attend popped into my brain. "It's possible that many of those people on that list would also be at the convention. We may be able to kill two birds with one stone."

My logic stopped his doubt in its tracks, and he pursed his lips. "Let me guess. You want to get your cards read, right?"

The thought had crossed my mind, and I had a few pointed questions I wanted to ask in the hope of getting some answers to my concerns about our relationship. I didn't want him to know that was the reason I wanted to drive the ten miles to Caston today, though.

Squinting from the sun, I stepped in front of him to avoid the bright light and looked him dead in the eyes to make my point. "I happen to be someone who keeps an open mind to the mysteries of the universe, unlike other people, who shall remain nameless, Alex. We need to interview self-proclaimed witches, and it isn't unheard of for witches to be tarot card readers. I don't think it could hurt, and it could help a lot."

"Well, when you put it like that, what choice do I have?" he asked with a grin.

The mocking sound of his voice told me he thought our trip to the tarot reader convention would be a colossal waste of time, but I appreciated the fact that he didn't say that.

"Great! Road trip!"

"But while I'm driving, I want you to tell me everything you know about Amy Perkins."

ALEX DROVE OUT of town toward Caston, which was about ten miles south of Sunset Ridge toward Baltimore, while I thought about everything I knew about our victim. As I considered what I'd learned about her during my work on that paganism article, I remembered he'd said he wanted to talk to Stephen about something but hadn't mentioned anything about it since. My curiosity being what it always was, I had to ask.

"So what did you want to speak to Stephen about?"

Without missing a beat, he answered, "I had a few questions about this case."

Okay. That didn't sound like he was hiding some alternative truth, like he had something to discuss with him that he didn't want me to hear.

"Like?" Sometimes I felt like a dentist trying to pull things out of his mouth.

He passed a car on the back road to Caston and pulled back into the right lane. "Like who called in the crime? Who found our victim? What did the report on the knife have to say?"

"All excellent questions," I mumbled, ashamed I didn't think of any of them before that moment. God, this problem with Stephen was blinding me to even the basic aspects of this case!

"I thought so," Alex said with a slight chuckle.

Staring out the passenger side window at the trees still full with green leaves on the side of the road, I asked, "So did he know the answers?"

Nodding, he passed another car but stayed in the passing lane this time. "Yep. Austin Mullen was the person who found our victim. He was also the person who called 9-1-1. He's not from Sunset Ridge, but he drove up from Frederick two nights ago to do some hiking in the woods out near my place. From what he said, he saw no one else the whole time he was out there until he came upon the clearing where Amy Perkins was found."

"Well, that wasn't very helpful."

"No, but it tells us something about the area where the crime happened. This guy had been out there for over a day and hadn't seen anyone, so it's likely whoever Amy was with wasn't out there camping."

I turned to look at Alex, wondering why he was following that train of thought. "True, but did you ever think the murderer was? That campsite didn't look to me like it had been used for cooking or anything else a camper would use it for."

Alex tilted his head back and forth and shrugged. "Well, no, but it's good to have that information from Mr. Mullen."

"What about the report on the knife? Did Stephen have that yet?"

I knew full well that it was possible he hadn't gotten the report from the lab yet since it often took them days or even weeks if they were busy. Even a basic report on the knife could very well take a day or so. It made me wonder why Alex would be asking him about it not even twenty-four hours later.

"No, he didn't. I told him I wanted to see it as soon as he got a chance to look at it."

His words contained a strange edge to them that I

couldn't place. Wanting to avoid any potential issues about Stephen, I didn't ask anything else about the report.

"Well, quid pro quo, so here's what I know about Amy Perkins. She was born and raised in Sunset Ridge, but she left for a couple years after graduating from Sunset Ridge High School. I wasn't close friends with her, so I don't know what she did or where she went when she was away, but she returned to town about five years ago and began reading tarot cards as a side job in addition to working at the Charming Cakes Bakery."

Alex looked over at me. "Charming Cakes Bakery? Is that where Prince Charming buys his pastries?"

I chuckled at his joke. "You haven't heard about Charming Cakes? It's only the best bakery around these parts. They make these little tart things that are to die for. How is it you've lived here for years and never had a Charming Cakes dessert?"

"I don't get out enough," he said dryly. "So what did she do at this Charming Cakes Bakery?"

I thought for a moment and said, "I think she was one of the cake decorators. Not a baker, definitely, since I don't think that was what her degree was in."

"She had a degree? Why was she a cake decorator if she had a degree?"

"I want to say her degree was in something in the health services area, but she never did anything with it."

"That begs the question even more. Who goes to school for a degree in a field that's exploding and turns their back on it? There has to be some reason."

"The plot thickens," I joked before continuing. "I don't know what happened, but I know she was never employed in anything related to health services since she returned to Sunset Ridge."

Alex drove the car down the exit to Caston and stopped at the bottom of the hill. Turning to look at me, he wore an expression of disbelief. "You never asked her when you were interviewing her?"

"No. Why would I? I was writing a piece on paganism, not a piece on people who had degrees in the health service industry who chose to abandon that profession."

He stared at me, still stunned that I hadn't pried into Amy Perkins' personal business until the driver behind us blew his horn and he pulled out onto Old Caston Pike. Alex said nothing as he drove, but I felt a little insulted that he thought I was no better than the old busybodies in town who routinely thought it was okay to invade other people's privacy.

We remained silent, Alex watching the road while I stared out the window at the line of older homes on my side, each one Colonial style with its order and symmetry. When he didn't say another word for nearly five minutes, I finally had to speak.

Twisting in my seat to face him, I said, "I can't believe you think I would ask someone about their private business, Alex. Is that what you think of me? That I'm like those awful old biddies who did that to me for years?"

Now my voice possessed an edge, and I saw the surprise register on his face as I spoke. Staring straight ahead and paying attention to the road that had gotten quite busy with other cars, presumably all heading toward the hall where the convention was being held on Broad Street, he said nothing for a few moments and finally when he did reply, he was nothing less than contrite.

"I didn't mean anything like that at all, Poppy. I just know you and people like to tell you things. It's one of the unique traits you possess."

"Well, she didn't tell me anything about her personal life. I didn't even get a lot of firsthand information about the pagan community, to be honest. Since she considered herself a Druid, she didn't feel that she could talk about paganism at large, so we mostly just talked about positive energy and how she believed in visualization as a powerful way of achieving things in her life."

"Okay."

He parked the car and pointed out the front window toward a red brick building with a plaque that read Jacob's Hall. Like so many places in this part of Maryland, it held some kind of historical value someone had figured out, so it had received a sign indicating that.

"Do me a favor and let me do the talking, okay?" I asked as we opened our doors to get out.

Alex slammed his shut and walked around the front of the car to stand next to me. Arching one dark eyebrow, he said, "They're going to know we're not here just to soak up the positive energy and get our cards read, Poppy. The uniform is going to clue them into that. I don't think they'll even need tarot cards to know we're here on official business."

I closed my door and scowled at his judgmental attitude toward what we were about to experience. "Again with the closed mind. I'm just saying that we might get further with these people if we keep the official thing to a minimum."

He twisted his face into an expression of irritation.

"Fine. We'll do it your way at first, but if we don't get anywhere, the badge is coming out."

"You know, the negative energy is coming off you in waves." I motioned around his body and added, "You can practically see it. Your aura is probably a dark brown or even a black at this moment. They're going to pick up on that."

Rolling his eyes, he said, "I don't know if I'm supposed to take you seriously or not. Let's just go and see if we can find any of the people on Tamara's list."

We walked toward Jacob's Hall and as we walked in, I stopped to read the historical sign hanging on the brick façade. "Members of the Second Continental Congress stopped at this building during their time in Baltimore at the Henry Fite House December 1776-February 1777."

I turned to look back at Alex and shook my head. "They never cease to amaze me with these things. It's highly unlikely anyone from the Second Continental Congress ever stopped here, then or at any time. But people do love these things. At least it's not the usual George Washington slept here ploy."

"So it's just a scam. Seems like a perfect place to hold this convention," he said with disgust lacing every word as he walked into the building.

"That's a lot of negative energy there, sir. Lot of negative energy," I teased as I followed him in.

I secretly couldn't wait to see how the very logical Alex reacted around an entire room full of people whose very beliefs flew in the face of his skepticism. Who would be more frustrated? Alex or the tarot card readers?

Either way, I intended on having a reading and knowing what they saw in the cards for me.

Chapter Six

WHATEVER JACOB'S HALL usually looked like, today it resembled something like a cross between a traveling carnival and a circus. A green and white striped cloth attached to the center of the ceiling flowed out to the walls to make the entire room look like the inside of a tent. Each tarot card reader had a table they sat at and a dark canopy for privacy during the readings, which made the whole area look like the fairway of a carnival.

Looking around, I elbowed Alex. "I didn't expect it to look like this. They really went all out. I like it! The place has a great feel to it, doesn't it?"

A surprising number of convention attendees milled about, traveling from table to table as they picked up brochures from each reader. I hadn't expected to see so many people there before noon, and Alex clearly looked shocked.

"I can't believe all these people are here. You know what they say. There's one born every minute."

I shot him a nasty glance to let him know how much I disapproved of his attitude toward the tarot readers. "For someone who thinks of himself as a good detective, you certainly do have a very closed mind when it comes to some things. Is it that you don't understand tarot reading and that's why you're so dismissive of it?"

Alex rolled his eyes at my judgment of him and sighed. "I know exactly what's going on here, Poppy. These people can no more see the future in their special cards than I can. The future can't be foretold, as much as we may wish it could be. This is just charlatans taking gullible people's money. Nothing more."

This man could be so frustrating! Balling my hands into fists at my sides, I tilted my chin up and looked him dead in the eyes, ready to blast him finally for his narrowmindedness. "It isn't just the future they talk about, Alex Montero. Many times, they just help people to see the situation they're in more clearly so they can make the right choice. Not all of us are able to see everything in black and white and cold facts. Sometimes feelings cloud things and it's just nice to have someone to help clear the fog."

For a long moment, he stared at me like I'd just said the dumbest thing he'd ever heard leave someone's mouth, but then he asked, "What are you talking about, Poppy? Is there something I should know?"

My frustration bubbled over, making me want to scream. "Nothing. Absolutely nothing that someone like you would care about."

I marched away toward the card reader at the farthest booth on the back wall, not looking back at Alex as I abandoned him. Hanging off the front of the table was a hand printed sign that said the woman sitting there went by the name Madame Cassandra.

"Hello, my name is Poppy. I'd like a reading," I said to a thin, older woman with jet black hair and startling silver streaks that framed her lean face.

She looked out at me from behind the table and studied me for a moment, pressing her lips together so they formed a thin deep red stained line across her face. Finally, after a few moments, she nodded. "Okay, but I'm not sure you're in the right frame of mind for a reading right now. It might be better if you come back in a few minutes after you clear your head of the anger you're holding in."

"I guess it's obvious, huh? Is my aura some horrible shade of baby poop green or something?"

My question elicited a chuckle from her, and she shook her head so those silver streaks swung back and forth across her face. "No, dear. I saw your disagreement with the officer over there right before you came over here to me."

Now I felt foolish. Hanging my head, I mumbled, "Oh, yeah. That."

"If it makes you feel any better, I don't do aura reading, so I have no idea what yours looks like. I just try to be as truthful as I can and help people by telling them what I see in the cards."

Taking a step toward her table, I said, "I'd really like a reading now, if you're willing to do it. I'm not really angry at my partner anyway, if that means anything. I just got frustrated with his closed mind on what you all are doing here."

Madame Cassandra smiled and waved me around the table. "Okay. Come back and we'll see what we can see."

I hurried through the space between her table and the back wall of the hall and sat down at a tinier table she had set up between herself and her customers. I hadn't even thought about asking how much she charged and hadn't noticed the amount mentioned on her sign, but now that I was sitting there ready for the reading to begin, I wasn't even sure I had more than a couple twenties on me.

Quietly, I asked, "I'm sorry, I know I should have asked this before, but how much is a reading?"

She picked up the deck of tarot cards and began shuffling. Focused on the cards in her hands, she didn't even look up when she answered, "Forty, dear."

Okay, that would probably be fine. If I didn't have enough, I'd just ask Alex to give me the money and pay him back later. That would give him a chance to pooh-pooh this whole thing again, though, but I didn't care. Let him dismiss it all he wanted.

She set the deck of cards in front of me. "Shuffle until you feel comfortable to cut them into three piles, dear."

I did as she instructed and shuffled until something inside me said to stop. Then I divided the deck into three nearly equal sized piles of cards and sat back in my seat for her to begin the reading.

But instead of starting, she looked at me intently, like she was studying me. She did this for so long I became uncomfortable, so I fell back on what I always did.

I talked.

"Is something wrong? Did I do the cutting wrong? I can do it again, if that's what you need me to do," I said, each word coming faster than the last as they all tumbled out of my mouth.

Madame Cassandra said nothing and didn't even shake her head. Uneasy about what could be going on, I opened my mouth to say something, but nothing came out. Maybe this was the way she did her readings. I didn't know, but what I did know is that any residual anger that had been left over from my disagreement with Alex was quickly replaced with a real sense of discomfort as I sat there waiting for her to begin the reading or at least say something.

Finally, after what seemed like an eternity, she said, "I prefer to do simple readings, using as many cards as I need to in order to get to the heart of the issue you're concerned about."

"Okay. That's fine with me."

She chose the stack of cards farthest to my right and moved the other two stacks with her other hand. I watched as she dealt out seven cards face down into a pattern that resembled a triangle on the right, a triangle on the left, and a single card in between them.

"Now, dear, what this will tell us is about you and your significant other and any issues there are between you that may be getting in the way," Madame Cassandra said as she turned over the first card.

"How did you know that's what I wanted to know about?" I asked as she tapped on the first card, the Queen of Cups. "What if I wanted to know about my career?"

She looked up at me and smiled. "Everything in life is based on relationships. Your significant other might refer to your boss at work or a co-worker, if you're wondering about your career."

"Oh. Okay," I said, examining the Queen of Cups and liking how she looked dressed in a long white gown sitting on a golden throne with a large gold cup in her right hand.

Madame Cassandra tapped on the card again and looked up at me. "These three cards represent you. This card, the Queen of Cups, indicates you're a compassion-ate and empathetic person. You care about others around you. In the upright position, like she is here, she's able to take care of the needs of others. She's the kind of woman any man would want for a wife or partner."

Her last words struck me, and I looked down at the card, surprised at how exposed I felt at that moment. I watched as she turned over the next card in the triangle that represented me and saw the Moon card that actually looked more like a sun with the face of a man inside it set against a deep blue background that represented nighttime.

Once again, she tapped her index finger on the card and looked up at me. "The Moon. You're prone to letting what happened in the past affect your present and your future. You worry that what happened before will happen again, so fear controls your thoughts and emotions."

The memory of Jared running off with Cicely and being left alone came rushing back, and I felt myself get small at the thought of that happening with Alex too. I'd never considered that he'd do that before, but now as I sat there in that tiny cubby at the back of Jacob's Hall staring at that Moon card, I began to worry.

Then she turned over the third card in my triangle and I saw the Three of Pentacles come up. Looking across the table, I waited to hear her interpretation to see if Alex and I were doomed or if there was some chance for us.

"The Three of Pentacles is all about collaboration. Working together is key. All the parts of a clock must work in unison for it to tell the correct time, and a relationship is very much the same thing. Both people must be working toward the same goal or they won't be happy."

I nodded and forced myself to smile at her, but so far, this tarot reading wasn't helping me much with my concern about my relationship with Alex and how I feared it had stagnated. Madame Cassandra smiled back at me and turned her attention to the other three cards that represented my significant other.

"Now these are all about the person who you're in the relationship with. Remember, it doesn't have to be a romantic relationship. It could be a work relationship too."

She winked at me and then turned over the first card, the King of Pentacles. "Ooooh, this is a good card for a potential mate or a partner. This represents a man who provides stability and comfort. He handles crises well, so as a partner, he's always grounded. He's a very strong opposite to the Queen of Cups, who is far more emotional and intuitive."

Well, that wasn't bad news, and Alex certainly would be considered as stable and grounded. King of Pentacles he was.

The next card she turned over made my stomach twist into a knot. A man lay on the ground with swords sticking out of his back. Was this death? Alex's death? Was he in danger?

Reaching her slender hand across the table, Madame Cassandra gently touched my arm. "Please don't worry. The Ten of Swords doesn't mean something bad is going to happen. It more than likely refers to a betrayal and loss that your significant other has suffered in the past. This loss was devastating, but he made it through. Does that make sense?"

I realized I'd been holding my breath since she turned over the card, so I let the air out of my lungs with a whoosh and looked over at her. Alex had been through a devastating betrayal with Ken and losing Helena had made him leave his life behind and come to Sunset Ridge.

"It does make sense. Thanks for explaining it that way. I got scared when I saw that card. It's pretty awful looking."

"Oh, dear, I know. It looks far worse than it actually is. In fact, none of the tarot is all bad. Each card shows us some part of ourselves and the situation we're in, good and bad."

"Let's see what the final card for your significant other shows us."

She turned over the last triangle card and I saw a man and a woman holding golden chalices with a lion head with wings on each side hovering over them and a caduceus between them. I had no idea what all that meant, but it looked positive, at least.

"The Two of Cups is an auspicious card, for sure," Madame Cassandra said. "It says that the relationship is important to the other person, which is always good news. This card can signify marriage or at the very least commitment. What it tells about your significant other is that they value what they have with you, be it work or personal."

That sounded great, except maybe the card referred to how Alex valued working with me instead of having a life with me. Maybe it wasn't as positive as I'd hoped.

Tapping her finger on the center card, she smiled at me. "This is the final card, the one that tells us what the conflict is and what the resolution is to that conflict. Let's see what the tarot has to say."

She flipped the card over and there was a picture of a man suspended by his foot from a single branch of a tree. Nothing about that looked good.

"Oooh, this is interesting. The Hanged Man is all about waiting and figuring out why you feel stuck in whatever position you've found yourself. Is it something from the past that's fixing you in that position?"

I had no idea what the answer was, but seeing that man hanging upside down disappointed me. I'd hoped to see something more positive as the answer to our issues. Unfortunately, all I saw was what I felt about our situation.

Reaching into my purse, I checked my wallet and found forty dollars. I handed it to Madame Cassandra and stood to leave. "Thank you for the reading."

I turned to leave, but she caught my arm by my wrist and stopped me. I looked down at her and saw she had more to say.

"Whatever is troubling you, try looking at the problem from a completely different perspective. You may find the answer staring you right in the face. Good luck, dear, and never let that passionate Queen of Cups in you dim. It's one of the things that makes you so wonderful."

"Thank you, Madame Cassandra. I'll try to do that. Thank you!"

I stepped out from behind her table and saw Alex speaking to a woman on the opposite side of the room wearing a red bandana on her head, a long, flowered peasant skirt, and a blue blouse. As I approached them, I saw large gold hoop earrings dangling from her ears too. She really had the whole gypsy thing going on.

I stopped next to him, and he gave me a brief smile before returning to his questions for her. "Now Miss Fox, when you say Miss Perkins and Miss Ridgeway nearly got into a fight, do you mean an actual physical fight with fists?"

The tarot card reader tucked a stray curl of blond hair under her bandana and shook her head, making her enormous earrings tug on her earlobes so they stretched out in what looked to be a very uncomfortable way. "Oh, I don't know about that, but I can tell you, they were both very angry with one another. Witches can be very passionate people, Officer Montero. Paganism is all about being in touch with ourselves, our feelings, and the world around us. Did you know that?"

Alex didn't respond but continued to write notes on her answer. He looked up to see her staring at him, waiting for him to say something to what she'd said to him. Clearly, he hadn't heard her and he looked confused for a moment, so I stepped in to save him.

"Hi, Miss Fox. I'm Alex's partner, Poppy. It's nice to meet you. We are learning a lot about pagans on this case."

She took my offer of a handshake and immediately turned my palm over so she could inspect it. Running her fingertip over the lines, she smiled and then looked up at me. "You have a wonderfully strong heart line, Poppy. So much love in your life. You're a lucky woman."

I stared down at the line at the top of my palm that ran parallel to my four fingers as she talked about how it had one tiny break but was solid otherwise and how fortunate that made me.

Lifting her head, she gave me a broad smile. "I

foresee a life full of love for you. So lucky."

Alex ignored everything she said and asked, "What were Tamara and Amy fighting about? Do you know?"

She shook her head again and made the earrings swing wildly next to her head. "No. I just heard them and knew they were fighting. I assumed it was because of Amy refusing to say she was a witch."

"Okay. One more thing, Miss Fox. When was the last time you saw Amy Perkins?"

She thought about the question for a moment as she let go of my hand and answered, "I think the last time Amy came to one of the Tuesday meetings at the center was the eighteenth. I didn't really know her outside of those, so that would have been the last time."

He jotted July 18 down in his notes next to her name and the words LAST TIME SHE SAW AMY before closing the notepad and looking up to smile at her. "Thank you for all your help, Miss Fox. If I have any other questions, I have your number to contact you."

"I hope you find out who did this to Amy. She was a wonderful person, even if she didn't call herself a witch."

"Good day."

I waved goodbye to her and thanked her for the impromptu palm reading. "Here's to hoping you're right," I said as I turned to follow him.

"Oh, I am. Don't worry," she yelled after me.

When I caught up to Alex, he was already near the door. I grabbed his shirt near his elbow to stop him and said, "Hey, did you get to talk to anyone else?"

He looked back at me but didn't stop walking toward the exit. "I spoke to two people on Tamara Ridgeway's list, including Miss Fox there. A third, Melody Chamberlain, was busy reading cards for someone, so I thought I'd step outside and get some fresh air while I wait."

His answer sounded workmanlike, almost emotionless without any of the usual kindness I was so used to hearing when he spoke to me. I had a sense he was angry with me for storming away before. I didn't know how I felt about that, though. He had been quite closed-minded about this whole event, and it had bothered me.

I followed him outside to the car where he stopped and leaned against the hood. Folding his arms across his chest, he asked, "So did you hear what you wanted to in there?"

"What does that mean?" I asked, instantly feeling defensive about his question about my reading.

"Poppy, they read body language and tell people what they want to hear. There's nothing supernatural about tarot card reading or palm reading or any of it. They sense you want to know about something and tell you about it so you'll feel good."

I took a step back away from him and leveled my gaze on his face. "And there's something wrong with me feeling good about myself or an issue that's on my mind?"

His expression showed he understood he'd gone to the wrong place with this discussion already, and he shook his head. "That's not what I meant. You know that. I don't begrudge you feeling good about anything. I just don't see why you would need one of them to feel that way."

"Maybe I needed some clarity. Some people find that with readings. What do you care anyway? It wasn't like you couldn't continue the investigation without me.

You didn't need me there to ask questions."

"That may be true, but I like having you around when I'm asking potential suspects questions. You get a sense from people that I may not. It's why we work so well together."

I thought about the Three of Pentacles in my triangle of cards and the Two of Cups in Alex's and how we really did work well together. And not only investigating crimes. I never doubted that he valued me personally and professionally, but to hear him say he did without any prompting made me happy.

"We do work well together. I'll be around for the final one."

Alex sighed and let his arms drop from his chest. "Good. I have to be honest. I find much of what these women peddle to be nonsense, but I did like what Miss Fox said about your heart line. I don't believe a word of it, but as the man who loves you, I like the idea of a happy life full of love with me, of course."

I took that step forward toward him and closed the distance between us as Madame Cassandra's words about looking at my problems from a different perspective ran through my mind. I still disagreed with Alex on the tarot readings being useless, but maybe that was just the stable, logical part of him talking.

And I had to admit, I found that part of him pretty incredible too.

"Well, you keep being the down-to-earth king you are, and I'll stay the emotional and intuitive queen I am, and I think we'll be fine."

Alex arched one eyebrow in confusion. "King?"

I waved off his question and winked at him. "Nevermind. It's just something I heard. Let's go in and see if Miss Chamberlain can fit us in now. On the way in, you can get me caught up with what the first two potential suspects had to say."

Chapter Seven

WHILE WE WERE outside, more people had arrived, so when we returned to the convention, the crowd of attendees made getting to Melody Chamberlain's booth on the left side of the hall difficult. Alex pushed his way through the people with me at his elbow, and as we arrived to her spot, I pulled him back from approaching her.

Confused, he asked, "What's going on, Poppy?"

"I was just wondering if we were going with me doing most of the talking this time. I know you had some success with the first two, but I am more accepting of what's going on here so maybe it would be better if I asked the questions."

A slow smile spread across his face. "I think I'll stay as the starter. Feel free to join in with any questions you have, like usual, though."

"Okay. Lead the way."

Melody Chamberlain stood on the far left side of the room at one of the tarot reader booths, and I noticed she didn't look like the other women in the room. While Madame Cassandra had a unique hair color that made her stand out and Miss Fox had gone full gypsy with her look, Melody simply looked like anyone you'd see on the street. She wore her medium brown hair to her shoulders, and her makeup resembled the way I wore mine.

She appeared to be a very average woman in a room full of far more theatrical characters. Dressed in a black skirt with a beige short-sleeved top and a few gold necklaces, she reminded me of what any office worker might look like Monday through Friday.

A woman and a man stood at her booth thumbing through a pamphlet she offered, so Alex walked up to her table and said in an authoritative voice, "I'm back for that conversation, Miss Chamberlain. I'd like to ask you a few questions."

The couple stopped reading the brochure and looked over at Alex and me as Melody Chamberlain said, "I have people here now, officer. Maybe later."

In that way Alex could make someone feel uncomfortable without saying a word, he turned to look at the two people and narrowed his eyes to match the serious look on the rest of his face. Whatever Melody thought she had in them she lost quickly as they hurried off with her handout to another part of the hall.

"Looks like you have time for those questions now," he said flatly.

I took my place at his side and watched Melody Chamberlain's expression fall. Answering a police officer's questions looked like the last thing she wanted to do.

She bit the inside of her mouth for a few seconds before she accepted Alex had no intention of going away without some answers. She sighed and her shoulders sagged. "Okay, since you chased away my customers, I guess now is as good a time as any. What would you like to know?"

Slowly, he pulled out his notepad and pen and flipped the cover and sheets of paper until he found a clean one. It was an intentional delay, and I'd seen him do it time and again with people to put them on the defensive. The whole action never failed to impress me with how effective it usually was.

But today it didn't seem to have much effect on her. She stood glaring at us, alternating from him to me in the time Alex spent looking for a spot to jot down his observations from their conversation. Something told me Melody didn't fear the police as much as I'd thought at first.

"This is my partner, Poppy McGuire, Miss Chamberlain. So, what can you tell me about your relationship with Amy Perkins?" Alex asked in his deep commanding voice.

"I know her. I mean knew her. It's so sad to hear what happened to her," Melody answered, choking up on the word *happened*.

Watching her like I was to see her reaction to his first question, something he'd told me was often the most telling since guilty people were often so eager to hide their guilt that they had to overwork to achieve it, he nodded. "Yes, it is. I take that to mean that you heard about her murder before right now. How did you find out?"

Melody seemed surprised to be asked that question and looked up at him with wide eyes. "Tamara. I mean, of course she'd tell the group. We used to see Amy every Tuesday, so it's not like it's strange that she'd let us all know."

Glancing over at Alex's notes, I saw him write

CLAIMS TAMARA TOLD THE GROUP—NO ONE ELSE SAID THAT. It seemed strange that the other two members of the group hadn't mentioned Tamara calling them to let them know about Amy's untimely death.

"Of course. Now how would you characterize your relationship with Amy Perkins, Miss Chamberlain? Were you close since you saw her every Tuesday and shared the same beliefs?"

I listened carefully to her answer since I knew Amy hadn't believed in the same religious ideas since she didn't see herself as a witch. Melody smiled broadly, which seemed like a strange reaction to his question and made me wonder what she found so amusing.

"I know you already heard about the issue between Tamara and Amy, Officer Montero. It's not that big a thing, though. Tamara can be a little over the top with her zeal for the witches' way, but Amy was accepted whatever she believed. We witches accept all. Blessed be."

Melody hung her head reverentially as she said those last two words and then lifted it to smile at me. "You know, I remember Amy saying that the last time I saw her. See, she really wasn't a Druid, or whatever she claimed she believed in. By saying blessed be, she showed how much she was like we witches."

I mentally corrected her grammar—us witches, us not we—and saw Alex look over at me like he knew exactly what I was silently saying to myself. The writer in me didn't take a day off, even when investigating a murder.

"So would you characterize your relationship with Amy as friends?" he asked, trying to ascertain how close they were for the second time.

"Oh, yes. All of us who are witches would be considered friends. We don't have a coven, but that doesn't mean we aren't close."

Alex jotted down a few words about her answer while I asked, "Are you part of a coven, Miss Chamberlain?"

Melody shook her head and gave me a smarmy smile. "Oh, no. Many non-witches think that all witches join covens, but it's just not true. Many of us are solitary witches, like I am. That's why I liked to attend the weekly witches' circle meetings. To give me a chance to spend time with others like me."

I jumped on her use of the past tense there. "Liked to attend? Have you stopped going to the Tuesday night meetings?"

Her smile faded quickly, and Alex focused his attention on her reaction. "Is something wrong, Miss Chamberlain? Is there a reason you've stopped attending the meetings at the Third Eye Mind and Body Center?"

She nervously tugged on the three gold necklaces around her neck, pulling them down in between her breasts until they must have been cutting into the skin on the back of her neck. When she realized I was watching her, she dropped her hands from the chains and shifted her gaze to the floor.

"I just meant that I enjoyed seeing Amy and the others. I still go. That hasn't changed."

Her answer didn't do anything to allay my suspicion that she had stopped attending the witches' circle meetings, and I knew it didn't dispel Alex's curiosity about her use of the past tense either. However, he didn't dwell on the issue and continued with his questioning.

"You mentioned Tamara Ridgeway's zeal about witchcraft. We've learned that this caused quite a rift between her and Amy. Do you believe that was their only disagreement?"

Melody looked up and her pale blue eyes grew wide. Shaking her head rapidly, she answered, "I don't feel right telling you this because I don't want to betray a fellow witch, but I know it wasn't their only disagreement. Tamara and Amy didn't agree on much, in fact."

"Like what?" Alex asked as I eagerly waited for her to explain what else the two women had fought about.

The voice in my head said *Ten bucks they fought over a guy*.

"Well, I feel wrong saying anything about it. It was a private matter between two consenting adults."

Maybe I was wrong. Had I been thinking jealousy over a man when I should have been going more direct with a love affair between them?

I looked to my left and saw Alex staring down at her with that patient look he had. I knew the expression on my face was anything but that.

"I...I mean, it's nothing, really. They just had a disagreement over someone Amy had been seeing a while back. It didn't last, and after they broke up it was all but forgotten."

She still hadn't said it was a man, but the alarm bells had already started to go off in my head. Hoping to make sure we all were clear about this, I asked, "Are you talking about a boyfriend of Amy's?"

"Yes. Tamara didn't like him much, I think."

I knew it. I knew there was a man in the middle of

this somewhere. Amy was an attractive woman, so it wasn't surprising that she dated a number of men. Tamara, on the other hand, was nowhere close to Amy's league, so I had a feeling she had been jealous of Amy.

"Do you know why she didn't like this man? Do you remember his name?" Alex asked.

"No, I don't. I'm sorry. I never really knew why Tamara didn't like him, but I heard them fighting one Tuesday night before a witches' circle meeting and I can tell you it got pretty heated. I heard Tamara say he was no good to any of us, but I didn't know what she meant by that. Then she said, 'You better be careful' and I hurried out to the meeting room before either one of them knew I was there."

"Do you know if Amy was dating him still when she was murdered the other night?" I asked, quite curious about the mystery man.

"I don't think she was. I think they broke up a while ago. That was the only time I ever heard Tamara and Amy talk about him, though."

Alex jotted down a few things about her answers and said, "One last question. Well, two, Miss Chamberlain. When was the last time you saw Amy Perkins and do you have any idea why anyone would want to kill her?"

Melody answered his questions quickly. "I saw her last at the meeting on July eighteenth. As for why someone would want to hurt her, I have no idea. Even Tamara's disagreement with her never seemed to be more than a philosophical difference of opinions to me. I mean, I could be totally wrong about that, but I just can't imagine a fellow witch hurting her. It's just inconceivable to me."

"And where were you last night, Miss Chamberlain?"

"Am I a suspect?"

Alex didn't answer immediately, but then he said, "We just need to know where anyone who knew Amy was last night."

"Oh. Well, I went to the movies to see *An Affair to Remember* at The Colonnade and I was back home by eleven since the movie started at nine."

A woman peeked her head around me and asked in a frantic voice, "Are you available for a reading? I have a question I must have answered today and every other reader is all booked up!"

A look of relief washed over Melody's face, and she smiled to the woman as she motioned for her to come around the table to join her. "Please, come here. We will start immediately."

The woman hurried around me to Melody's makeshift inner sanctum and sat down in one of the metal folding chairs that flanked a tiny TV tray table. Melody looked back at her and then turned her attention back to Alex and me, now much happier that she had a paying customer.

"You'll have to excuse me, Officer Montero. Destiny calls."

Alex stuffed his notepad into his shirt pocket and gave me a side eye look. "Certainly. If we have any more questions, we'll need to speak to you again. Please give my partner your number and address."

With that, he spun on his heels and walked away, leaving me with Melody and a very desperate woman dying to hear what the future held and practically shooting daggers from her eyes to let me know it was time for me to go. Melody seemed less upset by my continued presence and smiled as she picked up one of her flyers from the table in between us.

"My number is on there, so if you or your partner have any further questions, please don't hesitate to call," she said as she jotted down her address. Handing me the flyer, she added, "And if you ever want a reading, please don't hesitate to call. I can tell you have the right frame of mind for tarot, even if your partner doesn't."

I fought back a chuckle about how Alex truly felt about what Melody and her fellow tarot card readers did and thanked her as I took the pamphlet from her. "I'll definitely keep the reading idea in mind. I had one from Madame Cassandra earlier, though."

She looked across the hall toward her competition and wrinkled her nose. "Oh, she's good, but I think I'd be able to give you a clearer picture about how to get through to a man like yours."

"A man like mine? How do you know that's what I'd want a reading about?" I asked, surprised she had zeroed in on my concern without my even mentioning anything.

Melody looked over toward the door and then back at me. "It's quite obvious. Call me if you want to know the answers."

With that, she turned her back and began talking to the woman who sat impatiently waiting for her to tell her what the future held. Still a bit stunned that she'd known what worried me enough to have a tarot card reading, I headed out of the hall into the heat and found Alex standing near the car reading through his notes.

"Well, that was interesting, don't you think?" I asked as I joined him.

"Interesting? I guess you could say that," he answered without looking at me.

Using Melody's pamphlet as a fan, I tried to get some air moving around my head as perspiration began to form along my hairline. "She thinks you and I have problems."

That made him look up from his tablet, and he raised one eyebrow like he always did when he heard something he didn't appreciate. "Who? The woman who did your reading?"

"No. Melody Chamberlain. After you walked away, she said she could give me a reading and let me know how to get through to a man like you."

Now the second eyebrow joined the first up in his forehead. "Really? A man like me, huh? What kind of man would that be?"

I didn't want to get into this discussion there outside the tarot readers convention, so I waved the issue off and instead said, "I thought that part of what she said about Amy and Tamara having a problem over a guy interesting. I knew there'd be a man involved in this case somehow."

My change of topic caught him off guard for a moment, but when it became apparent I didn't plan to answer his question, he simply turned back to his notes. "Are we thinking they were both with him or something else?"

The memory of Tamara Ridgeway made me shudder. I shook my head at the thought of any man dating both her and Amy. "No way. Amy and Tamara aren't even in the same league. I'm not even sure they're from the same planet dating-wise."

Alex looked up at my assessment of the two women and smiled. "Have I ever told you how I love the way you describe things? Nobody pins it down as colorfully as you do, Poppy."

When he said things like that, I couldn't help but be happy. Even though they were small compliments, I knew he meant them, and that's why they made me feel so good.

"Just think of me as the color commentary portion of the investigation. I bring the whole thing to life, so to speak."

"Colorful and punny. Cute. So no to the idea of both women attracting the same man?"

"So much no I need a different word. Never. Impossible. Couldn't happen. No way, Jose."

My answer made him laugh. "Okay. Got it. So what do you think the problem was between Tamara and Amy concerning this man if it wasn't that they both were dating him?"

"Jealousy? Tamara liked him, but he was out of her league and she resented Amy dating him?" I suggested.

"Maybe. Jealousy is often a reason for murder. Until we know any more, that makes Tamara our prime suspect so far."

After our experience with her, I didn't mind the idea of Tamara Ridgeway being our main suspect. What an obnoxious woman she was! In truth, I could see her better as a victim than a murderer, though. That personality of hers could rub anyone the wrong way. I'd only spent a few minutes with her and she'd succeeded in insulting me more than once and making me wish I'd never have to speak to her again.

"What did you think of the three women from the convention here? They all knew Amy through being witches and spending time at the Third Eye Mind and Body Center, along with Tamara."

Reading off his notes, he said, "Susie Mitchell, interview number one, says she knew very little of Amy. She just joined the witches' circle in June and she didn't attend regularly until early July, so she never really got a chance to know the victim. She seemed genuinely upset when I told her about Amy's death, like she hadn't known before."

I stopped him as I remembered something Melody said. "Wait a second. Melody Chamberlain gave the impression that Tamara had alerted everyone to the news, so why didn't Susie seem to know?"

He quickly flipped through the pages of his notepad until he came to his notes on Melody and in big letters he'd written CLAIMS TAMARA TOLD THE GROUP—NO ONE ELSE SAID THAT.

"Interesting. So did Tamara tell everyone else and they didn't feel it was worth mentioning? And if so, that means Susie Mitchell was pretending for my benefit, but I didn't get that feeling."

I instantly regretted going to Madame Cassandra for my reading instead of helping Alex with the interviews. "I'm sorry. I might have been able to help with that if I wasn't off getting a tarot card reading."

He didn't say anything in response to my apology and continued with his explanation of what had happened while I was absent. "The second woman, Jerilyn Fox, you met just before my questioning ended."

"Big earrings that I worry are going to someday rip right through her earlobes," I said, remembering those enormous hoops dangling from her head.

Alex cringed. "So colorful. Sometimes too colorful."

"Sorry."

Recovered from my graphic description, he said,

"She heard Tamara and Amy fighting but assumed it was over the witch thing. She didn't really know Amy, but what she knew she liked. Said she brought coconut macaroons to the Tuesday night meetings a few times. She claims to have seen Amy last at the July eighteenth meeting."

"Another one who says she hasn't seen her for weeks. That begs the question of what Amy's been doing for the past few weeks, don't you think?"

Alex nodded and sighed. "Yes, and I'm beginning to think that's going to be the key to this case. The woman's been doing something since the eighteenth of July, yet none of the people who used to see her regularly knows what. We need to find that out."

"I agree," I said as a group of five women walked past us on their way into the convention. "And last, but not least, is Melody Chamberlain, who looks less like a witch and tarot reader than she does an office manager at a law firm. What did you think of her?"

"I think she's lying about something. What, I have no idea yet, but my gut says she's lying," he said as he watched the crowd of women walk into Jacob's Hall.

"Did you catch the way she nearly pulled those necklaces off her neck when you asked her if she'd stopped attending the meetings? I thought she'd either rip them apart or cut right through her skin."

He cringed again and then smiled. "I did notice that. Not exactly that way, but she seemed uncomfortable about something. And the way she said she attended the witches' circle meetings, like it doesn't happen anymore."

"I don't think asking Tamara about it will get us anywhere," I said, sure I didn't want to see her again anytime soon. "Maybe we should go back in and ask

Susie and Jerilyn."

"No, I think we got all we could from them, but I will be asking the other one on the list when we speak to them if Melody has stopped attending the meetings. For now, I think we're done with the tarot readers convention."

"Where are we off to now?" I asked as he walked around the car to get into the driver's seat.

"I want to see how Stephen and Craig are doing on the private life of Amy Perkins. Maybe they found out something about this boyfriend Melody mentioned her having. Let's head back to the station and meet up with them, if we can."

Alex pulled away from the front of Jacob's Hall and turned the car around to head back to Sunset Ridge. We said nothing for a long time, Alex because he tended not to talk too much and myself because my mind was full of what we'd learned from the witches who spent time with Amy on Tuesday nights and what I'd found out in my reading with Madame Cassandra. I didn't know if anything she'd told me was true, but I figured it couldn't hurt to try to see things from a different perspective.

"You're unusually quiet over there, Poppy. Did your chi get all thrown out of whack being around all those soothsayers?" Alex asked as he turned onto Main Street.

Sometimes even when he was being sarcastic he could be cute. "I don't think that's how chi works, but I'm fine. Just thinking about the case and enjoying the cool air over here."

He said nothing in response, but as he turned off the car in front of the police station, he looked over at me and gave me a smile. "You already know how to get through to a man like me, just so you know. You don't need those people to tell you how to do that, Poppy."

Chapter Eight

EVEN THOUGH WE still had one more name to investigate from Tamara Ridgeway's list, I had a feeling Alex had other things he wanted to check out. He hadn't overtly acted like he didn't believe Stephen and Craig could handle their part of the case, but his desire to return to the station instead of going to find our final person on the list told me he wasn't completely comfortable with the way the four of us had to work together.

Not that I was fond of this arrangement myself. While I didn't tend to be a lone wolf like Alex, four was definitely a crowd when it came to investigating crimes. And that didn't even factor in how uncomfortable just being around Stephen made me.

Alex held the glass door to the station open for me, and as soon as I stepped one foot into the building, my stomach began twisting into a tight, painful knot. It was ridiculous and I knew it, but there it was.

I literally dragged my feet, dreading the place I'd grown to call almost a second home since Alex and I began working together over a year ago. He ran into the back of me coming through the door, and I turned around to see a surprised look on his face.

"Sorry, Poppy. I must not have been paying attention there," he said as he gently pressed his hand to the small of my back to urge me down the hall.

"It wasn't you. I was just walking a little slowly," I whispered as we walked past the receptionist.

Leaning down, he said in a low voice, "Why are we whispering?"

He'd made it perfectly clear that he didn't care what his fellow officer thought of me, but I couldn't shake my insecurity about this whole Stephen thing. I wanted so much to prove that I was truly an asset to Alex's work on this case, but so far I'd done very little. What if he asked him about it? What would Alex say?

We reached his office, and as he sat down behind his desk, I shut the door. I needed to get this off my chest now.

The door closed with a click, making him look up from whatever he was looking at on his computer screen. With a sly smile, he asked, "Have something planned that requires the door being closed?"

"I need to talk to you," I said, pressing my back to the door in desperate need of something to steady me.

The twinkle in his eye that had been there a few seconds before disappeared as he drew his eyebrows in. "Okay. What's wrong, Poppy? You've been acting strange all day. Is something going on?"

I took a deep breath and tried to keep myself measured even as everything I felt began to unravel in my brain. Taking a few steps away from the security of the door, I stopped behind one of the chairs in front of his desk and gripped the hard plastic in my hands.

"I know you said the whole Stephen thing doesn't matter to you, but it matters to me. I'm happy that you don't pay attention to the things he does, but I do and they bother me. Now we're working with him on this case, and it's brought all the issues he and I seem to have with each other into sharpened focus."

He watched me carefully as I explained what was on my mind, his gaze never wavering as I spoke. Alex had likely thought this problem was solved by what he'd said earlier, but it wasn't for me. I could pretend for only so long, and my ability to ignore the fact that one of his fellow officers had no respect for me whatsoever had run out.

"Poppy, I don't care—" he began to say, but I cut him off by raising my hand and continuing.

"I do care, Alex. I care a great deal, in fact. I've tried to understand how you can be so comfortable with the fact that one of the people you work closely with is so disrespectful towards me, but I'm going to be honest here. I don't get it. Not in the least. He's been rude to me on virtually every occasion we're in the same location, even after you had a talk with him. It got better for a little while, but I can still see the disgust he has for me every time I'm near him, and he doesn't even pretend to hide it. How are you perfectly okay with that?"

"I'm not," Alex said quietly as a look of pain came over him, like what I said had hurt him.

Flopping down in the chair in front of him, I felt deflated by his answer. "Then why does it seem like you do?"

"What do you want me to do, Poppy? I'd give my life for you, but I can't make people like you. I know it bothers you that he's like he is, but he's nobody. Derek doesn't think much of him as a cop, and nobody really likes him on the force. Maybe that's why he dislikes you so much. In his mind, he's a real cop and we don't like him, but you're not and everyone here likes you. Well, everyone but him."

Now I felt stupid.

"You make it sound like I'm some fragile little thing who gets her feelings hurt all the time, Alex. I'm not. I've had to grow a tough skin living in this town with all its gossipy biddies looking at me like I was some loser, but I don't think I should have to defend myself to someone I've never done anything wrong to."

Slowly, the corners of his mouth turned up into a sexy smile and he folded his arms behind his head. "So what you're saying is you want me to kick his ass? You want me to go all Alpha male on him?"

"Now you're making fun of me, aren't you?"

"Only a tiny bit, but I just want you to remember that if anyone ever tried to truly harm you in any way, Poppy, I'd lay down my life to protect you. You know that, right?"

"I know. I just want to be respected for what I do with you, and nothing I've ever done seems to be enough for him."

"Why do you care what he thinks? He's one person who means very little to everyone around you."

I hung my head and spoke the words even I hated to admit were the truth. "Because I'm not a cop. I'm allowed to play at being one because the police chief is a friend from childhood and I'm dating a cop. Stephen's dislike of that makes me feel like a fraud."

Alex stood up and came around the desk to stand behind me. Putting his hands on my shoulders, he leaned down and kissed me softly on the cheek. I turned my head to see him looking at me with those dark eyes of his in that way that said he wished we weren't there in his office at that moment.

"Poppy, out of all the cops I know here and in Baltimore, you were the only one who was able to solve the case of Bethany's murder and Helena's. When everyone else thought I was guilty, you never gave up. You did as good a job investigating and clearing me as any cop or detective I've ever met. Your police work is the reason I'm standing here today. Don't let what one person thinks change the reality of what you've done."

"But he's right, Alex. I'm not a cop. I don't belong here."

Alex's lips brushed mine before he kissed me and pressed his forehead to mine. "Yes, you do. A badge only makes things official. I've known from our first case that you have good instincts. I wouldn't want to do this job without you. Remember that."

Looking into his soulful eyes, I felt like I could remember those things the next time Stephen shot me a nasty look or said something rude about me being on a case. "Okay."

"Good." He stood up and motioned toward the door. "Mind if I open the door now? People are going to start thinking something wild is going on in here."

"You know, for a serious guy, you sure do have a way of making light of a lot of things."

"Do you actually think I'm making light of the possibility of us having a middle of the day rendezvous right here in my office?" he said with a wickedly sexy smile I couldn't help but love.

"Just open the door and let's get back to work, Officer Montero."

He slowly swung it open and there stood Craig with his hand in the air poised to knock. His eyes shifted from Alex to me and then back to Alex again. "I just wanted to see if I could talk to you."

I quickly stood to leave. "I'll go. Maybe I'll make a coffee run."

Craig turned to look at me and shook his head. "Uh, actually, I wanted to talk to the two of you, if that's okay."

Alex and I exchanged surprised looks and he invited Craig in to join us. The most junior member of the Sunset Ridge police seemed hesitant, as if he was reconsidering his idea to come to speak to us, but then shuffled over to the seat I'd just occupied and plopped down.

I slid behind him and sat down next to him, curious as to what Craig wanted to speak to us about since I had the feeling it had nothing to do with the case. Alex sat back down behind his desk and waited for Craig to begin talking, but he said nothing and instead just stared down at his lap.

We exchanged another set of glances as we both wondered why he'd come in to talk and wasn't talking. Finally, Alex said, "Did you want to tell us something about the case? Would you rather wait until Stephen joins us?"

His immediate reaction showed he definitely didn't want that to happen. Shaking his head, he quickly answered, "No. I want to talk to you two only."

"Okay, that's fine. What's up?" Alex asked, but Craig still said nothing.

So I gently patted him on the forearm and leaned in next to him. "The first case is always a very exciting one.

I remember the first time I worked with Alex, and that was probably way less cool than what you're experiencing because I wasn't a real cop like you."

Craig turned to look at me with a wide-eyed stare. "It is exciting, but you're so much better at this than I am, Poppy."

"Oh, that's not true, Craig. You just need to believe in yourself."

He shook his head again. "Stephen obviously doesn't believe I'm any good. He said I should stay here while he went to speak to the victim's boyfriend. He doesn't even want me there when he speaks to people regarding this case."

I glanced over at Alex as Craig sat there dejected and wanted to help him. "Some people are just used to working solo. I'm sure he thinks you're a great person to be on a case with."

My supportive words didn't appear to be having much effect, if the frown deepening on Craig's face was any indication. I really wasn't the best choice to defend Stephen in any way, so I looked over at Alex and silently urged him to jump in to help Craig.

He cleared his throat awkwardly and said, "It's always tough to be a rookie, but you'll get the hang of it. You've been around here for a while, so you're probably more knowledgeable about how to conduct an investigation than you think. Give yourself a chance to learn the ropes."

"I guess. I just thought that I'd be doing more of what you guys do together. I mean, you never just leave Poppy behind, do you?"

"No, but we're different people than you and Stephen. I believe in you, Craig, and I know Poppy does. Just give it a little time."

I quickly moved to shore up Craig's confidence. "Oh, yeah. I totally believe in you. You're going to be fine at this. You just have to believe in yourself."

A smile lit up his face, and I saw that we'd done some good. "Thanks, guys. I will."

Craig stood up to leave, but Alex stopped him by asking, "Can you bring the preliminary report on the knife? Stephen told me he'd get it to me, but it would be a big help if you could while I'm here."

"Sure! I'll bring it right over. It should be ready by now," Craig said as he hurried out of the office to do as Alex asked.

Once we were alone, I quickly asked, "Why did you ask him about the report on the knife? I thought it wouldn't be ready until tomorrow."

He didn't answer but simply smiled. Was his distrust of Stephen so thorough that he didn't even believe that he'd get the report to him in a timely fashion?

I had no chance to press him for an answer before Craig reappeared with a sheet of paper. Handing it to Alex, he beamed, "Hot off the presses. It just came through the fax machine."

After one glance, my partner looked up at me and then said to Craig, "Can you help with something else? I have to find a woman named Crystal Sendona. I don't know if she lives in Sunset Ridge, but she lives in the area. Can you get me an address for her?"

I'd never seen Craig smile so broadly. Thrilled to be actively participating in the investigation, he nodded eagerly. "I'm on it. Just give me a few minutes."

He hurried out of the office, leaving us alone once again, and Alex handed me the forensics report on the knife. "Take a look."

I scanned the report and saw that the lab had found no fingerprints on the decorative handle of the knife or the blade. There was no residue from any medical gloves either.

Looking up from the paper, I joked, "So the murderer wore leather gloves on a hot August night or the knife magically ended up in her chest somehow."

"Maybe someone threw the knife at her like in a carnival sideshow?" he asked with a shrug.

I handed the report back to him. "What does it matter how it got there? There are no fingerprints on it, and in the end, that's not what killed her anyway. Were you looking for something particular in this report?"

He shook his head. "No. I was hoping there would be fingerprints we could use, but more importantly, I wanted to get a look at the report for myself. I didn't want to have to hear about it secondhand."

Now I was confused. "Why wouldn't you get to?"

A strange look came over his face. "Because I'm not the lead officer on this case."

Craig reappeared once again with another sheet of paper I suspected had the information about our next interviewee on it. "Here you go, Alex," he happily chirped. "She lives right here in town. Are you going to speak to her now?"

I knew by the leading sound of his voice that he hoped he could join us when we went to speak to Crystal Sendona. Not that I didn't want Craig to come along, but two police officers and me showing up at a woman's house might scare her half to death.

Thankfully, Alex picked up on his hopefulness and came up with a way to let him down easy. "Thanks,

Craig. We are going to see her in a little while. I'd say you should come with us, but I don't want to step on Stephen's toes in this. We all have to work together, and in the end, you are his partner. I know I wouldn't like it if Poppy joined someone else without my knowledge."

Craig nodded his understanding, I suspected mainly because he trusted Alex. "I get it. I definitely don't want to make him think he can't have faith in me even more."

Alex stood up and patted him on the back. "Don't worry. You guys will get used to working together. And the four of us are going to solve this case and you'll get to chalk up a win for your first investigation."

Those supportive words had the exact effect I hoped they would, and Craig left happy to be a part of his first case. When I knew he was out of earshot, I said to Alex, "That was nice of you. He's a good person. I'm glad you said those things. You meant them, right?"

"I did. Craig's a good guy. He has good intentions. He's green, but everyone is in the beginning. I think he'll get much better as he learns more, and that will help his confidence."

Turning around to make sure no one was outside in the hallway, I quietly said, "Why do you think Stephen is acting like he is toward Craig?"

"It's obvious. He doesn't think he needs to work with him since he's a rookie when it comes to investigating."

Hearing that made me feel bad for Craig. The guy had been dying for the chance to be more than crowd control at crime scenes and a traffic cop, and now that he had finally been given that opportunity, Stephen was cutting him out. It made me dislike Stephen even more than I already did.

"I hate that. That's not okay, Alex."

He looked down at me and shook his head. "No, it's not. But maybe I'm wrong. Maybe there's another reason."

"Like what? He's just a jerk?" I asked, my defensiveness for not only me but also for Craig rising inside me.

Alex didn't answer immediately, but I saw in his expression he had something else in mind than Stephen being just an ignorant ass. Intrigued, I stood up and closed the door.

Turning back to face him, I said, "You can't just leave me hanging like this. Please share with your partner so she has a clue as to what's going on, okay?"

He took a deep breath and let it out slowly, dragging the whole thing out and making me even more curious. Sometimes he could be so dramatic.

When he didn't speak up, I said, "Come on! Don't hold out on me. What are you talking about?"

"I have nothing concrete, so that's why I haven't said anything yet, but the way he acted at the crime scene made me wonder. Jumping to conclusions is one thing, but he was pushing that witch stuff pretty hard from the moment we got there without any evidence. Then it seemed very important to him for him and Craig to investigate our victim's personal life. He was adamant about it when I went to speak to him this morning. I didn't care that he wanted to choose that route and have us look into her professional life, but he was insistent on it because he wanted to give Craig firsthand experience with that facet of the investigation."

"What are you saying?"

"I'm not sure, but the fact that he left Craig here instead of giving him that experience in interviewing people in her personal life he was so adamant about strikes me as odd."

In my mind, I wondered what Stephen could be up to, but also I liked the idea that Alex saw him as someone he might not be able to completely trust. It wasn't a professional feeling at all, and I knew it. It was personal, and as much as I didn't want to be like that, that's how I felt.

Plus, his treatment of Craig rubbed me the wrong way. The guy just wanted to learn the job the best way he could, and it was his partner's responsibility to help him. That Stephen had pretty much abdicated the job irritated me.

I got lucky when Alex agreed to let me work with him as his partner, and this showed me how fortunate I'd been.

Alex opened the door and held out his arm. "We'll have to see what happens with that issue. For now, it's time to go talk to Crystal Sendona and see if she can shine any light on who this mystery ex-boyfriend of Amy's is."

As I passed him, I said, "Maybe we can also find out why Tamara had such a problem with her dating him. Maybe it was jealousy, but maybe it was something else."

Smiling, Alex walked with me down the hallway. "Maybe. Something tells me if we can find out his name, we might be able to figure out why she wouldn't have approved of him."

I still mentally placed my bets on pure, run-of-the-mill jealousy. After spending just a few minutes with Tamara Ridgeway, I could definitely see her as a jealous woman.

Chapter Nine

CRYSTAL SENDONA'S HOUSE sat on the corner of Rose Street and the street I lived on, Barn Street. We weren't exactly neighbors since she lived at the far end of Barn toward the Hotel Piermont and I lived closer to the center of town, but I still was struck with how close I lived to an actual witch.

Alex pulled the car up to the front of her house, a cute bungalow type of home painted green with dark purple trim similar to the much larger older homes over on Victorian Row, as my partner liked to not-so-affectionately call the area where the most prestigious members of Sunset Ridge society lived. Crystal's home had a far cozier look to it than those enormous Victorian homes, and I hoped we'd find its resident friendlier than the well-to-do citizens of town who routinely seemed to be the most difficult witnesses and suspects to deal with.

"I think I'm surprised to have a witch live on my street," I announced as Alex shifted the car into park.

He looked over at me wearing a silly grin. "Is that very open mind of yours closing just slightly now that you know one lives so close by?"

I didn't try to stop the scowl that came over my face. "Don't be ridiculous. Of course not. I'm not anti-witch.

I'm afraid you're going to have to stay in that closed-minded area you exist in without me."

"I'll try to survive. Ready?"

"Sure. Once again, do you think I should do the talking?"

Alex shook his head and frowned. "I think I can handle it. I haven't had a problem so far."

I opened my door and got out of the car. Looking across the roof, I saw him throw me a smug look. I hated when he was right like this.

The temperature had climbed to the low nineties, and it wasn't even noon yet. By the time I reached Crystal's front porch, beads of sweat already sat on my forehead, waiting for the moment when they'd roll down into my eyes. As always, Alex looked unfazed by the heat, even as he wore his dark blue uniform.

Fanning myself as he rang the doorbell, I asked, "Is this thing with you and the heat something they teach cops in the police academy? If there's a trick to dealing with the heat while wearing a dark, long-sleeved shirt, I think you should share it with me since I'm beginning to melt from the weather."

"There's no trick. Some people are just better in the heat than others. I think it's my Mediterranean ancestry. Between the Spanish and Italian, I have generations of people who were used to warm weather inside me. You've got one hundred percent Irish, and that doesn't help you with handling the heat."

More smugness, this time about his ancestry and why he could handle the heat better than I could. It might have been the scorching temperatures, but his coolness about all these things was getting on my nerves a bit.

The front door opened and a young woman in her mid-twenties with long, straight brown hair and stunning hazel eyes stood looking out through the screen door at us. Her gaze focused immediately on Alex in his official uniform and opened wide with a look of fear.

"Officer? Is something wrong?"

"Miss Sendona, my name is Officer Alex Montero. This is my partner Poppy McGuire. We'd like to talk to you about your friend, Amy Perkins. Do you have a few minutes for us to ask you some questions?"

I watched for her reaction to see if she knew about Amy's death, and it became obvious quite quickly that Crystal Sendona already knew what had happened to her fellow witch. The fear in her eyes faded away, replaced by sadness, and she silently nodded her head before opening the door for us to come in.

One step into her home told me she loved nature. Pictures of meadows and groves hung on the walls of her living room, and a wallpaper border of green and yellow flowers on a white background ran around the length of all four walls up next to the ceiling. In addition, vases full of purple and pink wildflowers stood on the end tables flanking her light green sofa on the far wall and on a cutout between the living room and dining room.

In addition to those clues, I immediately noticed her love of nature extended to her having no air conditioning in her house. Just my luck. We had one person to interview, and of course, her house would have to be as hot as a steam bath.

Crystal appeared to have been blessed by the same genes as Alex since I didn't notice a drop of perspiration anywhere on her face. Damn my northern European ancestors!

"Miss Sendona, we'd like to ask you about Amy Perkins. We're investigating her murder last night," Alex said quietly in a sympathetic voice.

"Yes, of course. I assumed someone would come around at some point since Amy and I were close friends," Crystal answered, her words laced with grief.

"We apologize for having to do this while you're mourning. It's just that the sooner we can find out anything that might give us a clue as to who her killer is, the sooner we can catch him or her," I explained, knowing what she was going through at that moment as she grieved the death of her close friend.

Clearing her throat, Crystal nodded and offered us a seat in the living room as she sat down in a chair opposite the sofa. "I understand. Whatever I can do to help the police find out who did this."

Alex and I sat down on the light green sofa that turned out to be much older than it looked and had practically no springs left under its cushions. He quickly caught himself before the piece of furniture sucked him in, but I wasn't as fortunate and within seconds, I found myself struggling to regain my ability to sit upright.

After my ab muscles performed a full workout in about three seconds' time, I got myself to the edge of the sofa with the help of Alex's hand on my back. Embarrassed, I hoped Crystal hadn't noticed my clumsiness, but she had and even through her sadness giggled at me.

"I'm sorry. I didn't mean to laugh at you. It just reminded me of Amy. Every time she came over, she'd sit down on the couch and would end up on her back just like you just did. And every time she'd say I needed to get new furniture."

"It's okay," I said as my cheeks grew hot from a blush of humiliation and sweat began to drip down the sides of my face. "When you've lost someone, it feels good to laugh at even the stupidest things. I know that."

"Thanks. Amy wouldn't want anyone to be all somber. She was a laugher. Did you two ever meet her, I mean before?"

Alex shook his head, but I smiled at my memory of interviewing her for that article as I wiped near my hairline. "I did. She was very nice and very sweet to help me with something I was writing for *The Eagle*."

"She would give anyone the shirt off her back if they needed it. Amy didn't have a nasty bone in her body. She made the world a better place," Crystal said, choking up on the last words about her friend.

"We've heard from a few other members of the witches' circle meetings you go to on Tuesdays at the Third Eye Center that she had problems with Tamara Ridgeway there. Can you tell us anything about that?"

Crystal's eyebrows drew in and she frowned deeper. "Tamara told you all about it, I'm sure. She tells everyone who is willing to listen about it. It wasn't that big a deal, at least not to Amy. Amy believed a lot of what witches like myself do. We practice a religion based on a respect for nature, and she did too. It's just that she considered herself a Druid."

As Alex jotted a note in his tablet, I asked Crystal a question I hoped wouldn't offend her but had been on my mind since this case had begun. "I mean no offense, but what is the difference between witchcraft and Druidism? When I spoke to Amy, it was for an article on paganism, but we never got into her own personal beliefs since I was going for a more general treatment of the topic. It sounds like what witches believe and what Druids believe is very similar, so why would Tamara have an issue with Amy claiming to be a Druid instead of a witch?"

Out of the corner of my eye, I saw Alex stop writing and glance over at me. I knew getting into discussions about religion generally wasn't advisable in an investigation, just as it was rarely a good idea to bring the topic up in conversation in most places, but my curiosity urged me to ask and Tamara's irritation over Amy's choice to identify herself as a Druid seemed to be an important area of inquiry.

Crystal said nothing for a few moments, and I worried that I had unintentionally offended her, but she smiled and nodded before answering my question. "I don't mind explaining the difference, Miss McGuire. Who knows? It might help find who killed Amy. I have to admit I don't understand everything Druids believe in, but from what Amy had always told me, there are several main differences between us, even though in general we believe in many of the same things. Both use magick, but she said Druids didn't use circles, like we witches do to perform magick. We use it to keep forces out, but for Druids, that isn't something they're concerned with."

"Keep forces out? What do you mean?" I asked, transfixed by her description.

"There is negative and positive energy, Miss McGuire. For witches, circles help us contain the positive energy around us and keep out the negative energy."

It seemed Alex was curious about what Crystal had to say too because he asked, "And Druids don't worry about negative energy?"

"Well, the way Amy described it to me, it's not about worrying so much as being willing to let the negative and positive join together. Does that make sense?"

"Yin and yang. Light and dark forming one whole. I understand," he said as he wrote something in his notepad.

His statement surprised me, though. I had never thought of Alex as a yin and yang kind of person. He'd always been more of a right and wrong kind of man to me, so the idea that he had knowledge of this type of thing seemed a little out of his wheelhouse.

"Exactly. Amy also told me that another big difference was witches tend to look to one deity, the Goddess, while Druids have many gods and goddesses. I'm not sure that's much of a difference though, at least to me, since I invoke various deities in my spell work."

As Alex noted this distinction or non-distinction in his notes, I thought about the knife someone had used to kill Amy and wondered if Druids used them like witches did. "Tamara Ridgeway told us that knives are called athames to witches. Do Druids use tools like that too?"

Crystal nodded. "Amy told me that's one big difference between Druids and witches. Tools like an athame are symbolic to Druids and can be used by any other Druid. A witch's athame is personal and infused with her own personal energy, so it wouldn't be used by anyone else."

I looked over at Alex and wondered if he was thinking the same thing I was. If a witch had killed Amy, or thought he or she was killing her with their athame, then it would have been a very personal attack based on what Crystal had just said.

"Tell me, Miss Sendona, do Druids believe in tarot readings?" Alex asked.

I gave him a side-eye glance as Crystal explained they didn't see the Tarot in the same way as witches did. "I don't know if they rely on them as much as the witches I know do. I can tell you Amy didn't, though. That I do know. But she read for extra money. She was a talented tarot reader."

"Can you tell me why you weren't at the Tarot Readers Convention in Caston today?" Alex asked, surprising me by his closed-mindedness. It wasn't like just because a person was a witch that she had to set up shop and read cards for people.

But she just laughed again, thankfully not offended by his question. "I don't read for money, Officer Montero. There's nothing wrong with doing it, and I'm not saying my fellow witches are wrong to, but I don't. To me, being a witch or specifically, a Wiccan, isn't so much about that kind of thing as it is just a way I live my life. I seek to live in harmony with the rest of the world, doing harm to none as I go about my life."

"Can you think of any reason why anyone would want to kill Amy Perkins, Miss Sendona?"

Alex's question ended any lightness we all may have felt at her kind answer, and Crystal frowned deeply as she shook her head. "No, I can't. Tamara disliked that Amy wouldn't call herself a witch, mainly because she thought Amy considered herself above us, but even that slight wouldn't be enough to make her kill her. I can't believe that. A disagreement, even on a person's beliefs, is one thing. Killing them is another thing entirely."

Every bit of Crystal Sendona's body language said she truly believed what she was saying and was genuinely sad about the loss of her friend. Unlike the other women we'd spoken to that day who had seemed surprised or unhappy in varying degrees about Amy Perkins' murder, Crystal appeared to be truly someone who would miss her.

Even more so, I believed what she said. Looking over at Alex's notes, I saw he did too. Whenever we interviewed someone he had real suspicions about, he tended to scribble question marks all over the page. He hadn't drawn one on Crystal Sendona's yet.

"We've heard about an ex-boyfriend of Amy's that supposedly Tamara and she had an argument over. Do you know anything about that?"

"Who said that?" she asked, narrowing her eyes.

"One of your fellow witches who attends the Tuesday night meetings, Melody Chamberlain," he answered. "Do you know anything about this argument and what the boyfriend's name was?"

A look of resignation came over Crystal's face. "I'm not sure Melody is the best person to give you any information. She's quite close to Tamara, so she's biased, to say the least. She mentioned the fight they had about the guy, but I didn't think much of it. Amy said that Tamara felt the guy was going to bring the center nothing but trouble."

"Why would he?" I asked, increasingly curious about this mystery man nobody seemed to want to mention by name.

Crystal leaned forward, as if to whisper a secret, and said quietly, "Amy dated a lot of people. She didn't see love like other people did. To her, it was an emotion that could be shared with anyone, regardless of race, beliefs, or even sex."

Her last word hung in the air for a moment, and Alex and I turned to look at each other. His expression looked like pure confusion. I didn't know if he picked up on what Crystal was trying to say, but I thought I had.

"So she and Tamara…?"

I didn't finish the rest of my statement, but Crystal filled in the blanks for me. "Had dated off and on for a while. They were done months ago, but Tamara has had a hard time letting go. It was never even very serious, according to Amy."

Next to me, Alex wrote in his notes TAMARA—AMY ? TOGETHER?

There was that all too familiar question mark. I didn't know if he didn't believe Crystal or didn't believe that the two women had ever been together in general.

"So this was a matter of Tamara being jealous that Amy had moved on and was dating a man?" I asked, still dying to find out if Crystal knew who this boyfriend had been.

"Yes, I think so. She was still hung up on Amy until the day she died, I think. And for Tamara, Amy dating men bothered her."

Alex chimed in after drawing another question mark in his notes. "Why would her dating a man bring trouble to the center? Is there a problem with men attending the Third Eye Center?"

Crystal looked at me and then Alex before shaking her head like in disbelief. "Men aren't a problem at the center. I'm straight and date men, and in fact, I've brought a few of my boyfriends there. It wasn't that she was dating a man but what he was."

Now even I had to admit I was confused. "What he was? What do you mean? That he wasn't someone who practiced witchcraft?"

Still looking like she couldn't believe the questions we were asking her, Crystal shook her head again. "No. Because he was a police officer."

My mouth dropped open, and out of the corner of my eye, I saw Alex show a rare moment of shock. A police officer? Amy had been dating a cop? That's who the mystery boyfriend was?

"Do you know who this police officer was?" Alex asked in a hushed voice, still clearly surprised by Crystal's bombshell news. "Was he local?"

"Amy kept her romantic life very private, even from me. She liked to live her life on her own terms as much as possible, and especially concerning who she dated. Tamara only found out because she saw Amy with the guy in Frederick one night and she recognized him from one time when she had to call the police about someone trying to break into the center late one night."

I literally sat on the edge of the sofa hoping to hear this officer's name. "So she never told you his name? Maybe she described him?"

Looking over toward Alex, I saw him holding his pen so tightly his knuckles were turning white. "A name would be very helpful, Miss Sendona. Do you know when this attempted break-in occurred?"

"I'm sorry. She never told me his name. She did say he had dark hair she liked a lot. Let me think about when the break-in might have been."

For a moment, it felt like Alex and I were hanging by a thread waiting for her to give a date. Even without a name, we would be able to figure out who it had been based on when the break-in had happened. All Alex would have to do would be to check the duty rosters for that time.

Crystal tilted her head back and forth like she was trying to debate on when it could have happened. Finally, she said, "I want to say it happened right after the holidays. Definitely not before Christmas."

My brain began spinning as I thought about who on the Sunset Ridge Police Department Amy could have been dating. A dark haired man. Images of every officer paraded through my mind. Alex had dark hair, as did Craig, Derek, Stephen, and if I was being gracious, the tiny bit of hair that Roger, the eldest officer on the force, had would be considered dark.

But I couldn't imagine Amy with Roger. Then again, I'd never imagined her with Tamara, not only because I hadn't predicted she dated women too but also because the owner of the Third Eye Mind and Body Center was such a less than appealing woman inside and out.

But then there were the part-time officers, some of whom I barely saw once or twice a month. Did any of them have dark hair?

Alex pushed his knee against mine, tearing me out of my deliberations as to who the mystery policeman Amy had been dating was. I looked at him and understood it was time to go.

We stood from the dangerous sofa to leave, but I had one more question to ask. "Did Tamara Ridgeway call you to let you know what had happened to Amy?"

Crystal nodded. "She called earlier, but I'd already heard the news from her father."

"Thank you for all your help, Miss Sendona, and we're very sorry for your loss," Alex said quietly as we walked outside.

Dying to know who he thought Amy had been with, I was barely able to wait until we were alone again to ask him his opinion. When Crystal closed the door behind us, I said, "Talk about stunning! I totally forgot about nearly melting into a puddle of sweat once she began talking about all that Druid and witch stuff, and then when she said Amy had been dating a cop, I actually had a chill run down the back of my neck."

Alex didn't seem as excited by this new development as I was. He said nothing until we got back into the car, but I knew as he turned on the air conditioning full blast that Crystal's news had shaken him.

He pulled away from the curb and began driving back toward the station, still not speaking. Desperate to hear if he thought he knew who Amy's boyfriend was, I finally said, "You're killing me here, Alex. You have nothing to say after all of that?"

Stopping at the end of Rose Street, he turned his head toward me and quietly said, "I'm going to find out who Amy was dating on the force, and if it's who I think it is, the entire police force may have a problem."

Instantly, a single name ran through my mind. If I had to place a bet on any one officer being Amy's boyfriend a few months ago, who would it be? Who was the poster child for dating virtually every single woman in town?

Derek.

Chapter Ten

A LEX MADE A beeline into the police station with me right behind him, but when he bolted down the hall to his office, I didn't follow him and instead headed directly for Derek's office. He had his way of finding out who the cop was who'd been dating our victim, and I had mine.

I found Derek's office door closed, so I threw it open with all I had and it slammed off the wall, making a loud booming noise. The police chief looked up at me wide-eyed, surprised by the noise and likely pretty stunned to see me standing there glaring at him.

"Damnit, Poppy. I think you nearly scared me right out of my skin." He stared at the wall behind the door and added, "That's nothing to say of what you've done to my office. What's with barging in here without even knocking and putting a damn hole in my wall?"

I saw the hole in the bland beige wall but at the moment, I didn't care. I had bigger things to worry about.

"Yeah, whatever. I need to know something, Derek. It's very important."

He screwed his face into a grimace that resembled the expression people made when they tasted something disgusting someone made and didn't know how to tell them the truth. Before my eyes, Derek morphed into the dictionary definition of dread.

"Whatever it is, Poppy, can it wait at least until I get through these reports? It's been a hell of a day already, what with the mayor calling me every hour asking if we have a witch problem in town. The last thing we need is some witchcraft hysteria in Sunset Ridge, but between him and the damn council talking about it nonstop, that's where we're headed," he grumbled as he returned to huddling over whatever the stack of papers were in front of him.

I took three giant steps toward his desk and slammed my hand on the end of it, once again startling him.

He looked up, his mouth hanging open. "For God's sake, Poppy! What is wrong with you today?"

Adrenaline rushed through me as I stood there looking down at Derek. "Alex and I were just interviewing one of Amy Perkins' friends and she said she was dating a cop at the beginning of this year and keeping it hush hush."

Derek's eyes narrowed to confused slits, and he scrunched up his face. "Who was dating a cop? The friend? Who is she, and why do I care?"

"No! Not the friend. The victim, Amy Perkins!" I exclaimed, already frustrated by this conversation.

My explanation did nothing to rid Derek's face of that confused expression. He added a head shake as he struggled to understand what I was getting at. "Amy Perkins, the woman from last night? She was dating a cop? One of mine?"

"Yes, one of yours. In fact, I was thinking it might be you she was dating, Derek."

He sat back in his chair and leveled his gaze on me. "What? Why would you think it was me?"

I couldn't help but roll my eyes at that question. Anyone with a brain would automatically think of Derek in this case or any other involving a pretty single woman secretly dating a cop in town.

"Well, you have dated nearly every single woman in town, and Amy Perkins was a beautiful woman and a definite free spirit. I could see you being attracted to her in a big way. Plus, the fact that she was keeping things on the down low says to me that her boyfriend wanted to keep his personal life private."

He held his hand up to stop me. "Whoa. Before you go any further, that's the best reason right there why it wouldn't be me. I haven't had a private moment in this town since before high school."

I jumped on his claim immediately, knowing that wasn't exactly true, and pointed my finger at him. "Ah ha! You can't say that, though. Nobody knew you were dating Solange because you were keeping it secret from nearly everyone."

Derek opened his mouth to argue with me, but then he closed it and hung his head for a moment. When he looked up at me, he appeared tired of our conversation. "Fine, that's true. But I never dated Amy Perkins, Poppy."

My theory shot to pieces, I stood there in his bland office disappointed I'd been wrong. "Then who was it? Crystal Sendona said it was a Sunset Ridge cop with dark hair who right after the holidays responded to a call out at the Third Eye Mind and Body Center."

"Nice to know you naturally jumped to the conclusion that it would have to be me," Derek mumbled.

"Well, I'm sorry, but you do have a history with women, you know. And you do have dark hair."

"So does Alex. Did you jump to the conclusion that he must have been Amy Perkins' secret boyfriend?"

"No, but I had a good reason for that. Alex is with me."

Derek rolled his eyes. "You know, you'd be much better at this if you didn't go into things blinded by personal prejudices. I know you like to think I'm the town gigolo, but you're wrong."

"Yeah, yeah. I know. Now you're a one-woman man. But just because you're all settled down now doesn't mean you were always that guy."

He sighed heavily and shuffled the papers in front of him. "I wouldn't say all settled down quite yet."

Something in the way he said that told me possibly things weren't all hearts and flowers with him and Solange, but that would have to wait for another time. At the moment, I had to figure out who this mystery man of Amy's was.

"I'm sorry I thought it was you, Derek. I need to go find Alex and see if he had a better theory."

I spun around, and as I began walking toward the door, he said, "I know my memory of her is her lying on the ground with a knife sticking out of her chest, but if I remember correctly, she had an innocent girl look to her. Not really my taste, but I bet it would be Craig's."

Stopping dead, I looked back at him as all of Craig's nervousness from the moment this case began played out in my mind. Had he been worried about us finding out about him dating Amy this whole time? Was that why he seemed to be such a mess instead of because it was his first big case?

"Then again, I don't think Craig would ever cheat on his wife, so that might be a dead end," Derek said with a shrug.

Just then, Alex came into the office and stopped as he bumped into me. "Derek, I think we have an issue."

Derek motioned toward the door. "If it's about witches, I think this might be something we want to discuss in private."

Alex closed it and said, "No, it's not about witches. I'd like to see the duty rosters from late December and January."

"Oh that. Poppy told me one of us was dating the victim. Since we know it wasn't either of us now, who are we thinking about?"

The two of us looked at one another, and I waited for Alex to say a name. Instead, he hedged and answered, "I'd prefer to wait until those duty rosters tell us who was on the schedule during those times. We know the officer went out to answer a call at the Third Eye Center sometime after the holidays."

Derek listened to Alex's explanation and then nodded. "I think that means I need to take a look at the record of that call. Give me a few minutes. I'll meet you in your office when I find out what I need to know."

Alex and I filed out of Derek's office and silently headed down the hall to his. He closed the door behind us and said quietly as I sat down, "Why did you go to Derek instead of coming with me?"

Sheepishly, I admitted my blunder. "I thought he might be the officer Amy was dating."

His eyebrows shot up into his forehead. "Really?"

"I know. I know. It sounds stupid now, but I figured

since she was a beautiful woman and Derek has been known to be a bit of a hound in town, he seemed like the logical choice. I guess in hindsight it wasn't very logical at all. You don't have to tell me about how bad it is that I jump to conclusions. Derek already chastised me about it. I got it."

"You just marched right into his office and accused him of knowing a victim he saw lying dead last night as if he wouldn't have told anyone?"

"Well, when you say it like that with that disbelief written all over your face, it makes it seem crazy."

Alex smiled and shook his head. "You're lucky he likes you, Poppy. If any of us did that, he'd chew us out and then give us overnight duty until the end of time."

I knew what he said was the truth. Derek let me get away with things I doubted he'd let another human being do without lowering the boom on them. Knowing someone since childhood had its benefits. That I took advantage of that didn't escape me.

"He can't give me overnight shifts. I'm not one of his cops," I said with a chuckle. "The worst he can do is yell, but Derek doesn't like doing that with me."

"The worst he can do is to forbid us from working together. I think you forget that, Poppy. One of these days he just might do that."

Alex was right. I knew it, but I sometimes forgot in my enthusiasm for the cases we worked on how much power Derek held over us and my working with the police.

Eager to change the subject, I asked my partner what I'd been dying to know since he showed up in his chief's office a few minutes before. "So where did you go when I went in to talk to Derek? Who do you think

Amy's boyfriend was?"

The door opened before he could answer. "I think I'll let the boss tell us who it is."

Derek closed the door behind him and sat down heavily in the seat next to me. "This isn't good. Why wouldn't he have spoken up and said he knew the victim?"

He and Alex exchanged glances, making me realize I was the only one in the room who didn't know who he was talking about. I waited for a few more seconds for someone to finally spill the beans before I asked, "Who?"

"Stephen," Derek said in a low voice barely above a whisper. "He was the cop who went out on that call to the new age place outside of town."

"Seriously? He dated Amy and he didn't mention that to anyone after being one of the two officers called out to the scene of her murder?" I asked, shocked that my nemesis had stepped out of line in such an incredibly unethical fashion.

It didn't escape me that he had disliked having me around since the first time I met him, right after the holidays. Maybe he didn't like having someone working on cases who spent half her time working for the newspaper. He may have thought I'd dig up his secret.

But who would have cared if he was dating Amy Perkins? She was an upstanding citizen in town and had never been in trouble with the law. She was beautiful and charming. Or was it because she was a witch that he wanted to hide his relationship with her?

My brain spun with thoughts about Stephen's behavior since the case had begun. Looking across the desk at Alex, I said, "Maybe that's why he wanted to make sure we were kept investigating anything but her personal life. While we spend our time talking to witches, going to tarot conventions, and heading to the Charming Bakery to talk to people and ask if Amy had any enemies, he made sure anyone who might be able to point him out as Amy's ex was interviewed by him."

"Don't jump to any conclusions, Poppy. We don't know anything other than one of Amy's friends claims she was dating an officer and Stephen seems to fit the description since he was the one who went out on the Third Eye Center call," Alex said in his very measured voice.

"It's not jumping to conclusions. Why would Crystal Sendona lie about a thing like that? And if it's him, that would explain why he left Craig behind when he went out to speak to Amy's family and her boyfriend after making sure you and I got nowhere close to them. If her family knew they dated, he wouldn't be able to keep that a secret with the two of us hanging around."

Derek sighed and let out an uncomfortable groan. "It does seem strange that he didn't want Craig to go with him, especially since it's his first major case and he's supposed to be learning from Stephen."

"I just don't think we should draw any conclusions before he explains himself," Alex said, quickly becoming the only person in the room who didn't think Stephen was up to something odd.

"I'm going to have to talk to him about this. You said he was out talking to Amy's family and her boyfriend? When does Craig expect him back?"

Alex looked down at his watch. "I talked to him when we got here and he said he thought he'd be back before one. It's about one o'clock now."

"Well, you two go see what you can find out at

Amy's workplace while I handle this matter," Derek said seriously. "When you get through with that, we'll know better how things are going to move on from here."

He stood up and silently walked out of the office, his shoulders slumped. Derek didn't have much experience dealing with things like this. Very few people in Sunset Ridge did. The police department was the embodiment of a small town organization. Everyone knew everyone, or at least we all thought we knew everyone pretty well in town.

Seemed we didn't.

Now he'd have to confront one of his own and Stephen, nonetheless. Of all the officers he had to deal with, he was the most antagonistic. Although I was the one who was usually on the receiving end of his rudeness, more than once he'd been difficult with his fellow officers and even the receptionist, and every time, Derek had deferred the problem to whoever had been disrespected.

Alex rose from his chair and motioned for me to join him. "Let's go. I don't think having us here is going to be helpful to Derek."

He hurried out of the building so fast that I had to jog to catch up to him. I did just as he reached the car parked out front and grabbed his arm to stop him. Alex turned to look at me and pointed toward the other side of the car.

"You're practically running away. What's going on here? Why do we have to leave so quickly? We did nothing wrong."

"Just get in the car, Poppy."

The concern in his eyes confused me. Why did we have to flee like guilty people?

I did as he said to and barely got the door closed before he pulled away from the curb. He remained silent, not explaining anything about his strange behavior and making me wonder what had happened to him. Alex wasn't the type of man to run away from a fight. He didn't go looking for problems, but he didn't shy away from dealing with issues when they came up either.

Nothing about this felt right.

Finally, when it became apparent he had no idea where Charming Cakes Bakery was located, I asked, "Do you plan to ask me how to get to Amy's workplace since it seems you don't plan to tell me what the hell all that was about?"

Alex winced and glanced over at me. "Poppy, we needed to get out of there because as of the moment Derek found out Stephen may have had a relationship with the victim, I became the lead officer on the case. I didn't want to run into Stephen and possibly get into a conversation about the case with him, so I got us out of there."

"I don't understand. Derek will just take him off the case. So what? He's probably going to give him a hard time, but if he was dating Amy at some point, he shouldn't investigate her death when there's another officer who can do it. Namely, you."

He turned the corner off Main Street and pulled the car into the first open spot on Foreman Street. Jamming the shifter into park, he turned in the driver's seat to face me, his face more serious than I'd ever seen it.

"You're not seeing the bigger problem, Poppy. I haven't had a chance to speak to the person who called in the crime. I only have his word that someone found her. What if that isn't true? What if in addition to lying about even knowing the victim, he lied about that too? I have no idea if he and Craig were together all night before that call came in."

What Alex was saying didn't sink in for a moment. What did he mean?

Then it dawned on me. What he meant was perhaps Stephen had played a part in her death.

"Oh, my God! Are you saying you think he may be a suspect?" I asked, stunned that I could even be saying that. I disliked Stephen, but I never thought he could murder someone.

"I don't know," he said in that somber voice he used whenever something truly upset him. "I don't know anything about this, but I thought it would be better to be careful. I have no idea what his relationship with Amy was. I don't know why it ended or if it ended amicably. All I know is if he was dating her, they were keeping it a secret and he omitted telling anyone he knew her when he saw she was a murder victim last night."

"What's going to happen, Alex? I don't think Derek has ever had to deal with anything like this. I doubt if the Sunset Ridge police force has ever had this problem. I mean, sure, everyone knows everyone in town, so many times you guys are investigating crimes that involve people you know from seeing them on the street or in the grocery store, but that's completely different than this. This isn't the possibility that one of our neighbors ran a red light or got into a fight with the person next door. He may have been in a relationship with someone who was murdered, and even worse, he may have had something to do with it."

Alex touched my hand and squeezed it gently. "I don't know, Poppy. For now, we just have to focus on our part of the investigation until we hear differently from Derek. We'll go to this Charming Cakes place and do what we always do, even if all that happens is we find out Amy was a cake decorator everyone loved and she didn't have an enemy at all at work."

"You know, I've never liked him ever since that first night I met him, but that was just because he was so rude to me. I never imagined anything like this could happen with him, though. I just hoped he'd stop being such a jerk to me so we could all exist in peace."

Alex squeezed my hand again and leaned over to kiss me softly on the cheek. "I know. Let's get going and see what we can find out about Amy at her work. Who knows? Maybe some disgruntled cake decorator who's always been jealous of her ability to make those icing flowers will confess and this entire case will be sewn up by the end of the day."

As he drove up Foreman Street, I gave him the directions to Charming Cakes Bakery and hoped we could wrap up this case today. I didn't like Stephen, but I hated seeing Alex so worried about the Sunset Ridge police. More than just fellow officers, they were his family in many ways, and I knew the idea that one of them could be guilty of a crime like this had shaken him.

Chapter Eleven

W E PULLED UP to the Charming Cakes Bakery building, and I saw Alex had clearly been expecting something else. Facing us was the vine-covered façade of what looked like an old and abandoned manufacturing plant, but the Charming bakery was actually more like a factory on one side and a storefront on the other. Whatever he had been prepared to see, Alex arched a curious eyebrow and then turned toward me.

"So this is where they make the best cakes?" he asked in a tone of disbelief.

"I know it looks like a run-down place, but give it a chance."

He shrugged and turned off the ignition. "I don't have to like how it looks. I just figured I'd see a different kind of place when I drove up."

"Don't judge a book by its cover," I admonished him, sure he had already made up his mind not to ever try a Charming cake.

Alex didn't respond to my teasing and simply got out of the car. I pointed toward the storefront and said, "I think we should start with the finished product. That's what Amy's job was, so it seems logical."

As we walked toward the glass front doors of the bakery shop, he mumbled, "Nothing about this case seems logical."

To him, that would be true. Alex spent his time believing in a few principles of life, and one of those things was that the men and women he worked with on the police force did good things. They worked hard to make sure the citizens of Sunset Ridge were protected, whether that meant answering nightly phone calls from one of them who simply couldn't abide by someone parking in front of her house, even if it was a perfectly legal thing to do, or solving the murder of one of their neighbors.

But Stephen's dishonesty had thrown that principle into chaos, and for Alex, nothing could be worse. The foundation of his life rested on being a cop, but now that foundation had been shaken by the revelation that one of their own had betrayed what they all believed in.

I wanted to make him feel better, to make him see that Stephen's behavior meant nothing compared to all the good he and every other officer did for our town every day. I just didn't know how to, and so far, nothing I'd said had done much to help.

He held the door open for me and we walked into the most delicious smelling place I'd ever been. If they sold coffee, I may have thought it was heaven right here on earth. The intoxicating scent of sugar and spices filled the air surrounding us, making me want to devour one of Charming Cake's famous delicacies.

I stood there inhaling deeply and closed my eyes to revel in the yumminess. I felt Alex push on my upper arm and heard him say, "You okay, Poppy?"

Opening my eyes, I took another deep breath and

nodded. "I just love the smell of this place."

"I can tell by the smile on your face. I don't think I've ever seen you this happy because of food."

Clearly, he didn't understand the love of a woman for her baked goods. "Food? It's not food. It's more like the ambrosia the gods on Olympus ate. To call it food is to diminish its deliciousness."

My effusive love for the wondrous delights of Charming Cakes made him chuckle. "And to think I thought you loved that muffin."

A middle-aged woman wearing white pants and a t-shirt and a hairnet over her short blond bob came out through a door that led to the factory and stood behind the glass display cases filled with freshly made Charming treats. "Can I help you two?" she asked sweetly, likely already knowing the answer by the way I was eyeing up the cupcakes and eclairs in front of her.

Since we were there on police business, I tried to stop myself from practically drooling and Alex answered her with a flash of his badge. "My name is Alex Montero and this is my partner Poppy McGuire. We'd like to speak to the owner."

"I'm sorry, but the owner isn't here. There is a shift supervisor on, though. I can get him for you."

"That would be great. Thank you," Alex said as he peered over at the door to the factory.

The woman hurried to get the supervisor as I stood gazing longingly at the goodies in the cases and wondered how anyone could work at a place like this and not eat their weight in sugary goodies every week. I thought about how fit Amy Perkins had been and didn't know how she managed to keep in such good shape working here.

Maybe something in being a Druid kept her thin.

"I swear, I don't think I've ever seen you so quiet," Alex said, breaking into my thoughts.

"Well, now you know what to get me for my birthday and every gift-giving holiday from this point on," I said with a smile, only half-joking.

As the woman returned through the factory door, he said quietly, "I'll keep that in mind."

She waved us around to her side of the counter. "If you'll come with me, I'll take you to Mr. Dixon. Please follow me."

We did as she instructed and found ourselves not in a factory but a room that resembled a kitchen, just the biggest kitchen I'd ever seen. Large cabinets with stainless steel countertops ran in three rows with space between them for workers. Ovens lined the two shorter walls, with racks taking up the one longer wall and what looked like large stainless steel boxes taking up the other long wall. Eight workers all dressed in white from head to toe like the woman who had brought us back stood at each countertop finishing cakes and pastries with frosting and other tasty touches.

A slightly overweight man with thinning brown hair and glasses approached us wearing a pale blue short-sleeved dress shirt and brown dress pants covered in flour handprints. Smiling broadly so his full cheeks puffed out, he wiped his palms on his thighs and extended his right hand to shake ours.

"I'm Walter Dixon. Officer Montero, I hope nothing's wrong to bring you here."

"I'm afraid there is, Mr. Dixon. Is there somewhere the three of us could talk in private?" Alex said in his serious way that instantly frightened the bakery supervisor enough to make his smile slide from his face.

"Yes, yes, of course. Please follow me," he said as he quickly led us to an office right off the kitchen area.

Closing the door behind us, he sat down in a chair at a round table and looked up in terror at us. Had he been that close to Amy? But the absolute fear in his eyes didn't make sense after the cheery greeting he'd given us just a minute before. Maybe he had something to hide.

"What's wrong, Mr. Dixon?" Alex asked as he took his pad and pen out of his pocket.

He stretched his mouth wide and tried to look relaxed, but the action only had the effect of making him look like he was in pain. "It's my ex-wife, isn't it? She told me she'd call the cops when I didn't get all of my things out of the house by Wednesday. I just didn't have the time to rent a truck. I do plan to get everything out of there as soon as I can. If you can just give me a couple more days, I swear, I'll get it all out and she can have the place all to herself."

I looked over at Alex and saw the briefest hint of disgust in his expression. That Mr. Dixon thought we were there to make him remove the rest of his junk from his former house was ridiculous. As if the police routinely helped exes out in their desire to rid themselves from their former spouses.

"That's not why we're here, sir. An employee of yours was found dead last night, and we need to ask you some questions about her."

As soon as the words left Alex's mouth, Walter Dixon jumped up from his chair, shaking his head frantically. "Dead? Who?"

"Amy Perkins. We were told she was employed here as a cake decorator. What can you tell us about her working here?" he asked.

Walter Dixon's shoulders sagged, as if the news he'd just heard about one of his workers depressed him greatly. "Oh, Amy. What happened? She was one of my best decorators."

"She was murdered, sir. Found out in the woods outside of town near Miller Road."

He slid his finger up under his eye to wipe away a tear and then adjusted his glasses. "Murdered? Oh, my God. This is terrible."

"Anything you can tell us about her would be helpful, Mr. Dixon."

"Amy was a wonderful person to work with. She kept to herself and didn't get involved in the spats that often happen with the other workers. She never missed her shift, and she made cakes everyone said were the best looking cakes they'd ever seen. I can honestly say she was one of my favorite employees."

Alex jotted a few notes as the man spoke, so I asked, "Can you think of any reason anyone would want to hurt Amy?"

Without giving it a second's thought, he shook his head. "No. She never bothered a soul here."

"Did anyone have any issues with her being a Druid?" Alex asked.

The supervisor's eyes flew open wide. "A what?"

Alex smiled and turned to look at me as if to say I could have the pleasure to getting into a religious discussion with the man. As he watched, I explained, "A Druid is a type of pagan. Amy considered herself a Druid. She tended to keep it private, though, so it's possible her co-workers wouldn't have known."

"I didn't know, but that doesn't necessarily mean

anything. No one ever complained about Amy for anything, though. I was actually the person who hired her four years ago when I was the HR person."

"Do you know why she chose to leave the health services field since she had a degree in that?" Alex asked as he jotted down the words DIDN'T TELL COWORKERS ABOUT BEING A DRUID in his notes.

"No, I have no idea. She never mentioned a reason why. I was just happy to have her after I saw how talented she was decorating cakes. I was happy to give her all the hours I could."

"Was she close to any of her fellow workers?" I asked, hoping Amy had confided in at least one person in her time at Charming Cakes.

Walter nodded. "There is one person I used to see her take breaks with. Her name is Marie Dondel. She's also a cake decorator. I can get her for you, if you like."

Alex didn't answer him, so I said, "Thank you. That would be wonderful. Can we speak to her in here so we can have privacy?"

"Yes, of course. I'll go get her right now."

As Walter Dixon ran out to the kitchen area to get Amy's only friend at Charming Cakes, Alex continued to write notes in his pad. Leaning over, I watched him put down KEPT TO HERSELF—LONER AT WORK.

"I hope Marie can give us a clue as to what Amy was doing for the past few weeks since she stopped attending those Tuesday night witches' circle meetings," I whispered when he finished his notes.

"Maybe she had to work Tuesdays. Or maybe all she did was hang out with her boyfriend, who I want to go see right after this."

Leaning away from him, I smiled. "That's a lot of

time with one person. Even you and I don't spend that much time together."

He didn't have time to say anything in return because at that moment, Walter Dixon ushered Marie Dondel into the room and we got to see the only person Amy had spent any time with at work.

The first thing I noticed about Marie was how brown her eyes were, probably because she stared so wide-eyed with a look of pure sadness in them. At any moment, she appeared on the verge of breaking into tears. Her dark hair hung in tight curls that bounced every time she moved her head. Thin like Amy, she clearly didn't overindulge on the treats they made either.

"I'll leave you alone," Walter Dixon said. "If there's anything I can do, please let me know, Officer Montero."

Once we were alone with Marie, she sat down and quietly began to sob, covering her face with her hands. "I can't believe this happened. Amy would never hurt a fly."

"Miss Dondel, is there anything you can tell us that may help us find who did this to your friend?" Alex asked as he sat down in a chair across from her.

She wiped the tears from her cheeks and took a deep breath before letting it out in a huge sigh. "Walter mentioned about her being a Druid. Do you think that had anything to do with it?"

"We don't know. We know she kept her religious beliefs private, so there might be something else that led to her death."

"Amy and I were close work friends. I knew Amy was into something different religiously, but she never brought that into our friendship. We went out a couple times over the years, but Amy usually had a boyfriend so she spent time with whoever she was seeing at the time."

I watched Alex's eyes light up at the mention of Amy's boyfriend. Hopefully, Marie would know something about him that we could take into our interview with him right after this.

"What can you tell us about the man she was dating?" he asked, holding his pen over the notepad, poised and ready to write whatever she said.

"Amy was very private about her personal life. I do know the guy she's been dating for the past three months is named Kellen Martin. I never met him, but I had a feeling that Amy wasn't exactly happy."

Alex jumped on that statement. "Why would you say that?"

"I don't know. She never seemed really thrilled when she mentioned that they did something together. I got the feeling he was controlling. One time she said she really wanted to go see some movie and he didn't want to go, so they didn't go. Sounded controlling to me, but I could be wrong."

The sadness in Marie's voice as she spoke about her friend made me wish I had gotten to know Amy better. She sounded like a great person to be around.

"What about any previous boyfriends? Do you know any of their names?" I asked.

"She never really talked about the men she dated. Other than Kellen, I never got the sense that any of them were very important in her life, though. She just liked to have fun. She was young, so that was okay."

I didn't want Marie to think we were judging her friend, so I quickly nodded and said, "Of course. We're just looking for any clues that can help us find who did this. Often, former boyfriends are likely suspects."

"No one stands out in my memory. I'm sorry. Amy wasn't the type of person anyone would want to hurt. At least, it never seemed like she was. She was fun-loving and sweet, and because of that, she hadn't really settled down until recently with Kellen."

"Is there anything else you can tell us about anyone here who might have wanted to harm her or anything about her boyfriend?" I asked, hoping for anything to give us a direction on who would have wanted Amy dead.

Marie shook her head slowly. "I wish I could, but other than Kellen, I didn't really know much about Marie's private life. The only reason I knew about him was I happened to see him waiting for her one night after work."

Alex looked up from his notes. "Was she supposed to work last night?"

"No. We both had last night off. Last night and this Sunday," Marie said quietly. "I wish I had suggested we do something together last night, but we weren't really like that. I guess you could say we were only work friends. I wish we'd been more."

Marie began to cry again, so I gently patted her on the shoulder hoping to give her some measure of comfort. "Thank you for helping us."

She stood to leave and sniffled. "Please get whoever did this. Amy didn't deserve anything like being murdered."

"We will do our best, Miss Dondel. Thank you for your help," Alex said with a sympathetic smile. "If you think of anything else, please call the Sunset Ridge police department."

After she left, I sat down in the chair, exhausted by everything we'd heard so far. Amy had been a good friend, a good worker, a good person, overall. So why had someone taken her life and left her lying there in the woods with a knife buried in her chest?"

"You okay, Poppy? You look depressed."

I lifted my head and saw Alex staring down at me with concern in his eyes. "I'm okay. I guess it's just this case. More and more, it's looking like the only thing anyone could hold against Amy was her being different because she was a Druid. I hate the idea of someone in Sunset Ridge being a bigot like that and killing her for believing in something they didn't."

"It might not be that," he said, trying to be understanding.

I knew he didn't see our small town in the way I did. He often thought I had rose-colored glasses on concerning the people in our town and what they did. Even after all the gossip I'd had spread about me, I still saw my neighbors in Sunset Ridge as good people.

"We still need to speak to Amy's boyfriend. We might find that her beliefs had nothing to do with what happened. It might be a simple case of love gone wrong."

Standing up, I tapped my fingertip on that notepad in his hand. "You better write something else down. First time Alex jumped to a conclusion." I looked up at him and smiled. "This is a red-letter day."

Unfazed by my teasing, he stuffed the notepad and pen back into his pocket and slid his arm around me. "Time to go, Miss McGuire. Comedy hour is over. We have a potential suspect to interview. First I want to check back at the station, but then we'll go see him."

As we rode back there, I thought about how compartmentalized Amy's life had been. "Alex, did you notice how Marie had no idea of who Amy really was. She didn't know about the Druidism really, and I don't think she had any idea she dated women at times."

"The murder of a more public person is far easier to investigate. Private people are, by their nature, hiding things, whether it's for some particular reason or just because it's who they are."

"Well, if it happened to me, it would probably be way easier than this case. I'm an open book. You, on the other hand, are like Amy. Your murder would probably remain an unsolved case forever because you keep to yourself so much."

Alex parked the car in front of the police station and turned to face me. "No, it wouldn't. You'd find out who did it. I know you, Poppy. You wouldn't leave any stone unturned. No chance of an unsolved case."

Knowing how bad this day had been for him, I leaned in and kissed him softly on the lips, even though I knew we were supposed to remain completely professional at all times when we were working on a case. He didn't pull away, though, and in his dark eyes as he looked at me, I saw he needed that small gesture of love.

I wanted to hold his hand as we walked toward the building, sure it would help him, but no sooner had we gotten out of the car Stephen came storming out the front door and walked directly at us, his face red with anger.

Pointing at Alex, he marched up to him and stopped just before the tip of his finger hit his chest. "Whatever you think, you're wrong. I'm a lot of things, but I'm not a murderer."

I wanted to tell him how Alex could never be someone who jumped to that conclusion. That his lying had been what made believing in him impossible.

But I said nothing, and Alex simply stood toe-to-toe with Stephen staring him down as he grew angrier and angrier by the moment.

Finally, Stephen lost his temper and barked, "Maybe if you didn't let your good cop instincts get clouded by what you feel for her, you would have seen that!"

Looking down, I saw Alex's hand curl into a tight fist and felt his rage radiate off him. Stephen had insulted me, but even more, he'd insulted Alex on the foundation of who he was.

And that he wouldn't take lying down.

Chapter Twelve

I RUSHED OVER to him just as he cocked his arm back to hit Stephen. I'd never seen Alex this angry before, and I knew when he cooled down that he'd regret it if he went through with doing this.

Grabbing his arm, I pleaded with him. "Alex, don't! Just let it go. Please, let it go."

He didn't lower his arm, not even flinching as I begged him not to hit him. His fist shook from anger as he stared straight ahead, almost looking through Stephen, who glared at me.

"Get the hell away from us," Alex said in a terrifying voice through gritted teeth. "I won't tell you twice."

Stephen turned his attention to face him, and for a long moment, the two men faced off with Alex still ready to hit him and Stephen angrily staring out from between slits for eyes. I didn't know what would happen next, but then he simply stormed away, leaving me standing there with my hands on Alex's bicep still shaking from how furious he was.

"Oh, my God!" I said quietly as he slowly lowered his hand still balled into a tight fist to his side.

Alex said nothing and walked away to go inside the police station. I watched him and knew by the stiffness of his body that every cell inside him still wanted to pound Stephen right in that nasty mouth of his.

I leaned against the car as my legs began to buckle from the reality of what had just happened. Looking up and down the sidewalk, I saw no one had stopped and seen their confrontation, thankfully. Things were strained enough with the police department. The last thing they needed was townspeople complaining about their officers brawling in the street.

Stephen still stomped down Main Street, and I thought about telling him how wrong he was myself. Alex hadn't been influenced by me concerning anything about him. If he had, he would have threatened to beat the snot out of him months ago. How dare he accuse an officer like Alex of being blinded by anything.

In truth, I'd often wanted Alex to do more about the problem Stephen had with me, but he always kept his distance, preferring to remain professional. If that fool thought just because we dated that I'd convinced Alex that he was a murderer, he was even dumber than I thought.

A hundred things I wanted to say to him ran through my head, but what was the use? He wouldn't listen to me or anything I had to say. As I got angrier by the moment about how insulting Stephen had been, I felt my temperature begin to rise. As Alex often said, my Irish began to show itself.

In the moment, I'd forgotten all about the stifling heat, but now as I stood collecting my thoughts after the incident, sweat began to drip down from my scalp. If I spent any more time out in the scorching temperatures, I might melt into the sidewalk, so I hurried inside to find Alex.

Hopefully, the air conditioning had helped him cool down by the time I caught up with him.

I made a beeline to Alex's office and found him talking to Derek, the two of them long-faced and serious. The chief left immediately without saying a word to me, and I wondered if that was because this problem with Stephen had gotten to a point that it meant that the arrangement allowing me to investigate crimes would have to end.

Worried that had already happened, I sat down in my usual seat in front of Alex's desk and looked over at him still wearing that expression that made my stomach knot. "Are you okay?"

Alex's face looked like pure anguish and I wanted to make him feel better, but he merely nodded and said in a low voice, "I'm the lead officer on the case now."

Ordinarily, this would be a reason to congratulate him, but I knew that wasn't the case now. Before I could say anything, he picked up the phone and called Craig to tell him he needed to speak to him and please come to his office.

He hung up, and I finally asked, "What happened out there?"

Drawing his eyebrows in, he frowned but pressed his lips together as if to stop himself from talking. I knew Alex well enough to understand how much this whole thing bothered him. If only there was a way to get him to talk.

While I tried to think of something to say, Craig showed up and knocked on the Alex's door. "What's up?" he asked in a forced chipper voice.

Alex held out his arm toward me and pressed a smile on his face. "Take a seat, Craig."

The junior officer did as he was told and looked over at me with such fear in his eyes that I thought he might break down at any minute. I didn't know if he had heard about what just happened between his former partner and his new partner or if he was just terrified about this whole thing of being promoted to more than traffic control.

Far more sternly than I knew he intended, Alex began explaining what we would do from now on with the case. "You'll be working with Poppy and me from now on, so here's a rundown of what we know so far. Tamara Ridgeway out at the Third Eye Mind and Body Center seemed to have an issue with our victim because she wouldn't say she was a witch. We spoke to three other witches at the tarot convention in Caston this morning who knew Amy Perkins because they attended meetings with her every Tuesday until last month at the Third Eye Center. Poppy will clue you in on all we learned. A friend of Amy's named Crystal Sendona was the one who clued us into Stephen being an ex-boyfriend Amy used to see."

Alex took a deep breath after that last part of his speech and looked away for a moment before continuing. "Finally, we spoke to a co-worker of Amy's named Marie Dondel who seemed to think there might be some problems between Amy and her current boyfriend, a guy named Kellen Martin. That's what we have so far. Poppy will give you all the details, and we'll meet up again here in my office in an hour."

Poor Craig had begun writing down everything Alex was saying just about the time he mentioned the tarot readers convention, but his attempt was futile. No matter how feverishly he moved the pen across the piece of paper he took from his shirt pocket, Alex simply spoke too fast. Even the pause after mentioning Stephen's part in the case didn't help Craig, so by the time Alex had finished speaking, all he'd gotten down were some badly misspelled versions of the names and the words *tarro cards*.

I sensed Alex wanted to be left alone for the hour, so I nudged Craig's arm as he tried to write and said, "Hey, it's okay. We'll hash it all out and you'll have a chance to get it all down."

Craig slumped down in his seat and shook his head. "I can't believe Stephen lied to all of us. I mean, I get why he lied to me, but you and the chief, Alex?"

Alex said nothing, but I didn't want Craig to go on thinking any of it had been acceptable. "It's not okay that he lied to you either. Now you get to see how a real team works together."

"Thank you so much. I won't let you guys down. I swear."

Somber and still unhappy from what had happened outside, Alex said, "I don't know all of what Stephen found out, so I'm going to have to check that out now, but I want you to find out everything you can about the three witches from the tarot convention. Poppy will run it all down for you."

I got up and motioned for Craig to follow me. "Let's get a cup of coffee and talk over the case like we always do."

"Coffee? In this heat?" he asked, as if the heatwave should stop anyone from drinking the best drink in the world.

"Sure! How do you take your coffee?"

Quietly, Craig admitted a sorry truth. "I don't drink

coffee."

With a smile, I tugged on his arm to leave. "Well, we need to change that right now. Let's go to The Grounds and get you started on your caffeine addiction."

AFTER LETTING ME get him his first coffee, Craig grabbed a handful of creamers and sat down with me at the table Alex and I liked to refer to as ours. I watched him pour one after another creamer into his coffee until it looked like watered down chocolate milk in his cup.

"So you and Alex drink this all the time when you guys are working on a case?" Craig asked, hesitating as he lifted the coffee cup to his lips.

I lifted my cup of French Roast in the air as if to make a toast to one of mankind's greatest creations. "I have coffee from the minute I wake up in the morning. It's literally what keeps me going. I bet if a doctor drew blood these days, they'd find coffee in my veins."

My nectar of the gods tasted delicious as it hit my tongue, and I savored the flavor as I watched Craig gingerly take a tiny sip of his first ever coffee. "Alex drinks his black most of the time these days."

As he swallowed that sip, Craig grimaced. "Black? I can't even imagine. I'm having a hard time getting this down, and it's more cream than anything else. I guess I'm just not a coffee drinker."

"Oh, I don't buy that. Everyone is a coffee drinker. Some people just don't know it yet," I said with a smile.

He gave me a tepid smile I suspected was an indication of how this case made him feel more than his apparent dislike for my favorite drink. Craig deserved better than to be kept in the dark, as Stephen had done to him. I needed him to know that and how real partners treated one another.

"So now that we have our coffee, we can start talking about the case. Alex and I do this for every case. It helps to talk things out."

"You two are so great together. Even though you're complete opposites, you work together so well."

I took a drink of coffee and chuckled at how right Craig was. "Opposites is exactly right. I think he could go an entire day without saying a word, and you know me. I'm always talking. I'm a regular chatty Cathy."

He nodded and tilted his head, staring at me like he used to back in high school. "You've always been that way, but that's one of the reasons why everyone likes you. You have a way of making people feel comfortable around you."

"You're like that too, though, Craig. We're a lot alike. I think you're going to find that when you start talking to people in cases that you do fine."

He looked across the table at me, and I saw worry in his eyes. "I hope so."

Reaching over, I touched his hand, hoping to comfort him. "You have to believe in yourself. Trust me. You believe in you and others will too."

Craig looked down at where my fingers rested on his hand and then smiled up at me. "I always had a crush on you, but you knew that. I used to watch you when we were in high school."

What I knew was that Craig had always been staring at me with puppy dog eyes back then. I'd catch him near my locker, hanging around like he belonged there when his grade's lockers were a floor below in Sunset Ridge High School. Sometimes I'd see him at lunchtime giving me moony eyes from across the cafeteria. I never had to doubt what he thought of me. He was a younger boy who had a crush, and at that time, I didn't see him as anything but a boy.

However, now that he sat across from me in The Grounds about to discuss his first big case with the Sunset Ridge police department, Craig was all grown up. He wasn't just that boy with the big blue eyes who liked me anymore.

"I didn't have to be a detective to know that. You were pretty obvious with how much you liked me," I answered with respect for how sweet he'd always been, even back then when he was a teenage boy three years younger than me with romantic ideas.

His cheeks got pink from blushing. Looking down at his cup of coffee, he said, "You know, you were never rude or nasty to me, even though I was so much younger than you and always running around giving you googly eyes. You always gave me a smile, even though I was practically stalking you. I never thanked you for that, but it was a nice thing to do."

"I've always believed no matter what, if a person likes you and lets you know about it, you have a responsibility to be gracious. You were too young for me, but that didn't mean you didn't have feelings."

"I did, and I wore them right on my sleeve. Other girls would have had a field day with me, but you didn't. And then I found Katy and she didn't either, thank God."

Katy, the woman he married right after she turned twenty-one, was a petite girl two years younger than Craig when they met in his senior year of high school long after I'd graduated. She had big blue eyes just like his, and I imagined if they ever had any kids that they'd be the most adorable things ever with beautiful eyes just like the two of them. Unfortunately, fate hadn't decided to bless them with any children, despite the fact that they'd been married for years.

"Katy must be thrilled that you've been promoted."

"Well, she worries. You know how she is. I told her I couldn't stay as traffic officer forever, but she's concerned that working real cases will put me in danger."

I knew what he meant. My father had worried from the moment I began working with Alex. "As I told my father, this is Sunset Ridge. You'll be fine."

"I said that to her, but she said a murder case is a murder case, no matter where you are."

"Well, tell her not to worry because you're working with Alex and me now, and we watch out for our partners."

Craig fell quiet, and I sensed he was more worried than he wanted to let on. "I'm serious. We take care of one another, and that includes you now. You're partners with us, Craig."

"I just don't want to let you two down. I know you'd be okay with me, but Alex is so serious, and I'd hate to fail on the very first case I get," he said with a deep frown etching into his handsome features.

"No way. You and I are going to talk about the facts of the case, and when we're done here, you're going to know exactly as much as I know about the case. Trust me. Alex doesn't expect anything but your best. That's all he looks for in people."

Craig's shoulders relaxed. "You really do look up to him, don't you?"

Without even thinking of how to answer, I said, "I do. He's so intelligent and cares so much about right and wrong and the truth. I find that so incredibly good. I mean, truly good."

"I see that. I want people to look up to me like that, Poppy. I want to do a good job starting with this case."

Putting my coffee down, I reached across the table and took his hands in mine. "Then let's get down to business."

Craig took a deep breath and nodded. "Okay. Alex said he wanted me to find out everything I could about the three witches? Are they real witches? Like witches from Halloween?"

I couldn't help but chuckle at the way he said that. He'd likely be disappointed by the reality of the three witches. No brooms. No pointy hats. Just different religious beliefs than others.

"No, not those kinds of witches. The three women we met at the tarot readers convention looked very much like me and you. Well, more me, but the point is, they looked perfectly normal, like anyone you'd see on the street. They just happen to believe in a goddess instead of the God Christians believe in and do spells and read tarot cards to tell the future."

"Is that for real? Can they really see into the future?" Craig asked, obviously curious about the idea of seeing into the future.

I shrugged, unsure what witches could actually do. "I don't know. I had my cards read this morning, though, and a lot of what the woman said made sense."

"Hmmm…"

"Let's get to the facts. First off, we spoke to three women there. The first was a woman named Susie

Mitchell. She spoke to Alex alone, and he said she had nothing to really say about the victim. The second woman was named Jerilyn Fox. She didn't know much about Amy because she didn't really know her, except from the witches' circle meetings every Tuesday at the Third Eye Center. She did say she heard Amy and Tamara Ridgeway, the woman from the Third Eye Center, fighting one time. She didn't know what they were fighting about."

"So we're thinking this Tamara Ridgeway is a suspect?"

"Good question. I would say yes. Alex tends not to make those kinds of pronouncements this early, though."

"Would he have a problem with me saying she was a suspect?" Craig asked, worry filling his eyes once again.

I quickly moved to quash that concern. Holding my hand up as if to stop any worry from festering, I shook my head. "No, don't worry about that. I proclaim people to be suspects way before Alex ever does. He likes hearing opposing views. He may not always agree with what I say, but he respects it."

Craig let himself smile and relaxed in his seat. "Oh, okay. I don't want to start out on the wrong foot with him."

Waving off his fears, I said, "Don't worry. It's all good."

I reached into my bag and dug out the pamphlet I picked up from Melody as I was leaving the tarot readers convention. Handing it to him, I said, "Now onto the third woman from the convention. Her name was Melody Chamberlain. She also was around when Tamara and Amy had an argument. So that's a second person who says she saw them fighting. Now, Tamara doesn't claim to be Amy's biggest fan, but she never mentioned this particular fight these other two women are talking about, so we're going to have to look into that."

Craig remained quiet for a moment and then said, "I noticed you didn't describe her like the first two. Is she a suspect?"

His picking up on that impressed me. "That's good. I don't know if I consider her one, but I can say that Alex asked her if she had an alibi for last night."

Leaning forward slightly, Craig looked at me like he couldn't wait to hear about that alibi. "Did she?"

"She did. She went to see a movie and says she was back home by eleven."

Instead of being deflated by her having a valid alibi, Craig moved on to another great question. "What was this fight everyone seems to be talking about? Do we know why Tamara and Amy fought?"

"I'm very impressed, Craig. That's a first-rate question. From what we've found out, Tamara and Amy had been dating before she began dating Stephen. When Tamara found out Amy was dating a cop, she told her that he would bring trouble to the Third Eye Center."

The mention of his former partner made his shoulders slump, like merely hearing his name deflated his enthusiasm. "I still can't believe he lied, Poppy. Is Stephen a suspect?"

That was the question, wasn't it? I had no idea how to answer it, though.

"I'm not sure, Craig. There's nothing so far to say that he was involved in Amy's murder, so I would say no right now."

"Do you have a favorite suspect?"

His question threw me a little. Normally, I would have no problem proclaiming which suspect stood out to me more than the others. But this whole Stephen thing made my thinking muddled.

"I don't have anyone in mind right now. I would say we shouldn't jump to conclusions."

He nodded his agreement, even as I knew it was pretty hypocritical of me to warn against jumping to conclusions since I routinely did just that. But the difference between Craig and me is that he needed to know how a real officer worked.

I knew I should act more like that too, though.

After I drank the last gulp of my coffee, I stood up from the table and said, "We better get back."

Craig tossed his nearly full cup of coffee in the garbage as we walked out of The Grounds, and as we crossed the street to the police station, I asked, "How was your first coffee?"

He smiled and said, "I feel as jumpy as a cat on a hot tin roof, but maybe that's because I'm on my first official case."

Poor guy. He barely took three sips of his watered down coffee and already he felt jumpy from the caffeine.

I looked at him and gave him my best supportive smile. "You'll be fine with the coffee drinking and the investigating. I believe it and so should you."

"Thanks, Poppy. I hope you're right."

He didn't have to hope. Craig may have spent nearly all his time on the Sunset Ridge police force as the traffic cop and the officer responsible for crowd control, but things had changed. He'd do fine, and I knew Alex would make sure to show him the ropes the right way, like a fellow officer should.

Chapter Thirteen

W E GOT BACK to Alex's office in time to hear him talking on the phone with Donny. I'd hoped in the nearly hour we were gone that his mood would have improved, but if his tense expression was any indication, things had only gotten worse, not better.

I listened as he asked Donny, "Are you sure of that time? This isn't something you might be off a couple hours with?"

As he heard the coroner's answer, his somber face morphed into one that told anyone seeing him that the news wasn't good. This case was going to make those worry lines between his eyebrows permanent.

Alex frowned and mumbled, "Okay. Call me if you get anything new."

With that, he hung up the phone and sighed like he had the weight of the world on his shoulders. He didn't seem to notice Craig or me standing in front of him for a moment, but when he did, he pressed a smile onto his lips that fooled nobody.

"Craig, after you find out everything you can about those tarot reading witches, text me with what each one of them was doing between eight and ten last night. Make sure you take notes on everything."

"Oh, oh, okay," Craig stammered out, suddenly nervous again.

I leaned in next to him and whispered, "It's okay. Remember, you just have to believe in yourself. You've got good instincts. Trust me."

His big blue eyes filled with worry, and he looked away toward the floor. "I will. I promise."

But he didn't look like he had an ounce of belief in himself. He looked as if he'd just been told by his idol that he was a bumbling idiot.

I looked over at Alex, who seemed confused by Craig's sudden insecurity, and mouthed, "Say something."

Not that my partner looked like he could cheer anyone up. Alex's expression resembled one a mourner wore at the funeral of a dear friend.

But he nodded and in his cheeriest tone asked, "Everything okay, Craig?"

He didn't answer and looked like he wanted to say something but couldn't find the words, so I asked, "Is something wrong? If you have any questions, trust me. Alex doesn't mind. You could never ask as many as I do."

My attempt at being self-effacing barely brought out a tiny smile from him. Something was definitely wrong, but what could have changed between our talk at the coffee shop and now?

"What's up, Craig?" Alex asked.

Craig didn't say anything for a moment, but then he said, "Stephen and I were on duty last night, you know. We were pretty much just hanging around the station here for most of the shift. I spent most of the time looking at Sports Illustrated and he was on the computer nearly the whole time."

Alex and I exchanged looks. Where was he going with this?

Then he continued. "At about nine o'clock, he said he was going to check something out about Mrs. Henderson's complaint about someone parking in front of her house every night. You know how she calls every single night and demands that we do something about it?"

Alex nodded and smiled at him. "I'm sure Mrs. Henderson liked that."

Shifting from one foot to the other, Craig said, "Yeah, I'm sure she did. But here's the thing. He was gone until right before the call came in about Amy Perkins' body being found out in the woods outside of town."

Now I understood. Craig was worried that Stephen had something to do with the crime. I looked over toward Alex expecting him to tell Craig that the times probably didn't work out, but he said nothing like that. Instead, he merely looked at him and nodded.

"I'll keep that in mind, Craig. Make sure you get the information on those three women and message me when you do, okay?"

Craig nodded in return but still looked upset. "Okay."

He immediately left, and I sat down and leaned over Alex's desk. "You didn't say anything when Craig mentioned Stephen being gone for that time. Why?"

In a low voice, Alex said, "Because Donny says he can put the time of death between eight and ten last night."

I practically fell into the seat next to me. "Is this really happening? Is Stephen really a suspect in Amy

Perkins' murder?"

"We need to go through every possible suspect in this case. Other than Stephen, I'm counting Tamara as a suspect. Hell hath no fury like a woman scorned seems to fit the bill with her."

"I think she's permanently scorned, Alex. I don't know if I was thinking of her as a suspect, though. Other than that, I think we need to speak to Amy's current boyfriend, Kellen."

Alex jumped at the chance to go do just that. "There's no time like the present. Let's get going and see what we can find out from him."

He didn't even wait for me before bolting out of the office, so I ran to catch up to him again. When I finally reached him, I said, "You know, I admit I probably need more exercise, but this constantly making me run to catch up with you today is wearing me out. Maybe we could do this a couple times a day and be good with that?"

Alex stopped at the car and hung his head before letting out a huge sigh. "I'm sorry, Poppy. I guess I'm stuck in my own head right now."

I hated seeing him like this. I reached out and touched him on the arm. "I know how much this is bothering you. It's bothering me too. For as much as I disliked him, I never wanted anything like this to happen. I'm sure we'll find out he had nothing to do with the case, Alex."

"I hope so. It doesn't look good now. He's been suspended until the case is solved. Derek is dealing with the town council and the mayor, and the entire force looks bad. They think we should hand this over to the state police. They don't even believe in us because of this. I need to get this case solved fast."

"We," I said, correcting him. "We have to get this case solved fast."

A look of pain crossed his face and settled into his eyes. "I'm worried it's only a matter of time before they say you can't do this with me anymore. Everything's a mess right now."

The idea of the council forcing me to stop working with Alex sent a stab of fear through me. I wasn't a cop, so they'd have every right to, but I loved working with Alex on cases.

"Well, they haven't done that yet, so let's get this case solved and show them there's no reason to."

A smile brightened his glum expression. "There's that Irish stubbornness I love."

I gently tapped him on the arm for that comment before walking around the car. "Great. I get stubbornness while you got the ability to keep cool on days like this. I think my ancestors gave me a bum deal."

Alex looked at me over the car's roof and smiled in that sexy way I loved. "Maybe, but that Irish lass thing is something that speaks to my Spanish blood."

He could be so cute at times.

"Just make sure the air conditioning is on full blast, Spanish blood. This Irish lass is already starting to melt."

AFTER A TEN minute ride in pure cool bliss, we arrived at Kellen Martin's house in the newer section of Sunset Ridge. 489 Lee Drive looked like virtually every other house in this part of town. New construction, two-story townhouse cookie-cutter design with the front door set off to the right with a window next to it on the left and the garage located on the other side of the home's façade. Every house resembled the one on each side of it, with little variation. Compared to the older section of town, this part lacked style to me.

Turning to face Alex, I lifted my hair to let the cool air hit my neck one last time before we got out. "It never fails to amaze me that anyone would want to live in a place with so little charm. Say what you want about Victorian Row, but those homes have real character."

"With real characters living in them," he joked, taking a shot at the town's upper crust who owned those older homes.

"Well, of course. Any home that contains a conservatory has to have, by law, a unique person living in it," I said with a chuckle.

He arched a single dark eyebrow at my claim, leveling his gaze on me. "By law, Miss McGuire? I don't think that's true."

I let my hair fall back down onto my neck and shrugged. "You know what I meant. Anyway, we know from experience that this part of town has its own set of characters too."

My memories flashed back to the case of poor Lee Reynolds, the local shock jock found dead after his on-air shift one afternoon. His house had been just a few blocks away from Kellen Martin's.

"Ready to head out again?" Alex asked as he turned off the car.

I dreaded the very idea of standing out in that heat. Maybe Mr. Martin would be nice enough to invite us in while we questioned him about his recently murdered girlfriend.

Then again, I'd worked enough cases with Alex to

know the chances of that happening were about fifty-fifty. If he had nothing to hide, he very well may invite us in and try to help with the investigation. But if he had anything to feel guilty about concerning Amy, chances were he'd give us very little and make us stand out in the stifling heat on his front porch while he did it.

"No, but I want to hear what he has to say, so let's go."

Alex tapped the gold door-knocker twice on the dark red painted front door while I examined the front porch area we stood in. A large green potted plant stood to the left side of us with two cute brown and white rabbit figurines who held a sign that said, "Welcome!" in front of it.

"I'm thinking he has to live here with his parents. No self-respecting guy in his twenties would have those bunnies on his front porch."

Looking down at the plastic woodland creatures meant to greet people, Alex smirked. "Amy didn't seem to be the type of woman who'd date a man who still lived with his parents. Kellen Martin is supposed to be twenty-seven years old."

"Now I have to see this guy," I said, astounded that the person we'd come to know as Amy would be with someone like that.

The words had barely left my lips when the door opened and there stood a very attractive man with sandy brown hair, green eyes, and a body that showed undeniable evidence that he spent some serious time in the gym daily. Wearing white shorts and a black t-shirt, both of which accentuated his tanned skin and muscular body, he looked much younger than what a twenty-seven year old man would look like.

He looked more like a teenage boy. A very good-looking teenage boy.

"Yeah? What can I do for you, officer?" he asked in a cocky voice that instantly grated on my nerves.

Two thoughts instantly raced through my brain. First, why would someone like Amy, a woman in her late twenties who lived on her own, date someone like this guy? And second, he didn't look too broken up by the fact that she'd been found murdered less than twenty-four hours before.

"I'm Officer Alex Montero and this is Poppy McGuire. We'd like to speak to you regarding the death of your girlfriend, Amy Perkins."

I watched Kellen Martin's face for a reaction to Alex's mention of Amy's murder and saw nothing. He didn't flinch or wince or even blink. Not a hint of surprise moved his expression. He simply stared at Alex like he'd just said that we found a dog wandering the neighborhood and wanted to know if it was his. In fact, he probably would have reacted more to that.

"Oh, that. Did you find out who did it?"

"No, not yet. In fact, we'd like to ask you a few questions."

I felt the coolness of the air conditioning float through the open door and hoped Kellen would invite us in. Unfortunately, he didn't react at all to Alex's explanation of why we were there. Disappointed, I looked to my right and saw confusion on Alex's face as he took out his pad and pen.

"Okay, Mr. Martin, when was the last time you saw Amy?" he asked, sidestepping Kellen's silence as my hopes for a cool interview faded quickly.

Scrunching up his face, Kellen seemed to think

about the question for a moment before answering, "I think it might have been Wednesday night. Yeah, I want to say Wednesday sounds right."

Alex intentionally said nothing, letting silence hang in the overheated air as he wrote down Kellen's answer. After nearly a minute, he looked up and asked his next question.

"So you didn't see her at all yesterday?"

Kellen shook his head so his straight brown hair fell into his eyes. Pushing it back off his forehead, he said, "Nope. Not at all yesterday."

Again, Alex said nothing for a long time, trying to get Kellen to fill the empty space in the conversation, but it didn't work. Curious about his oddly disconnected reaction to the death of his girlfriend, I finally couldn't help myself from saying something about it.

"You don't seem too broken up over losing Amy, Kellen. You know, someone stabbed her in the heart with a knife and left her to die alone in the woods."

I didn't care that my tone sounded indignant. Even if they were only casually dating or had gotten into a huge, relationship-ending fight on Wednesday, Amy deserved more than this deadpan act Kellen Martin had going.

"Well, she and I were sort of just spending some time together lately. It wasn't like we were a huge thing or anything. I'm sorry this happened to her, but I was home all night last night."

This guy was a real piece of work! I had to hold myself back from letting him have it with both barrels about how callous he was being about the loss of someone's life. I could only hope that Amy knew what Kellen was all about and was just spending time with him because he was eye candy. I hated even entertaining the idea that she may have really cared about this joker.

Alex remained calm in the face of Kellen's dismissal of the gravity of the situation, though. Seizing on his claim of an alibi, he asked, "Is there anyone who can prove you were here all night?"

That question finally elicited a reaction from Kellen. His face seemed to drain of all color for a moment and he stuttered out, "I...I have to have someone prove I was here? Why? I would never hurt Amy. We were having a good time. That's all it was. I had no reason to kill her!"

"It's an easy question, Mr. Martin. Can anyone corroborate your alibi?" Alex asked flatly.

Flustered, he shook his head and huffed out. "No. I was alone. My parents are out a lot."

"Interesting. Thank you, Mr. Martin. We'll be back when we need answers to more questions."

"Fine. I'll be here. You can come back whenever you want, but there's nothing proving I had anything to do with this. I know I'm innocent."

I wanted to say he might be innocent but he was a thoughtless clod, but he slammed the door in our faces, leaving us standing in the heat and me wondering how any decent woman would be with that guy.

"He's a real prize," I said as Alex placed his notepad and pen back into his pocket.

"A real big-hearted guy," he said rolling his eyes. "I almost hope he is guilty because I think it would be nice slapping cuffs on him and hauling him off to jail."

Hearing Alex express any feelings about a potential suspect surprised me, and as we walked back to the car, I said, "It's so unlike you to comment like that. I think I might be having a bad influence on you."

He frowned at what I said, and I realized it sounded like I was saying what Stephen had accused him of not two hours earlier. We got back into the car and its air conditioned splendor and headed back to the station in silence. I wanted to tell him that Stephen had been dead wrong, but I knew Alex well enough to know that he'd talk about it when he was ready.

The car rolled to a stop, and after he put the car into park, he stared straight ahead. He'd worn a frown all the way back, and now it looked more deeply entrenched in his expression than ever.

"Nothing you do has ever been a bad influence on me, Poppy. I never want you to think that. You make me a better cop. Period."

His anguished expression tore at my heart. Taking his hand in mine, I held it in my lap so no one would be able to see my tender gesture. "I'm sorry this is happening. He had no right to accuse you of being anything less than the consummate professional you always are, Alex. No right at all."

He turned to face me and lowered his gaze to our joined hands, nodding sadly. "I know. I just wanted to make sure that you know having you on cases has never compromised my judgment. What you bring to our cases is a different perspective. It isn't anything that clouds my instincts or anything ridiculous like that."

"Is that why you were going to hit him? Because he said that about me being a bad influence on your ability to be a cop?"

Alex looked up into my eyes and smiled. "No. I wanted to hit him because he's been a real S.O.B. to you for months and I finally saw how disrespectful he was to you. I'm sorry I didn't see it for what it was before today, Poppy."

I wanted to throw my arms around his neck and give him a huge kiss, but I never wanted to put him in any position that anyone like Stephen could ever use against him to say he wasn't the professional he so earnestly tried to be at all times he was representing our town.

Squeezing his hand, I told him what I knew to be true. "I know you always wanted to believe he was the kind of cop you are. It's just how you think. But he wasn't and never will be, Alex. I don't care if he's completely innocent in Amy Perkins' murder. He still could never be the man or the police officer you are. I believe that with all my heart."

"Thank you. It means more than you can know that you see the man I really am and the man I strive every day to be. When he said that about you having a negative effect on my ability to be the cop I believe I am, that was an insult to both of us. He was wrong, though. I need you to know that."

I looked into those dark soulful eyes of his and loved him even more than I thought I could. "I love you, Alex. You're the most honorable man I've ever known, other than my father, and that says a lot."

Alex squeezed my hand and took a deep breath before letting it out slowly. "I love you too, Poppy. Being with you has made me a better man and a better cop. No matter what happens, don't ever forget that."

Chapter Fourteen

"IT'S NEARLY FIVE o'clock," Alex said as he sat down behind his desk. "Where'd the day go?"

I dropped myself into the chair in front of him and rolled my shoulders. "We've been working all day on this case. I could go for something to eat. I think we forgot to get lunch in all of this."

He considered my claim and nodded. "I think we did. How about this? Let's see where we are on this case right now and then we'll go home and I'll cook you something great that will make you forget all about this day."

"It's a deal! I picked up some chicken and some turkey cutlets the other day while I was at the store, so that's about all you have to work with. Think you can whip something up with either of those?"

A sexy grin lit up his face. "Challenge accepted."

I knew cooking dinner for us would be more therapy for him than just making something that would fill our stomachs. Alex loved to make what he called his "special meals" for me because they let him escape into a place where he didn't have to think about anything but what temperature to cook the meal at and how long it should stay in the oven or the frying pan.

Some people painted or gardened. Alex cooked. Thankfully, he was quite a talented chef.

On the other hand, while his getting lost in creating culinary delights helped him, it had led to my gaining at least ten pounds since we began dating. However, I knew the benefits for his peace of mind far outweighed my extra padding I'd collected around my hips and behind.

And the truth of the matter was if I'd get myself back on the treadmill, both of us would benefit from his delicious cooking. When that would happen, however, I couldn't say. I always had the best of intentions, but then something always came up.

Like work at *The Eagle*. Or a case. Or the desire to sleep late instead of jumping on the machine in the corner of my dining room before the day started.

Alex cleared his throat to get my attention. I stared across the desk and saw him looking at me with a curious expression. "Were you just daydreaming about what I'd cook for dinner? You looked like you were a million miles away there."

"No. I was silently chastising myself for not exercising more. Let's get down to work so we can get home to that meal."

"Okay, boss," he said with a wink before beginning our discussion. "We need to run down who our suspects are. First up is Tamara Ridgeway. She has no alibi for the time Donny says Amy was killed. On top of that, the Third Eye Center is right near where she was found, so in theory, Tamara could have done the crime and gone back to the center without anyone being the wiser."

I rolled my eyes at the memory of that awful woman. "You won't get much argument from me about Tamara

Ridgeway being a good suspect."

"Okay," he mumbled as he put a check mark next to her name in his notepad. "Onto the next one. First, let me see what Craig has found out."

Craig answered the call quickly, and Alex said, "I'm putting you on speaker so all three of us can be on the same page. What did you find out about our three witches?"

"I'm just getting into the car to leave Jerilyn Fox's house. She and Susie Mitchell both have people who will testify that at the time Amy was killed they were nowhere near the woods. Jerilyn was at her mother's in Caston from six o'clock on, and Susie had eight-thirty dinner reservations with her husband Jonas at an Inner Harbor restaurant called Finnegan's. They had crab cakes and toasted to all the success she had at the tarot readers convention that day," Craig explained, sounding like he was reading off a sheet of paper in front of him.

Alex jotted down the highlights in his notes, so I leaned over the desk so my face was close to his phone and asked, "What about Melody? Did anyone at the theater see her there while she was seeing *An Affair to Remember* at The Colonnade?"

"I spoke to the only man working there in the afternoon—a man named Dick Montanga—and he said he recognized her from the picture on her pamphlet you gave me. Said he remembered seeing her come in because only three people saw the movie last night and she got a huge bucket of buttered popcorn."

"Okay, thanks Craig," I said into the phone's speaker. "Hang on. Alex probably wants to tell you something."

Sitting back in my chair, I mentally crossed off each

of the three witches from the suspect list in my brain. That left Tamara, Kellen, and Stephen.

"Call if you need backup for any reason, Craig. Good work," Alex said with a smile.

I knew his enthusiasm for the job Craig had done would thrill him. Through the phone, his happy voice said, "Thanks, Alex! If it's okay, I'm going to go home for the day after I get back to the station. Katy has a pot roast she texted me about, and it's been cooking all afternoon. I can practically smell it from here."

"Go enjoy that delicious pot roast, Craig. We'll see you tomorrow morning," Alex said cheerily.

After he ended the call, he leaned back in his office chair and stretched his arms behind his head. "That takes care of the women in our rogue's gallery. Now for the men."

I knew how hard talking about Stephen as a suspect was for Alex, so I quickly brought up Kellen Martin. "Amy's wonderful boyfriend Kellen, who is so overcome with sadness and grief? He has no solid alibi and he's a real winner."

"Being a terrible person doesn't necessarily mean he's a murderer. If that were the case, this job would be a lot easier. We could just go looking for the rotten ones out there," Alex said with a sly smile.

"Well, he's on the top of my suspect list," I said, still disgusted by his behavior when we asked him about his relationship with Amy.

"Above Tamara Ridgeway?" Alex asked in a shocked voice.

I put my hands out in front of me and pretended to weigh each suspect's chances at being the killer. "She is a complete shrew and her obsession with Amy calling herself a witch may have been more about her being a jealous former girlfriend than a difference in religious beliefs. On the other hand, Kellen Martin is possibly the world's worst boyfriend and a real putz, so if he turns out to be the killer, I won't be sorry to see him go away for good."

Sighing, he looked up toward the ceiling and quietly said, "That leaves Stephen. I think we need to talk to Mrs. Henderson and find out just how long Stephen was out on that call."

"Do we know how long he claims to have been handling the issue with her?" I asked.

Flipping through his notes, he stopped on a page filled with details and said, "The report he filed says he was gone from right after nine, like Craig said, to quarter after ten. The call about Amy being found came in at ten twenty-five."

I instantly did the math in my head and knew that even though it would be difficult, Stephen could have done the crime and gotten back to the station in time. I didn't say anything, though, because I saw by the sad look on Alex's face that he knew how long it took to get from where Amy was found to the police station too since he'd driven that distance hundreds of times.

"Let's go talk to Mrs. Henderson," he said, nearly jumping up out of his seat, clearly eager to get out of the office.

As soon as we opened the glass front doors to leave the station, the late afternoon heat hit us like we ran into a brick wall. But instead of going to the car, he began walking in the opposite direction toward my house.

"Let's walk since Mrs. Henderson only lives a few blocks away on Poplar Street."

Was he insane? Walk in this heat?

I wanted to say no more than any other word in the entire English language, but I had the sense that he needed this to clear his head, so I said yes, even while I silently wondered if I would still be able to stand up by the time we got there in the stifling heat.

After ten sweaty minutes, we arrived at Mrs. Henderson's blue house at 455 Poplar Street, just a block away from Victorian Row. While her house wasn't a grand home like those in the more exclusive section of town nearby, it certainly wasn't a character-less cookie cutter type of house either. Painted the color of a robin's egg, the Craftsman style home had a large front porch and nicely trimmed deep purple Rhododendrons landscaped around it.

We stopped on the sidewalk in front of her house and I wiped the sweat from my forehead and my neck under my hair. Of course, Alex looked like he had just stepped out of delightful air conditioning, all crisp and fresh, while I looked like a wrung out dishrag.

"God, I hope she's home. If we walked all this way in this heat and she's gone out, I'm going to be more than a little peeved."

He smiled at my frustration. "You look beautiful, even when you're all sweaty like you are now."

I wiped my damp hands on my dress. "Thanks. I feel like someone dunked me in a pool of salty tepid water."

His smile slid from his face, replaced by a look of disgust. "Again, with the vivid descriptions. Let's see if Mrs. Henderson is home."

As we made our way up the front walk, I said under my breath, "If she has her air conditioning on and invites us in, she will be my new favorite person of all time."

Mrs. Henderson spent most of her time complaining about traffic in front of her house and people parking in the spot she considered hers, despite the fact that she had a perfectly good driveway and garage on the side of her house. Other than that, she had a tendency to be a bit more strident than I preferred in a person. My father believed that came from her working as a nurse for nearly forty years. I didn't know if that was true. I just knew every time I'd ever seen her, she looked like she'd just sucked on a lemon. Even when she smiled, it was always tight-lipped, as if she had to force herself to be pleasant.

But her defining feature to nearly everyone who ever met her was her height. Nearly six foot tall, she towered over every woman in town and some of the men. It only added to her severe look.

We hit the first stair to the porch and saw her sitting in a white rocking chair fanning herself with a magazine. She would not be my favorite person today, unfortunately.

"Mrs. Henderson? My name is Alex Montero. This is Poppy McGuire. We'd like to ask you a few questions about the complaint you made to the police last night," Alex announced as we stepped onto the porch painted blue to match the house.

She stood up and met us before we reached her, and I saw the surprise Alex felt at meeting her. Tilting my head back, I watched her slowly stretch her lips into one of her tight smiles.

"Officer, I hope you aren't like the one who came by last night. My, he was rude," she practically spit out.

"We'd just like to ask you some questions about that,

if that's okay, Mrs. Henderson," I said in my nicest voice, hoping to use charm to make her forget how ignorant Stephen had been to her.

She lowered her gaze and looked at me for a moment like she had to go back into her memories to figure out who I was. Then after a few seconds, I saw the recognition in her eyes.

"Poppy McGuire. You're Joe's daughter, aren't you? I remember you from my time at the hospital."

With a chuckle, I nodded as Alex looked over at me. "I had a habit of getting pretty scraped up as a child."

Mrs. Henderson smoothed a few steel grey hairs into her tight bun. "I was thinking of when you would come visit your mother."

There was that severe personality that matched her look. Nothing like bringing up the memory of when my mother was dying to put a damper on our visit.

I felt Alex tense up next to me, but we had a job to do, so he asked, "About the officer who came out last night, Mrs. Henderson. We just need some information."

Looking like she didn't care about why we were there anymore, she grimaced and sat back down in her rocking chair. As she stretched her long legs out in front of her, she said, "Other than his being rude and doing nothing about the problem, I'm not sure what else there is to say."

Alex knew how to handle Sunset Ridge's most cantankerous citizens, so I knew he'd do the same with her. Turning on the charm, he smiled down at her in that way all the elderly women found so appealing and softened his tone.

"We want to make sure the problem is taken care of,

so if you can answer just a few questions, I'm sure we can solve this issue to your satisfaction."

Silently, I translated his borderline smarmy statement. You call all the time and will probably continue to call about this nonsense issue, but since we need your help, I'll be as nice as pie in the hope that you'll be less prickly and give me the answers I need.

As if on cue, her icy tone warmed, and that tight smile loosened up a tiny bit. "Well, I am happy that the police department is finally taking my complaints seriously. Would you two like a glass of homemade lemonade?"

Alex politely declined her offer, but I nearly jumped onto her lap at the thought of a cool glass of anything in this weather.

"Oh, yes, thank you, Mrs. Henderson. That would be wonderful," I gushed as she turned to grab the pitcher of lemonade from the table next to her.

She handed me the glass that at that very moment became the most important thing in the world to me. Parched from our walk there, I gulped down the entire glass, not even caring that it was too bitter and needed about a cup of sugar to make it taste good, while Alex began to ask his questions.

"So about the officer who came out last night. Can you tell me what time he arrived?" Alex asked.

"He got here right after nine, and he was rude. So short with me. He didn't care one whit about what I had to say. He gave me a lecture about the road being public parking and walked away."

"How long was he here?" Alex asked, obviously nervous about hearing her answer.

Mrs. Henderson rocked back and forth in her chair

as she thought about the question and said, "My favorite show Cross Country hadn't finished yet before he left. I know that. He was outside doing nothing, as far as I could gather, and he interrupted my show to tell me he was going before it finished. Other than that, I'm not sure. I was just so angry that he did nothing."

"What time does Cross Country come on?" I asked.

"Nine to ten every weeknight. It's really a wonderful show. Have you ever seen it?"

Alex wrote down her answers in his notebook, and I shook my head to answer her. "No. I don't watch much TV anymore."

Nodding, Mrs. Henderson agreed. "Oh, I don't either. Everything good has been done before. These days, most of what they're putting on are just redos of shows from the past. It's like creativity has gone dry in Hollywood nowadays. But Cross Country is different. It's a talk show and cooking show all in one."

I didn't know if I was supposed to pretend to think that sounded interesting. It didn't. Neither talk shows nor cooking shows were entertaining, in my opinion, and the idea of them being mashed together into one sounded like something I'd never want to see. Did the people being interviewed eat food while they were speaking? I had the vision of pieces of food spraying from between guests' lips as they talked about their newest book or movie they were promoting.

Yuck. No thanks.

Alex looked up from his notepad and asked, "So the officer was gone by ten o'clock, ma'am?"

"Yes, but he was incredibly rude before he left. He acted like doing his job was an inconvenience. Like he had somewhere else he wanted to be and couldn't be bothered with my problem."

"There's no chance that he was here until the end of your show?" Alex asked in a hopeful voice that tore at my heart. He so wanted to hear that Stephen had been here long enough to make getting out to the woods near his house and killing Amy impossible.

Mrs. Henderson's mouth tightened into a thin line that stretched across her face. "Young man, I know when my favorite show comes on each night. Cross Country airs from nine to ten every weeknight. Since it wasn't a weekend night, that meant it came on channel forty-five at exactly nine. I'm old, but I'm not senile, Officer Montero."

Quickly, he tried to smooth her ruffled feathers with a smile and an apology. "I meant no offense, Mrs. Henderson. I'm sorry. I just wanted to make sure I had all the details so we can solve this problem as soon as possible."

Like it usually did, Alex's charm offensive succeeded in its objective and Mrs. Henderson's anger melted away in seconds. Waving away his apology, she said, "I would appreciate that. I'm not asking for much. I just want the parking spot in front of my house clear each night, but invariably, someone arrives right after dark and parks in it."

"Well, we'll be sure to watch for who's parking there and have a little talk with them. I'm sure it will all be fixed this week. Thank you for your help, Mrs. Henderson."

He turned to leave even as I hoped she would offer me more of her sour lemonade that while tart still quenched my thirst. Since it looked like I wouldn't be getting any more, I placed the empty glass on the table next to her and thanked her for her help.

"If we have any other questions, we might have to come back. I hope that's okay."

With one of her tight-lipped smiles, she said, "I'll be here just enjoying this beautiful day."

I hurried down the stairs to catch up with Alex, who had already made it to the sidewalk that ran alongside the street in front of her house. I knew what she said hadn't been what he'd wanted to hear.

"Next time, let's forget the walking and go with the air conditioned car, okay?"

He slowed down his walking and looked over at me. "Sure."

"Are we still doing that wonderful meal tonight?" I asked, hating how unhappy he looked after hearing the truth that Stephen had lied.

"Sure. I just want to stop back into the station for a minute. I won't be long, and then we can get home to some lemon chicken and rice. Sound good?"

I smiled up at him and wished I could do something to make him feel better. "That sounds fantastic. A nice meal and some time relaxing tonight will do us a world of good."

He didn't respond to my suggestion, and as we crossed the street to head toward the station, I knew the fact that Stephen now absolutely had to be considered a suspect weighed heavily on his mind.

And I doubted cooking some chicken and relaxing on the couch with me would change that. The only thing that would change his mood would be solving this case and hopefully finding out that Stephen wasn't the one who had killed Amy Perkins.

Chapter Fifteen

I OPENED MY eyes after Alex rolled over for the fifth time in ten minutes, his arm knocking into my side with each turn. Looking over at the alarm clock, I saw the time in bright red numbers.

3:38.

This was the third time that night that he'd awoken me with his tossing and turning. I knew what was wrong, but I had no idea how to fix it.

"Alex? You okay?"

He sighed but said nothing, so I rolled over and saw him in the moonlight lying there staring up at the ceiling. That frown that had been a semi-permanent part of his face since the moment Stephen came under suspicion in this case looked even deeper.

"I'm fine, Poppy. Did I wake you up? Sorry," he said in a low voice devoid of emotion.

But I knew his emotions about this case were exactly what was keeping him up tonight.

Propping my head up on my hand, I let myself wake up for a few moments, worry about the man I loved uppermost in my mind. Finally, when I could think clearly, I asked him, "You haven't gotten to sleep yet tonight, have you?"

Alex turned his head and groaned. "Not really. I didn't mean to wake you up, though. Go back to sleep and I promise I won't do it again."

I ran my hand over his chest and let it come to rest over his heart. "I hate seeing you so torn up like this. I'm worried that this case is going to drive you crazy."

He covered my hand with his and smiled at me. "I won't let it make me nuts, Poppy. I'll be fine."

"It's quarter to four in the morning and you've been tossing and turning all night. I think you might have reached nuts level already."

My assessment made him laugh, and for a moment, he looked happy like I loved to see him. I wanted to see his face light up like that more. This case had only been active for a day and already he was battling insomnia because of it.

"Oh, this isn't nuts level. Trust me. I've had cases that nearly drove me out of my mind until I could solve them. I'm still okay."

I didn't believe that whatsoever, but I didn't want to argue with him either. As his partner, I was the person who needed to be by his side during the hard times, and having to investigate one of your fellow officers definitely qualified as hard.

Leaning over, I kissed Alex's lips lightly and whispered against them, "I love you, so I'll be right here for you the whole way."

He looked up at me with eyes filled with worry. "Good. I can't do this without you."

"That's ridiculous. Of course you can," I reassured him, knowing that at any time the town council may decide that I couldn't be his partner on cases anymore.

Alex pulled me down so my head rested on his chest

and kissed the top of my head. "I don't want to do this without you. How's that? Better?"

"Well, since you put it that way…" I whispered against his neck.

I breathed in the masculine scent of his skin, loving the very essence of who he was. Strong, steady, caring. He knew full well he could investigate any case he encountered without me and do a better job than most cops. Whatever I brought to cases, it wasn't expertise. I would never delude myself into believing that.

If anything, working with Alex helped me far more than it helped him. For the first time in my life, I had been given the chance to learn how to truly investigate like I'd always wanted to. If the Sunset Ridge town council took that away, I'd be the one who suffered. Alex would still go on doing what he did best—solving crimes. My absence on cases would just mean he would get a partner that probably wouldn't jump to conclusions as easily as I tended to and was a real cop.

We lay there in each other's arms, each of us knowing when we returned to the world outside my bedroom in a few hours that the case would be there with all its problems. Alex held me and squeezed my body to his like he was afraid I'd slip away if he didn't keep me in his arms.

He didn't have to worry. I wasn't going anywhere. He wasn't only my partner in crime. He was the man I loved, and at times like this when he needed me most, I knew my place was at his side.

I listened as his breathing slowed and felt his chest move up and down more slowly, hoping my being there for him would help him finally get some sleep. After a few minutes of lying there in silence, I lifted my head and saw he'd finally drifted off.

Tonight would be less than three hours, but at least he'd get some sleep before returning to the case in the morning.

ALEX SAT AT the kitchen table drinking his first cup of coffee of the day and writing notes in that pad he kept with him at all times. I poured myself a cup and sat down across from him as I prayed to the coffee gods to wake me up.

Lifting his head, he spoke for the first time that morning. "I don't want to believe a fellow cop did this, Poppy. I can't."

The betrayal I saw in his eyes made my stomach twist into a tight knot. Alex wasn't a naïve person. He saw people for who they were, not who he wished they might be. He knew in his gut, just as I did, that what we'd learned so far couldn't rule Stephen out.

And his behavior didn't help to make anyone think he was innocent.

"Tamara and Kellen are still very solid suspects too, Alex. Don't forget them."

I took a sip of coffee and relished its taste, letting it slowly make its way into my body and begin to work its magic. I still believed Kellen could be our killer. At the very least, he was a distinctly unlikeable person and someone who didn't care much about Amy. For those reasons alone, I wouldn't be bothered in the least if he turned out to be our murderer.

But my reminder of those other two suspects didn't ease Alex's mind. He took a drink of coffee and set his cup down on the kitchen table shaking his head and wearing that frown that seemed to never leave him on this case. "I've tried, but I can't get past the fact that he must have lied about how long he was at Mrs. Henderson's house. She's a pretty strong witness against him."

I wanted to play devil's advocate, but in this situation, I didn't know how to. Mrs. Henderson had been sure of when Stephen arrived and left. Her certainty left little room for doubt. If it hadn't been for that ridiculous TV show of hers, maybe there could be some wiggle room.

But there wasn't.

"Where was he for at least twenty to thirty minutes after he left Mrs. Henderson's house?" Alex asked and then sighed.

"Maybe we're missing something here," I said weakly, knowing we weren't. Time didn't lie, no matter how much he may have wished it would.

"If he went somewhere else after her house, why wouldn't he say so?" Alex asked, his voice full of stress as his mind raced to find a good reason to explain how Stephen couldn't have killed Amy, a woman he knew and lied about even to his fellow officers.

He finished his coffee and stood up to take his cup to the sink. "That would be enough time for him to commit the crime and get back to the station. He knows this and still he hasn't given any explanation after he lied about knowing the victim. No matter which way I think about this, it's not good, Poppy."

I heard the frustration mixing with his anguish at the situation, but I had nothing that would help. For as many times as Stephen had been a thorn in my side, I hadn't wished this on him, and even more, I hated how unhappy this was making Alex. But I had no answer for how he could be innocent yet Mrs. Henderson could still remain correct in her assertion of when he left her house that night.

"We better get going. I want to check out every one of our potential suspects again. I want to make sure we're not missing something."

Drinking the last of my coffee, I quickly washed my mug and set it in the dish drainer. "Okay. I'm ready to greet the day now that I've had my first cup of coffee. Lead the way!"

Usually, my chipper attitude made Alex smile, even though he didn't feel the same way about mornings, but today he was too much in his own head to even give me a perfunctory smile and pretend that he was amused by my gung-ho attitude courtesy of caffeine.

WAITING FOR US right inside the doors of the police station were Derek and Stephen. I saw them through the glass as we walked toward the building and knew Alex did too. I wasn't even touching him, but I felt him tense up next to me.

We'd barely made it through the doors before he began questioning Stephen. Without even pulling him aside, he asked, "Where did you go after you left Mrs. Henderson's? Did you go anywhere before you came back here?"

His words were laced with hope, but Stephen didn't seem to hear it and immediately reacted defensively. Narrowing his eyes, he glared at Alex and snapped, "I told you I came right back here. Check my report."

That answer didn't deter Alex, though. He

continued looking for a way to help his fellow officer, even if he didn't seem to want that help.

"She says you were gone before her show ended, and that was at ten. If you went anywhere else, just tell us," Alex said, practically pleading for him to give him anything to work with.

Stephen's face turned red with rage. He exploded with anger and barked, "She's nothing but a doddering old fool who can't remember anything other than people parking in front of her house! I can't believe you trust her over one of your own!"

Before Alex or Derek could do something to diffuse the situation, he stormed down the hall toward his desk and disappeared out of view. Rude as usual, he was doing nothing to help himself. I wish I could say I was surprised, but I wasn't.

Alex shook his head but said nothing. Derek simply nodded, as he often did when people behaved just as he expected them to. Never a huge fan of Stephen's, he may not have believed he was a murderer but he knew very well how difficult he could be.

"I need you to come into my office, Alex. We need to talk."

As much as I wanted to participate in the case, the look of worry on Derek's face told me now might be a good time to head across the street on a coffee run. Touching Alex on the arm, I said, "I'm going over to The Grounds. Want me to get you anything?"

"No, I'm good. Just come back when you're done and we'll start on going over everything we know about our suspects."

With a smile, I said, "I will." Turning to look at Derek, I asked, "Get you anything? A danish?"

Unlike most other days, Derek just shook his head. Something had to be really wrong because he rarely turned down the offer of a danish. It was probably about Stephen looking guiltier by the minute, but I'd find out when I got back.

As I headed toward the door, I heard Stephen banging things around back at his desk like some kind of spoiled child having a tantrum. The contrast between how Alex acted when he was accused of being Bethany's killer and how Stephen acted now couldn't have been clearer, and something inside my brain pushed me to finally say what was on my mind.

I marched back to where he sat and found him opening drawers and slamming them shut. He didn't notice me standing next to his desk, so I waited until he looked up to say my piece. When he finally did see me there, I could barely hold back the words from tumbling out of my mouth.

"You should know that even thinking you might have anything to do with Amy Perkins' murder is agonizing for Alex. He spent most of the night wide awake tossing and turning, unable to come to grips with the possibility that one of the people he's believed in all this time wasn't the person he thought he was."

Stephen just looked up at me with an angry glare, like what I said irritated him, but he said nothing in return. I wanted to smack that nasty expression off his face he made me so angry.

"I just thought you should know that while you're accusing him of falling down on the job, he's hoping every clue that turns up shows you had nothing to do with any of this."

Once more, he said nothing but sneered at me

before he returned to slamming the metal drawers in his desk. I turned on my heels and marched down the hallway to leave him to act like a child. As I passed the receptionist, I rolled my eyes and she did the same in return.

He deserved all the dirty looks he got.

By the time I hit the heat outside, my blood pressure had skyrocketed and the beginning of a whopper of a headache was forming just above my eyes. I needed a coffee and something sweet. Hopefully, that would help ease the pain in my head dealing with Stephen for just two minutes had created.

The line at The Grounds extended almost to the front door, so I waited as patiently as possible for my favorite drink and snack. Pam had told me she was looking to hire some new people part-time because business had picked up so much in the past few months. Leaning around the person in front of me, I saw a young man working behind the counter who I'd never seen there before. That explained the long line and crazy slow service.

Ten minutes later, only three people remained in line in front of me. As the first person told the new hire her order and waited for him to make two cappuccinos and bag up three cheese danishes, the man and woman in front of me began discussing their favorite cooking shows. I listened for a moment, curious about running into more people this week who enjoyed watching others make food.

"I just love cooking," the woman cooed. "I'm so glad cooking shows have become so popular."

The irony of someone standing in line at a coffee shop to get food and drink easily made at home while she professed a love for cooking wasn't lost on me. Amused by this, I chuckled quietly and tried to tune the woman out as she went on and on about her favorite meals I seriously doubted she ever cooked.

"...I was so angry when I went to watch Cross Country and my DVR didn't get it all. I swear, that machine has one job and it doesn't seem to be able to get it right. Every time I DVR a show on TV Land, it either cuts off the ending or I get the first fifteen minutes of the next show. It's ridiculous!" she complained as we waited for those two cheese danishes to find their way into a bag for the woman at the counter.

The man with her asked, "What happened to Cross Country? I didn't think that was on TV Land. Is it?"

Shaking her head, she huffed out her answer. "It's not. I have no idea what happened. Something preempted it and my DVR didn't catch the second half of the show. I'm so irritated. I love that show."

My mind raced at hearing this. Was it possible Mrs. Henderson had been mistaken on the time she thought Stephen left?

I jumped out of line and bolted out the door. I ran the four blocks to her house in the already sweltering heat of the day, drenched in sweat by the time I got there. Huffing and puffing, I struggled to catch my breath and fought a stabbing pain in my side after my dash there, clearly out of shape and needing to work out more.

That would have to wait, though. Now I had more pressing issues to deal with.

I knocked on Mrs. Henderson's door and she answered seconds later, giving me one of her tight smiles as she approached me. Through the screen door, she said, "The police really are taking this issue seriously, aren't they? Good. But where is your policeman friend today?"

"Hi, Mrs. Henderson. Yes, I think they are. I wanted to ask you some more questions about that show you love. Cross Country, right?"

"Yes," she said, clearly confused by my newfound interest in a topic I'd clearly shown not an iota of caring for just a day earlier.

"You said you DVR'd the show, right?"

"I did. Why do you care about the shows I record, Poppy?" she asked, her tight smile arching down into a frown.

"Have you watched it yet?" I asked, eager to find out if what I suspected might be true.

"No. I was going to tonight. What's this all about?"

"Would you be willing to let me see what you recorded, Mrs. Henderson? It would help with a case. I'd really appreciate it," I answered with my most sincere smile.

She didn't appear to fully understand why someone she barely knew would want to come into her house and watch a recording of her favorite show, but she opened the screen door for me and we walked into her living room. Thank God for the trusting nature that ran so deep in the citizens of small towns.

Grabbing the remote, she began to press buttons to get to her list of recorded shows. "I'm not sure how this could help with a case. This certainly won't help with getting those people to stop parking in front of my house every night," she grumbled as she scrolled through the list.

I watched the screen carefully, and when she found

the most recent episode of Cross Country, I read the information about when it recorded. It should have said Thursday's date and nine o'clock, but as I stared at the TV, I saw it said nine-thirty instead. Mrs. Henderson's DVR had done the same thing that woman in the line at The Grounds had complained about.

Holding my hand up, I said, "Mrs. Henderson, don't go to the show yet. This says that it began recording at nine-thirty that night. I thought you said your show ran from nine to ten every weekday night."

The elderly woman leaned in toward the TV and stared at it for a minute reading the details on the screen. "It does. Why does it say it started at nine-thirty?"

I had no idea what had preempted the show. She shook her head for a moment before it dawned on her what had happened.

"Oh yes, that's right. There was some man giving a press conference on something nobody cares about, so they had to move the show back. But we got to see all of Cross Country, thankfully. If not, I would have called up the cable company and given them a piece of my mind."

"So do you have any idea when the officer who came over here that night left?" I asked, my heart beating wildly at the possibility that I may have found out something to help Alex clear his fellow officer.

"I think the show was about halfway through, so I'd say very close to ten."

And with that, I had something I could give to Alex.

"Thank you so much, Mrs. Henderson. I'll be sure to tell my partner that the police definitely need to take care of that parking issue for you. Have a wonderful day!"

I got a genuine smile from her before I took off

toward the police station, running for the second time that day. I reached my destination in a few minutes, even more exhausted and sweatier than I was just a few minutes earlier, but none of that mattered.

As I came through the doors and felt the wonderful air conditioning hit me, I stopped and saw Alex still in Derek's office meeting with him. I was eager to give him my news, but I didn't want to interrupt them.

Derek saw me standing there and called out, "Poppy, I want you to come in here too."

The frown Alex wore made me think something more had happened, so I wanted to give them my information and hopefully cheer them up. I walked into his office and immediately said, "I have great news, guys! I think I found a clue that's integral to the case."

Joining his officer, Derek frowned too. "Poppy, I'm sorry I have to say this. The town council and the mayor have decided you won't be able to work with Alex anymore."

Chapter Sixteen

D EREK'S WORDS SLOWLY registered in my brain, and I felt like I'd run headlong into a wall. Every day since I started working with Alex, I'd wondered when the word would come down from on high that it all had to end. They'd done him a huge favor when he joined the town's police force by agreeing to let me partner with him on cases, but I always had a feeling it couldn't last.

Now that day had come, and as the reality sunk in, I knew no matter how I felt I had to respect Derek and his superiors. I couldn't lash out, even if I wanted to, because I knew Alex had to work with them after I was out of the picture.

But my chest hurt as I began to accept that my time as his partner had ended. I stood there in Derek's bland office feeling like someone had just taken away an important part of my life. Alex stared down at the floor shaking his head.

Taking a deep breath, I let it out and came up with something to say that sounded professional so he wouldn't be embarrassed. "I understand. I just have something to tell you guys about Mrs. Henderson and then I'll head out."

"No. This isn't right," Alex said in a low voice, still looking down at the floor.

Derek gave me a sad look and shrugged. "I don't have a choice, guys. I hope you know that. I fought them on this, but they had their minds set."

Looking up, Alex glared at him. "Then fight them more. Poppy shouldn't have to stop working with me. Nothing that's happening with this case warrants that."

I stood there stunned that he had pushed back on Derek's claim that he had tried to change the council's mind. Alex never did that. If anything, he was the quintessential team player. No matter what Derek assigned him, he never complained. He had more experience as a detective than the rest of the Sunset Ridge police force combined, yet still he never mentioned it, even as Derek scheduled him for overnight shifts and assigned him minor cases like missing garden planters or neighbor disputes over where a tree's leaves should fall while officers like Stephen were assigned more important cases.

I wanted to make this as easy on him as I could, so I faked a smile and waved the situation off like it didn't bother me to have what I loved taken away. "It's okay. I'm probably a pain most of the time anyway, right?"

Expecting Alex to force a smile too, I stood there stunned once more when he spoke again, this time in a much louder and angrier voice. "Derek, this isn't right. Poppy shouldn't be shoved out because Stephen has made this entire police force look bad. If anything, she's done more to help all of us than he ever has."

"Well, he made a big stink when they met with him and claimed that she was a problem. They're looking to get rid of anything that could make the town look bad."

"So instead of firing a cop who kept his relationship with a victim a secret and could very well be her killer, they're going to bother with Poppy?" Alex asked, his voice getting louder and louder.

"It's not a big deal. Really. It's okay," I lied, just wanting to diffuse the situation.

He spun around to face me and shook his head violently. "No, it's not okay! It's not okay at all."

My mouth hung open at Alex's outburst. I'd never seen him so angry. His eyes flashed fury, even at me. Taking a step back, I tried to speak but nothing came out.

"Alex, there's nothing I can do," Derek said weakly. "She's not a cop, so there's nothing that can be done officially."

And there was the real truth of this whole situation. No matter what Stephen had been accused of, he was a cop and I wasn't. He got the benefit of the doubt until it could be proven he was or wasn't guilty. I'd done nothing against the law, but in their attempt to make sure nothing else could hurt the police reputation in town, I was easily expendable because I wasn't a cop.

I was just someone who tagged along with a cop.

Alex shook his head again and pointed at me. "This woman is the reason I'm still working here. The only reason. When everyone else thought I was guilty of killing Bethany, including you, Poppy worked day and night to prove that I wasn't. She's helped me with every case since we started working together in ways that no other partner has ever done for me. I'm not going to let you stand there and claim that because she doesn't wear a badge that she's somehow less important than Stephen. He lied to all of us!"

Derek looked at his officer in shock. When Alex finished, he stared at the chief waiting for him to answer, but he said nothing.

I couldn't let Alex do this. His career meant the world to him, and barking at his boss was wrong. Derek wasn't to blame for this.

"Please, Alex. Stop this. I found out from Mrs. Henderson that there was some change of programming the other night and that favorite show of hers didn't come on until nine-thirty instead of at nine. Now she thinks Stephen might have been at her house until just before ten."

Both men focused on me for a few moments, but I saw by the anger still in his eyes that my news hadn't swayed Alex from his position that forcing me to stop working with him was wrong.

"See what I mean?" he said to Derek. "There was no reason to question that woman's claim that he had left her house in enough time to do the crime. This is what Poppy brings to our cases. Because she's not a cop, people say things to her that they wouldn't say to us. And that's just one of the many ways we benefit from her help."

Derek looked over toward me, his brows knitted. "So you're saying Stephen couldn't have killed her?"

I shook my head. "It doesn't seem like he would have had enough time."

Preoccupied with this news, he sat down behind his desk like the whole conversation had exhausted him. "I'll have to tell him and then the council. Make sure you give me all the information before you go, okay, Poppy?"

As he handed me a pen and paper, Alex slammed

his hand down on the edge of Derek's desk, startling both of us. "Before she goes? Why does she have to go now? Stephen is in the clear, and it's because of what Poppy did that we know he couldn't have killed Amy Perkins. Just tell the council and the mayor that everything's fine and we'll call them the next time we need money for uniforms or to get the cruisers fixed for the hundredth time."

I opened my mouth to once again say this wasn't a problem, but Derek bolted out of his seat and stepped toward Alex until they were toe-to-toe. He tilted his chin up and leveled his gaze on his officer with a look like I'd never seen Derek give anyone before.

"This isn't open for discussion anymore, Alex. They've made their decision, and that's it. It's settled."

But Alex obviously didn't agree. Setting his jaw defiantly, he drew his eyebrows in until they looked like two angry dark slashes on his forehead and narrowed his eyes.

"I've done everything this department has asked of me since I became a cop in Sunset Ridge. I've done the dog and pony show for the town council every time you asked me to so we could get what we needed from those five men who couldn't give a damn if we even have a building to work out of. I've paraded around ice cream socials and church picnics on my time off dressed in my uniform because you said it was good PR for the force. I've kept my relationship with Poppy almost completely behind closed doors, avoiding almost all public displays of affection and all in the name of being a cop this town can respect, even though my being happy in love with her and wanting to show her that outside her house or mine has nothing to do with my job or how well I do it."

Relenting for a moment, Derek quietly said, "I know, Alex."

But Alex wasn't finished. "I've never once even argued with you when you haven't assigned me to a case I'd be a hell of a lot better at and gave it to another cop who had almost no experience. I've done everything I can to make sure the people of this town see us as a police force they can trust and believe in. Ask yourself if you can say that about all of your officers. I'm asking you to go to bat for me with the council on this one thing, Derek."

I stood listening to this amazed at every word. I'd never complained about how we had to conduct our relationship because I'd always believed Alex wanted it that way. I knew him to be a private man, so naturally, it came as no surprise that he didn't like public displays of affection. I'd never been the type of woman to hang all over her boyfriend, so it wasn't like he ever denied me anything I ever needed.

When we were alone, he made sure I never had reason to doubt how much he cared for me. That had always been enough for me, and I'd thought that it had been enough for him too.

Now I realized his behavior had all been for the job. Not that this surprised me. Being a police officer was everything to Alex. He believed the life of a cop was a calling he'd had for so long he couldn't remember a time when he didn't want to serve.

It was everything to him. What he thought about twenty-four hours a day. Above all else, Alex Montero was a dedicated public servant who believed in the job he'd devoted his life to. Whether he was wearing the uniform or not, he was still a cop.

Derek hung his head and said what I knew bothered even him. "There's nothing more I can do, Alex. They've made their decision."

"Then you can put Stephen back on this case as the lead officer because I'm done. After all I've done for this department and the one time I need you to stand by me you can't…"

His voice choked up, and he cleared his throat before continuing and stunning both Derek and me.

"You'll have my official resignation within the hour."

A feather could have knocked me over as my brain processed those terrible words that hung in the air. Derek lifted his head and stared at him, his mouth hanging open as the news that he'd lost his best officer filtered into his consciousness.

Alex didn't wait for his response, though. Turning toward me, he held out his hand and motioned with his chin toward the door. "Let's go, Poppy."

I wanted to ask if he was sure of what he was doing. Being a cop meant the world to him. Why would he do this because of some stupid decision by the town council? It's not like we weren't still going to be together like we were now after work.

But I didn't say a thing. We'd have that conversation later in private. For now, I'd stand by him and his decision like I always did because I loved him.

I placed my hand in his and smiled when he closed his fingers around it. It wouldn't have been surprising if I felt it shake as we walked out, but I didn't feel anything but the steady strength I always found in Alex.

Behind us, Derek yelled, "Alex, wait! Don't do this! You're a good cop. We can work this out!"

Alex squeezed my hand gently and looked back at him. "The only way we can work this out is if you convince the council that Poppy stays. Period. If that can't happen, then there's nothing more to talk about."

We waited to hear what Derek would say next, and for the first time, I worried that Alex had played this all wrong. He didn't have to put his job on the line for me like this. I wasn't sure it was worth it in the long run, and what if the council refused even knowing he wouldn't return if they didn't agree to his condition?

Before I could whisper to him that he didn't have to do any of this and that I was okay with what they'd decided, Derek came out into the hallway and said, "Let me talk to them before you go making any final decisions. I won't take your resignation until I hear from them. Give me a couple hours, okay?"

"Fine. I'll wait to hear what you find out."

With that, we walked out hand in hand into the blazing heat that had settled in for the fifth straight day in a row and began walking toward my house. Confused and more than a little disappointed that we weren't going toward his car, I tugged on his arm to get his attention.

"Hey, your car is over there, Alex. Where are we going?"

He looked down at me and shook his head. "I need to blow off a little steam, so I hope you'll be okay with walking. Anyway, I think it's time this town saw that we're together as a couple. I'm tired of hiding what I feel for you because of this uniform."

"Are you sure? You don't have to do that for me. I know how you feel about us, and I don't care who else knows."

He smiled in that sexy way that never failed to make me crazy about him. "Well, I do. Maybe the town council wouldn't feel like they can do this if they knew how I felt about you. I've done everything I can for this town from the moment I agreed to help you on that first case, and I expected better from them. They seem to want to make Stephen happy even after he lied, then Derek can assign this case to him. Let him solve it. Or let Craig. I don't care. I'm done if they won't let you stay."

We walked down Main Street together as people walked toward us, and I noticed not one of them even bothered to look down at where we held hands. They smiled at Alex, saying, "Hello, Officer Montero," or said hi to both of us with a pleasant "How are you two today?"

Not a single fellow Sunset Ridge citizen frowned at the sight of us so obviously displaying our relationship. True, we weren't exactly draped over one another or pawing each other as we walked down the street, but we were holding hands like couples did and nobody cared.

Except the two of us. We cared.

I basked in the happiness of knowing that we could be seen together this way and not have to keep all our feelings to ourselves and behind closed doors. It was a small victory, but a victory nonetheless.

We crossed Main Street to head toward my house, and when we were alone again, I asked him, "Why was it such a big deal that the council said I couldn't work cases with you anymore?"

I expected him to say that they'd agreed when he took the job that I could partner with him and reneging meant he'd have to take on a new partner. I knew Alex well enough to know the loner part of him preferred not to have a fellow cop to work with.

But he didn't answer like that. And the way he answered my question made all my worries about the future of our relationship and where we were going with it disappear.

Alex stopped and turned to face me. He looked down at me with an expression of love in his eyes that I usually only saw when we were alone at one of our homes.

"Poppy, what I said back there to Derek about you being the only reason I was still a Sunset Ridge police officer was true. Even more true is that you believed in me when no else would. You fought for me when I needed it most. How could I not fight for you when the mayor and council wanted to just cast you aside?"

As tears welled in my eyes, I looked down at where our hands joined together. "Are you sure this is a hill you want to die on?"

Lifting my chin with his finger, he smiled sweetly at me. "You're the most important thing in my life, Poppy. Disrespecting you is disrespecting me."

"But I'm not a cop, Alex. It's just a fact."

"You care as much about our cases as I do. You worry about what clues mean and think about each and every suspect as much as me. I don't care if you're not a cop. You're an investigator and my partner. I made it clear when I agreed to take the job that you were part of the deal. That's the hill I'm willing to die on."

I smiled up at him, even as I worried that at some point he'd regret what he'd done. "I love you, Alex. Thank you for saying all of that back there to Derek. It meant more to me than you could ever imagine."

"All I did was say the truth. Nothing more and

nothing less. Since I first met you, I thought the people in this town underestimated you. Today told me they still are. As the man who loves you, it's my responsibility to show them how wrong they are."

I wanted to tell him how foolish I'd been for worrying for the past few weeks about where we were going and what kind of future we had together, but I kept that to myself for the moment. We had more important things to talk about anyway.

As we started walking again, I brought his hand up to my lips and placed a kiss on his knuckles. "So Officer Montero, what about this case? Now that we know Stephen likely isn't the killer, we're left with Tamara the shrew and Kellen the awful boyfriend. Have you thought about which one you think is our murderer?"

Alex smiled and shook his head. "No, I haven't. In fact, I have no intention of thinking about that case for the rest of the day."

I couldn't believe what I was hearing. How could he ignore the Amy Perkins case?

"What do you mean?" I asked, stopping and tugging his arm as he continued to walk.

Turning around, he shrugged. "What? Don't I deserve a day off?"

"Yeah, I guess, but the case. You aren't just going to stop thinking about it. How can you?"

He flashed me a sexy grin. "I figured I'd have something else to occupy my time. The case will be there tomorrow, and if Derek doesn't convince the town council to let you come back, then there will be no tomorrow at all for that case and me. Stephen will handle it. In the meantime, I want to relax in your cool house with a glass of something cold and think about nothing but the woman I love by my side. Are you in?"

Of course I was in. It wasn't every day that Alex and I got to have a day together without either one of us worrying about work. I just hoped I could be like him and not think about who killed Amy Perkins, even if I wasn't officially a part of the case anymore.

"Air conditioning and you in relaxation mode? I'm all in," I said with a smile.

Pulling me toward my house, he winked at me. "Good. Let's make the most of today, Poppy. Whatever happens with the town council and this case, it can happen tomorrow."

I loved that idea as much as I loved him.

Chapter Seventeen

I STRETCHED MY legs under Alex's as we lay on the couch watching TV for the fourth hour in a row. Looking up at him, I saw even though he hadn't said a word since telling me he had to get a drink two episodes ago, he wasn't asleep. He just stared at the TV like he was completely engrossed in the show.

"This is nice," I said quietly, really thinking I might go stir crazy if we did this for much longer.

Alex lowered his gaze to look at me and smiled. "It is. I can't remember the last time we just relaxed like this."

Disappointed he was actually enjoying just lying around in the middle of the day, I forced a smile and nodded. "Yeah."

"If only you weren't so fidgety. It's like you're going out of your mind when you're supposed to be appreciating this day off," he said with a chuckle.

"No, no. It's not that at all."

He arched his right eyebrow like he did whenever he heard something that didn't seem right. "No? Good."

Turning his attention to the TV, he settled back into his relaxation mode while I quietly wondered if he'd get tired of this soon. I certainly hoped he would.

Less than five minutes later, my need to do something—anything—overwhelmed me, and I jumped up from the couch. Alex looked up at me with worry in his eyes.

"What's wrong? Are you okay?"

I spread my arms wide to punctuate my point and finally told him the truth. "I can't lay around anymore. I'm going crazy! I know you're loving having an afternoon off, but I think if I watch another episode of that show, I'm going to lose it."

Whenever I said things like that, he always listened patiently and then chuckled at my outburst. Sitting up, he stretched his arms above his head and yawned big.

"Well, I guess we have been lounging around for a while. Do you want to do anything, or were you just bored?"

"I guess I'm not very good at relaxing. I can't seem to do it for more than a few minutes, unless I'm sleeping."

"That's not relaxing then. That's sleeping."

I rolled my eyes at his need to make that distinction. "Okay. So now that we've established that relaxation isn't my thing, do you want to do something?"

Alex stood from the couch and dipped his head to kiss me. He cradled my face in his palms and pressed his forehead to mine. "Your hyperactivity is one of the things I love best about you. Give me time to grab a shower and we'll go for a ride or something."

Rubbing my hand along his still mostly smooth jaw, I said, "Great! You don't have to shave, so about fifteen minutes?"

He kissed the top of my head and laughed as he walked away toward the stairs. "Make it twenty. I might want to enjoy my shower."

Not five minutes later, my phone vibrated across the top of the coffee table. I picked it up and saw it was my father. I hadn't spoken to him in almost three days and had a feeling he was calling to check on me to make sure I was still alive.

Answering it, I bypassed hello and immediately launched into my apologies for being such an absent daughter. "I'm sorry, Dad. I just realized we haven't spoken for the past few days. I've just been busy with this case and a bunch of other things. How are you doing?"

My father's deep voice came through the phone and I knew he understood. "It's fine, honey. I'm good. I just figured you and Alex were involved in a case, but I just saw Derek at the end of my bar again and I hear Alex isn't a cop in town anymore? He wouldn't say much, but I think this might be the cherry on top of the awful cake our police chief has been forced to eat lately."

"What do you mean?"

What else was Derek dealing with beyond the issue with Alex? What was this awful cake my father was talking about?

"Nothing. I'm more interested in what's going on with you and Alex? Did he really quit his job? What happened?"

I heard the genuine concern in my father's voice and quickly worked to let him know everything was okay with the two of us. "He did. Well, sort of, I guess. It's not a big deal, though, Dad."

"It sounds like a big deal, Poppy."

My father didn't ask again what had happened, but I knew he wanted to know. I wanted to defend Alex just in case my father thought he'd been rash in his decision too, so I gave him the Cliff notes version of what had happened on the Amy Perkins case.

"I don't know if he's going to never be a cop in Sunset Ridge again, Dad. There have just been issues with this case we're working on. Well, a case we were working on, emphasis on were. Because of the issues, the mayor and town council told Derek that I couldn't work with Alex on any more cases. That's when he told him that if I was out, he was resigning. It's all very up in the air, though, but he did it because he wanted to support me, Dad."

"You don't have to defend Alex's decisions to me, Poppy. It's none of my business why he does what he does, except when it comes to you. I've never doubted that he would do anything to protect you, but I'm curious why the mayor and town council suddenly didn't think it was all right for you to work with him on police cases. You didn't do something illegal, did you?"

Leave it to my father to ask that question. I knew he loved me as much as a father could love his child, but while he always saw Alex as honorable, he naturally jumped to the conclusion that I'd done something wrong in the eyes of the law.

At least I knew where I got my tendency to jump to conclusions from.

"No, Dad. I did nothing illegal. One of the other cops has never liked me, and when he got caught lying about a case, he naturally looked for a way to get the heat off himself by bringing me up."

My father growled and said, "It was Stephen, wasn't it? What is that man's problem with you? Did you break his heart in high school or something?"

The very thought that at any point in my life I could

have been involved in anything romantic with Stephen made me cringe. "No! I have no idea why he's never liked me, but I can tell you that the feeling is definitely mutual."

"I haven't talked to him much, but I don't like anyone who does that kind of thing to my daughter. So Alex told Derek you stayed or you both went? No wonder Derek wouldn't tell me much other than Alex had quit."

"As police chief, I don't think he's supposed to say anything about it, Dad," I teased, knowing full well that rule had never been followed by any police chief in the history of our town.

"Don't be ridiculous, Poppy. Derek leaks more than a boat full of holes. He didn't want to tell me what happened with Alex because it was more about you than him. I understand. Derek knows how close we are, so he probably expected I'd give it to him with both barrels if he told me what actually happened."

That was my father in a nutshell. He would naturally ask me if I'd done anything illegal since he knew better than anyone else in the world my propensity for getting into trouble, but have anyone else say a peep against me and his Irish got up full tilt. I had to love him for it, though.

"Go easy on Derek, Dad. As you said, he's been going through some stuff lately. I got the feeling talking to him yesterday that things weren't all hearts and flowers with his girlfriend."

"I'd say not. They broke up. He's been a permanent fixture at the end of the bar. If you ever came around the bar anymore, you'd see that. He's been having a rough time of it in the past couple weeks and he's taken to drowning his sorrows."

Had it been that long since I spent time at McGuire's?

"Broke up? I had no idea. I thought they were in it for the long haul. I feel bad for him now."

Dismissing Derek's heartbreak, my father groaned. "He'll be fine, Poppy. Our police chief has broken enough hearts in town to be due at least one himself. You watch. He'll be back to his old self in a few weeks and dating like he always has. Some people never change."

I didn't want to argue with my father, but I had the sense that Solange had been different than all those other girlfriends. Something told me Derek would miss this woman.

"I wonder what happened."

"By the way Derek has been talking, I think it was a matter of things happening at the wrong time. He wanted to get married and she wasn't ready. I think he may have pushed too hard. Something he said gave me the impression that he gave her an ultimatum."

So Derek had found the right girl, just at the wrong time. That made me sad.

"When am I going to see you and Alex in the bar again? Since you stopped bartending for me, it's like we never see each other anymore."

Guilt coursed through me, settling into my heart. I had been a neglectful daughter recently, and I knew he missed me when I didn't come around like I used to. It's just that Alex and I had been enjoying the summer months, and the few scant hours we got to spend together after his shifts and my work at the paper we liked to have to ourselves.

But that was no reason to ignore my father. I needed to rectify that and soon.

"I promise we'll be by as soon as this whole thing blows over, Dad. I'm not even sure Alex is really off the police force officially, but as soon as it gets straightened out, we'll come over and have a drink. Just the three of us."

"Okay, honey. Promise me you'll stay out of trouble," he said in that wise old owl tone he took with me whenever he had a feeling I was in the middle of something that most certainly included trouble.

"I'll try, Dad. You know me, though," I joked, poking fun at his overly cautious way with me.

"I do, Elizabeth. That's why I said to stay out of trouble. Love you, honey. Tell Alex I said hello too."

"I will, Dad. I love you too."

As I placed the phone back on the table, I heard a knock at my front door. Wow, I sure was popular today. Two people in one day who wanted to talk to me.

Peering through the peephole, I saw Derek standing on my front porch looking glum. After what my father had just told me about the demise of his relationship with Solange and everything that had gone on today with Alex, I didn't have to wonder why.

I opened the door wearing my brightest smile. "Derek? What are you doing here?"

He tried to smile back at me, but the corners of his mouth never quite made it high enough to equal more than a half-hearted smirk. "Can I come in? I want to talk to you and Alex."

Derek was always welcome in my home, no matter what differences we might have, so I stood back and waved him into the living room. As he passed me, the strong smell of liquor from his breath wafted toward me.

"How are you doing, Derek? I have a feeling you've started early today," I said as I closed the door and sat down on the couch.

He chose the dark blue wingback chair across from me and smiled. "That's not good since I just went to see the mayor. Hopefully, he doesn't have the nose of a bloodhound like you do, Poppy."

I shrugged. "It's a gift and a curse. Actually, I think my nose has been trained to smell alcohol from working at my father's bar all these years."

Derek swiveled his head left and right. "I thought I'd find Alex here. I saw his car back at the station still, but I figured you guys had come here. Is he around? I want to talk to you both."

"He's upstairs taking a shower. He should be down soon, though. In the meantime, do you want a drink or maybe a coffee? Not that I'm saying you need to sober up, but who knows who you might have to go talk to after us."

I chuckled as the last words came out of my mouth, and Derek finally managed a real smile. "No, I'm fine. I think I've had enough to drink for the day."

Settling back into the couch cushions, I sat there in awkward silence for a few moments and finally said, "So how are things going?"

Not my smoothest segue, but I meant well.

Derek sighed deeply. "I've had better days. Well, I've had better weeks. Months, more like it."

He definitely sounded like a lost man, but I didn't know if it was because of work or his personal life. Or a combination of both. I didn't want to pry, so I returned to uncomfortable silence and hoped Alex would come downstairs soon.

After a few minutes without a word that felt like hours, he quietly said, "I laid it on the line with the mayor. I told him I can't afford to lose my best officer because of all of this."

Too curious to wait for Alex to join us, I continued the conversation. "What did he say?"

"You're back, if you want to be."

His news made me happy, but if he liked what the mayor had decided, it didn't show in his face. His mouth seemed fixed in a frown.

"You don't look happy about that, Derek. Have I done something wrong?"

He blew the air out of his lungs slowly and shook his head. "No. I'm fine with you working with Alex, Poppy. I've just got a lot on my mind right now."

"Anything you want to talk about?"

Sighing again, he frowned deeper. "This job is a lot tougher than most people realize. Hell, I didn't realize it when Dominick was the chief. I just thought he was a hard ass because that's who he was, but the more time I spend as chief, I see the job probably made him even worse. I don't know. Maybe I'm just not cut out for this."

I hated seeing Derek doubt himself. True, he'd never been the sharpest tool in the shed, but he'd worked hard to do his best since taking the job as police chief for our town.

"You're a good chief, Derek. Don't get down on yourself like this. Stephen's lying isn't your fault. There's no reason the town council or the mayor should blame you for that problem. That's on him, not you."

He nodded, but it didn't look like he truly believed

what I said. "I know. It's just one more thing I've had to deal with."

His voice trailed off as he finished his sentence, and I guessed he wasn't talking about the job of police chief anymore. Quietly, I broached what I had a feeling was really bothering him. I wouldn't have done so with other people, but Derek and I were friends for long enough that he deserved to have a sympathetic ear offered to him.

"I heard about Solange. I'm sorry, Derek. I know you cared a great deal for her. She'll come back, I'm sure."

He shook his head sadly. "No, it's over. The irony of this is that all those years when women wanted me to settle down and get married, it was me who didn't want that. Now that I have the chief job and want to start a family, the one person I wanted to do that with doesn't."

I couldn't help wish things had turned out differently for him. I didn't know if Solange was the woman for Derek, but he clearly thought she was. They just were at different places in life, unfortunately.

"I'm so sorry, Derek. You're a good man, and if it makes you feel any better, I have no doubt that nearly every one of those women you said no to marrying would jump at a second chance now."

A smile slowly spread across his face. "Well, since most of them are already married, that could get tricky. But thanks, Poppy. I appreciate it."

Alex walked into the room at that moment and looked surprised to see me sitting there with Derek. Taking a seat next to me on the couch, he took my hand in his and gave it a gentle squeeze.

"What's up, Derek? I didn't think you'd be here

when I came back down."

His voice contained an edge to it that I hadn't expected. Glancing over at him, I saw he wore a stern expression too.

"I was just telling Poppy that I told the mayor I couldn't afford to lose my best officer, so Poppy had to stay. He agreed, thankfully, so we can go back to the way things were starting right now."

While Alex had sounded cold and guarded, Derek sounded downright hopeful. Turning to face my partner, I said, "That's good news, right?"

When he didn't answer, I asked, "Alex, isn't this great? Isn't this what you wanted?"

But the look on his face said it wasn't.

"Yeah, but what about the next time, Derek? I'm sure the mayor is going to expect me to keep doing everything I have been, but what assurances do I have that he and the council aren't going to jerk us around whenever they want?"

Holding his hands up as if to surrender, Derek shook his head. "They won't. I promise. I won't let them do that. You're my best officer, and I told him that having Poppy with you is a line you won't cross. As long as you want to have her as your partner, that's how it will be."

Still Alex refused to say he'd come back. I leaned over to whisper in his ear, "What's wrong? I thought this was what you wanted."

He looked at me with those brown eyes so sweet and whispered, "I liked having the time to enjoy with you this afternoon. I'm not sure I want to go back."

I knew him well enough that what he enjoyed for an afternoon would soon drive him insane from boredom like it already had begun to for me. "I liked it too, but you love being a cop and even though it was nice to lay around for a few hours, you'd miss the job."

Derek interrupted us and said, "I'll throw in Saturday or Sunday off every week."

Alex looked over at him and smiled. "Or?"

"I can't promise both. That will leave Craig working every weekend, and you know something seems to happen every weekend."

"What about Stephen?" Alex asked, practically reading my mind.

"Stephen quit about two hours ago. The council decided that his record would have to include his lying, even though he had no part in Amy Perkins' death, and he refused to agree, so he quit."

Stunned, I looked at Alex and whispered, "You can't leave the Sunset Ridge police in a lurch like this. I know you. You care too much."

After a moment, he nodded and said to Derek, "Okay. I'm back. Saturday or Sunday off each week and no Stephen. How can I say no?"

His answer made Derek happy for the first time since he got there. Smiling, he stood up to leave. "Okay, good. I don't think I can take any more upheaval for today, so I'm going to leave before something else happens. If anyone wants me, I'll be locked in my office with the phone on silent."

Alex walked over to him at the door and offered his hand. "Thanks, Derek. I appreciate you going to the mat for Poppy and me. I won't forget this."

Chucking Alex on the shoulder, Derek said, "Good. You're going to have to keep working with Craig too. I forgot to mention that."

"I knew there would be some catch," Alex said with

a laugh. "I'll see you back at the station first thing tomorrow morning."

After Derek left, I walked up to Alex and wrapped my arms around his waist to hug him. Looking up, I saw he was happy with how things had turned out too. "All's well that ends well, right?"

"I guess, but we still don't know who murdered Amy Perkins, so the case hasn't ended yet." He pressed a light kiss onto my lips and continued, "But we can leave that for tomorrow. Tonight, I thought we'd have a date night instead of me cooking lemon chicken. Dinner at Diamanti's and maybe a movie sound good?"

Holding his face in my hands, I smiled. "It sounds perfect to me."

Chapter Eighteen

D INNER AT DIAMANTI'S impressed as always, with Alex claiming the chef made his bourbon pork chops better than ever before as he pushed the plate away from him. My entrée choice of roast beef with red wine gravy tasted delicious, and both Alex and I raved about the garlic mashed potatoes and steamed green beans served with our meals.

I finished my Cosmo and considered having another one, but as Alex drank the last of his scotch neat and placed the glass next to his plate, I saw the clock behind the bar said it was nearly seven-thirty. If we had another drink, we might be late.

"We better get going. The movie starts at eight, and I'm worried there might be a huge crowd tonight."

Alex narrowed his eyes in disbelief and leaned back against his chair. "A huge crowd? Poppy, if all of Sunset Ridge decided to go to the movies tonight, The Colonnade would still only be half full. The place is the biggest theater I've ever seen, and that's saying something since I lived in an actual city before."

The Colonnade was large, especially for a small town movie theater. Built in the 1950s, it had shown movies every day, except for holidays, since its grand opening when a movie ticket cost something like twenty-five cents and people drove cars the size of the QE2. My father liked to tell the story about when he was just a kid and snuck into the movies with his friends to see a special showing of Alfred Hitchcock's *Psycho* when he was thirteen years old. The group was caught halfway through the movie crouched down in one of the four loges at the top of the theater and thrown out after the manager called each of their parents.

Why The Colonnade had been built so large always baffled people outside of Sunset Ridge, but for those of us who'd always lived here, we never thought about it. It was just The Colonnade, the place to see movies.

"Well, I don't want to miss the previews. And I love that old timey thing they have with the dancing hot dog jumping into the bun."

Alex shook his head and smiled. "I've always thought that whole thing was very sexual."

Sometimes he said the strangest yet most intriguing things that I had to wonder what else he kept locked up in that mind of his. As I stood from the table to leave, I grabbed my purse and said, "I may never look at that cartoon the same way again, you know."

He found my reaction amusing, like he often did when he said things that caught me off guard. On our way to his car, he ribbed me about never picking up on the sexual aspect of the dancing hot dog cartoon, not believing I'd never noticed not even once that it had to be more than just a hot dog jumping into a bun.

"You know, Poppy, of all the people in this world, I would have thought you would have seen that," Alex said as he slid into the driver's seat and turned the key in the ignition.

"Why? Why on Earth would you think I, of all people, would see that in a children's cartoon?"

He stopped at the corner and turned left to head toward The Colonnade. "Because you always see things that aren't there."

"What does that mean?" I asked, quickly becoming annoyed that I didn't understand him.

"Don't get angry. I'm complimenting you. Whenever everyone else sees the surface of something or someone, you see what's below, the truth of the situation."

Flattered by his assessment of me, I gave him a love tap on the upper arm. "Oh, well, that I'll admit to. But I think it's more a female thing than it is a me thing. Females tend to overanalyze everything, so it's second nature for us."

Alex glanced over at me and smirked. "Then why didn't you pick up on the hot dog and the bun thing?"

"Because I'm not a perv."

Throwing his head back, he laughed out loud. "A perv? I think I object to that."

He pulled the car into the parking spot and turned off the car. Leaning over, I kissed him sweetly and said, "Well, object all you want. The overanalyzer didn't see all that sexy stuff in the hot dog cartoon. Ready to go?"

For one of the first times in public, Alex and I walked hand in hand down the street to the front door of the theater. Like earlier in the afternoon, people saw us and had no response whatsoever.

Being ignored never felt so good.

The Colonnade had an old fashioned ticket booth in the front of the building, and thankfully, the line to buy tickets wasn't long since the previews would be starting at any minute. We reached the window within five minutes of arriving and saw a man sitting there. His dark hair hung in his eyes even though it had been cut short everywhere but on the top of his head. It had a very eighties look to it.

He seemed engrossed in a card he was reading and didn't see us waiting, so Alex tapped on the glass to get his attention, startling him. Looking up, his eyes flashed shock at being interrupted.

"Can I help you?" he asked in an irritated voice, like we'd done something wrong by wanting to be waited on.

"Hi, Richard. Didn't mean to scare you. We'd like two tickets to the eight o'clock show," Alex said in a tone far nicer than the man had given us.

I wondered for a moment if Alex knew him, but then I saw his nametag pinned to his shirt said Richard with the words *How Can I Help You Today?* just below his name. Too bad he wasn't as friendly as what was hanging off his clothes.

Alex turned toward me and whispered, "I think we interrupted him just as he was reading a love letter. See the card? It says, 'Love, M.'"

Craning my neck, I tried to see what he was talking about, but the movie clerk had covered it with his arm. Sorry we broke up your romantic moment, Richard.

He shoved the tickets out to us through the hole in the window and gruffly said, "That'll be fifteen dollars."

For a moment, Alex did nothing. He didn't say a word or even reach for his wallet. He just stared into the booth.

"I think he wants us to pay," I joked as I nudged his arm. "Do you want me to get this?"

As if my touching him pulled him out of a daydream, he looked over at me blankly and shook his head as he hurried to get out the money to pay for the movie. "No, I'm fine. I got this."

We walked into the theater, and I had the sense something was off with Alex. I asked him what was wrong, but he just put a smile on and told me he'd been deep in thought, but he wouldn't say about what, so I didn't ask.

He'd tell me when he wanted to.

"THAT STILL STANDS as one of the best movies ever," I declared as we stood to leave the theater. "I don't usually go for scary movies, but *Rosemary's Baby* is one of the greats. I'm so glad The Colonnade does these oldies movie nights."

Alex shrugged as we hit the outside and the lights from the lobby suddenly seemed too bright compared to what we'd been used to for the past two hours. Squinting, he looked at me and said, "It's not one of my favorites, but as long as one of us enjoyed it."

He preferred action flicks to oldies and the chick flick rom-coms I liked, so his blasé attitude toward the film didn't surprise me. Taking his hand in mine, I said, "Next time, we'll find a theater playing something you like if this place is showing something you don't want to see."

Although I never expected a lot of talk from Alex, knowing the type of man he was, his lack of any response surprised me. Clearly distracted, he didn't even look over at me to acknowledge he'd heard me speak.

Just as I went to ask him what was wrong, in my peripheral vision appeared Amy's boyfriend Kellen and a young blond woman in a pink sundress practically hanging off him walking into the theater. I tugged on Alex's arm and discreetly pointed toward the couple.

"I'd heard pink is the new black. He sure looks like he's in mourning, doesn't he?" I mumbled.

Instead of avoiding us, Kellen directed the girl toward where we stood and walked right up to us. Wearing what looked like a gloating expression, he flashed a smarmy smile and pulled the girl to his body so there was no wondering if they were on a date.

"Officer Montero, I didn't realize someone like you would like a horror movie like *Rosemary's Baby*. I pegged you for more of a serious flick kind of guy," he said, almost taunting Alex.

Refusing to take the bait, he smiled and said in his most professional voice, "I don't. My partner does, though, and she got to pick the movie tonight. I prefer films that involve bad guys ending up in cuffs and in the back of a police cruiser."

The blond girl in the pink sundress with a tan I worried would one day end up in a horrible case of skin cancer cooed at Alex's description of his kind of movie. "Oooooh, I love those movies too. Kellen says they're bour...bourgee..."

Turning to look at him for help with the word she wanted to say, she waved her hand as if to cue his help. "What do you call those movies, Kellen?"

"Bourgeois," he answered smugly, adding more information ostensibly for her benefit and anyone else's who didn't understand his insult. "Pedestrian and common."

Her face lit up like being talked down to thrilled her. "Yes, that's it! Bourgeois. Kellen knows all about movies, don't you?"

No longer even focusing on her, he stared directly at Alex and answered, "I have always enjoyed films. It's one of the things I know a lot about."

Disgusted by him and his new girlfriend, I asked, "Did you see a lot of films with Amy?"

His smug façade slipped for a just a moment when he glared at me before turning his attention back to Alex without even answering my question. "Are you making any progress finding out who your murderer is?"

I so wanted to slap him for how callously he acted regarding everything about Amy. What would it take to show a little compassion for someone who he'd spent time with?

"We're getting closer and closer every moment, Kellen. I expect to have a break in the case any time now," Alex said with a confident, full smile I knew hid the truth.

We hadn't even worked on the case all day. How could he truthfully claim we were close to anything like a break?

Kellen's eyes grew wide in surprise at Alex's news. "Really? You guys work fast. I figured it would take the Sunset Ridge police weeks to solve it. I mean, these local yokels aren't exactly crack investigators."

This guy was infuriating! Could he be any ruder? For the second time in this conversation alone, I wanted to smack his smug face.

Alex said nothing to his taunt, but I couldn't let it just pass, so I said, "You underestimate the police in our town, Kellen. And Alex here isn't from Sunset Ridge. He cut his teeth in solving crimes in Baltimore, so he's no local yokel."

For a split second, I thought I saw concern creep

into smug Kellen's eyes, but he simply plastered a smile on his face as his girlfriend began to explain to no one in particular how much she loved the club scene in Baltimore. Nobody was listening to her, though.

"Well, good luck with that whole thing, Officer Montero. I'm going to enjoy a good film with Candy here, so have a nice night."

And with that, he turned on his heels and pulled Candy, the blond girl with an IQ I suspected hovered around that of a houseplant, toward the theater. We watched them walk away and then began to walk to Alex's car.

"Please tell me he's our murderer. I want to see him hauled away in handcuffs and forced to wipe that self-satisfied expression off his face before someone else does it for him. I was barely able to stop myself from smacking him."

With a shrug, Alex kept my hopes alive that one day that guy would get his comeuppance. But he said nothing more about Kellen, so I asked, "Why did you tell him you expect to see a break in the case at any moment when we haven't done a single thing on the case all day? You were bluffing, right?"

We reached the car and Alex opened the passenger door for me, still not answering. I looked up at him for some kind of answer before he closed the door, but he simply said, "You know better than anyone else that we don't have to be actively discussing the case to be working on it."

Intrigued, I waited for him to get into the car and put his seat belt on before I said, "I'm serious, Alex. Is something happening on the Amy Perkins case that I don't know about?"

After a moment of suspense, he admitted what I already knew, sadly. "No, there isn't. You're right. We haven't worked on the case all day because we've been preoccupied with relaxing." Tapping his finger to his forehead, he added, "But just because we haven't spent all day running around looking for clues or sitting in my office doesn't mean we haven't been working on it. Much of investigative work takes place right up here."

I had spent a lot of the time thinking when we were supposed to be binge watching episode after episode of whatever that show was that afternoon, but I hadn't found any real answers to who had killed Amy Perkins. Stephen and the three tarot readers from the convention had been cleared, so that left Kellen and Tamara.

"But nothing points to either one of them, other than the fact that they're both pretty awful people."

Alex turned to face me with a look of confusion. "What?"

"Sorry. I was just thinking about our suspects and no matter what I do, it always comes back to those two awful people—Kellen, Amy's heartless boyfriend, and Tamara, the shrew who also dated her and had a problem with Amy not calling herself a witch. But neither one seems to really have had a reason to stab her in the heart out there in the woods."

"Ah. Okay. Well, on that subject, let's take a ride over to Kellen's parents' house while we know he's at the movies. Maybe they can give us a little insight into their son we've been missing so far."

As we drove there, I tried to imagine what kind of people they were to have brought up a child to be such a thoughtless and rude person. Before I even met them, I disliked them for what their son had already shown himself to be.

Alex once again knocked on their front door, and while we waited for someone to answer, I leaned close to him and said in a low voice, "How much are we betting one or both of them is as obnoxious as their kid?"

"Sometimes kids just turn out bad, Poppy. It isn't always the parents' fault."

I waved away his excuse and shook my head. "You can't plant peas and get corn."

The porch light came on and the door opened just as I finished talking, and there stood a woman I guessed may have been around my father's age. The early signs of crow's feet around her eyes said she may have been in her late forties, but the deep creases like parentheses coming down from her nose and the lines that extended from the edges of her mouth making her look like she was permanently frowning said she had to be at least in her mid-fifties.

"Can I help you?" she asked in a voice laced with fear.

Alex quickly showed her his badge and worked to allay her worries. "My name is Officer Montero, ma'am. This is my partner Poppy McGuire. We need to ask you a few questions about a case we're investigating."

Her round eyes opened wide, and she pressed her face to the screen. "Is it about Kellen? Is my son in trouble? He's okay, isn't he?"

"He's fine, ma'am. In fact, we just saw him at The Colonnade. No, the case involves his ex-girlfriend, Amy Perkins. Do you have a few minutes for our questions?" Alex asked.

She stepped out onto the porch and folded her arms across her chest. "I can't imagine who would have wanted to hurt that girl. She was just the nicest thing."

While Alex fished out his notepad and pen from his pants pocket, I took the opportunity to ask a question I'd wanted the answer to since the first time I met her son. "Mrs. Martin, how serious was their relationship? They weren't going out that long."

She thought about her answer for a moment and said, "Not too long, but Kellen was crazy about her. She was older, you know, so I think he might have been more infatuated with her than she was with him. She was only around for a little while, but we liked her almost as much as Kellen did."

Alex looked over at me and subtly raised his eyebrows before turning to ask Mrs. Martin a question. "Kellen says he was home alone with no one else who can verify that the night Amy was killed. Is there anyone who can help us eliminate him as a suspect?"

"He's a suspect? That's impossible! Kellen would never hurt Amy. Never!" she shrieked.

"Unfortunately, when we spoke to him, he didn't seem very bothered by the fact that she had been killed, and since we just saw him at the movies with another young woman, it doesn't seem like he's missing her much."

Alex wasn't usually so blunt with people's mothers, but either Mrs. Martin had no idea of the kind of person her son was or she was intentionally portraying him as a much nicer person than we'd experienced in the two times we'd spoken to him. For whatever it was worth, I didn't feel like she was lying. At least not intentionally. I had a sense that she believed her son had truly cared for Amy.

"Oh, that's not proof that he isn't missing her. He's

just like that." She turned to face me and continued. "You know how men are. They don't like to show their real feelings. I promise you he's heartbroken, even if it doesn't seem like it."

Alex began to say something, but I stopped him. "Men are definitely not very good with emotions, are they? If there was anything to show us he couldn't have done it, that's all we'd need. We don't want to investigate someone who is simply missing someone."

She grimaced and raised her eyes toward the porch roof for a moment, and then she held up her hands and excitedly said, "I called him on the home phone that night! He was here alone and he answered my call here. You can get the phone company to give you records or something, can't you? I called the house here before ten."

Alex wrote down in his notes and looked up as she continued to speak.

"I was worried that he hadn't fed my cat and wanted to make sure he did. Please, check the records and you'll see."

"Can you tell us the exact time you made the call and how long you spoke to him?" I asked, sympathizing with her.

"It was quarter to ten and we spoke for at least two minutes. Please check the records. If you need me to sign a waiver or anything, I will. Just give it to me and give me a pen."

"We'll check into that, ma'am," Alex said in his best polite voice. "Thank you for your help."

After swearing that her son could never do a horrible thing like murder, Mrs. Martin left us standing on her porch and wondering who the real Kellen was. Could the person we'd met really be just a front for the person his mother believed him to be?

As we walked back to the car, I asked Alex, "Do you really think Kellen was here all night?"

He laughed at the disappointment in my voice. "It's possible that awful guy isn't our murderer, Poppy. We'll have to see once we get the phone records."

I stopped at the end of the sidewalk and sighed. "I'm not buying that this guy is truly heartbroken. I think what we saw there is a mother who has no idea what her son is really like."

"What is that you said before? You can't plant peas and get corn? Maybe Mrs. Martin wishes the corn that grew was really peas like her," he said with a smile.

"I don't know. What I do know is that I like her more than her son."

Alex nodded and opened my car door. "On that, I agree one hundred percent."

Chapter Nineteen

CRAIG SAT BEHIND what used to be Stephen's desk tapping a stack of papers on the top and grinning like the cat who just swallowed the canary. I liked seeing him happy, and while I couldn't admit it out loud right there as I stood in the big office where everyone but Derek and Alex had their desks, seeing him in that chair instead of Stephen because of his promotion thrilled me as much as it did Craig.

Maybe even more since Stephen had been a thorn in my side for months.

"How's it going?" I asked him as he began to straighten out the stapler, tape dispenser, and pencil cup in front of him.

"Good! I'm ready to go as soon as you two are." Craig stopped fidgeting with his office supplies and leaned over his desk toward me. Looking up with his big blue eyes wide, he said, "I want you to know that I'm happy you're still going to be around and that Alex is staying on. It wouldn't be the same here without you guys."

"Thanks," I said as a smile spread across my face. "I'm happy to be staying too, and I know Alex loves being a cop."

"Yeah, but he could be a cop anywhere. I'm happy he decided to stay in Sunset Ridge."

I patted him on the shoulder for that compliment. "Thanks, Craig. I'm sure Alex would appreciate that."

"How long before we get our day rolling?"

Looking down the room toward Derek's office, I wondered the same thing. Alex had gone in to speak to the chief as soon as we arrived this morning, and for the past forty minutes or so, they'd been in the office with the door closed. Even I had no idea what they were discussing, so like everyone else, I was in the dark about what would happen next.

"I'm not sure. Whatever they're talking about, it seems pretty important. Maybe I'll make a coffee run while we're waiting. Want one?"

Craig's expression morphed onto a look of disgust and horror that said the last thing in the world he wanted was a coffee. I may not have understood his dislike of the best drink in the world, but I understood that face he made.

I laughed at his reaction to my simple question. "Got it. Can I get you anything else? Tea? Soda maybe?"

The muscles in his face relaxed, and he shook his head. "No, I'm good."

"I sometimes get Alex a danish. Would you like one too?" I asked as I turned to leave.

"No, but thank you so much for offering. I appreciate that, Poppy."

Looking back, I saw a huge smile lighting up Craig's face. Happy that I had put that there, I said what I knew would make him see that he was a welcome addition to our partnership. "You're with real partners now, Craig. The danish and coffee are just perks that come with it."

I didn't think it possible, but his smile actually grew bigger until it was nearly an ear to ear grin. "Thanks, Poppy. That means a lot to me."

With that bit of workplace kindness accomplished, I walked toward the exit and saw Alex coming out of Derek's office just as I passed by. A quick study of his face and body language told me whatever they'd been talking about for all that time hadn't been anything negative. While he wasn't grinning like Craig, he did look generally pleased with whatever the meeting had been about.

"I was just about to go for a coffee and danish run. Are we heading out now?"

Alex nodded and waved for Craig to join us. "Yeah. I want us to all go over every single clue we have so far and every suspect we can either count in or eliminate from our investigation. It's time to get back to work."

Okay, so maybe his conversation with Derek wasn't that wonderful. I heard frustration in Alex's voice and wondered if the whole Stephen issue had made this case more difficult on him than others. Just another reason to dislike him.

"Everything okay? You seem a little stressed," I said quietly so no one else could hear.

"No, I'm fine. Yesterday put me a little off my game, so I want to get back to working on this case and get it solved. Amy's father called Derek last night because someone told him the case was in disarray after Stephen left, so there's a little more pressure now. We'll get it solved, though. I told Derek that."

Jumping to Alex's defense, I said, "In disarray after Stephen left? It wouldn't have been in disarray, which it isn't, by the way, in the first place if he hadn't lied about knowing the victim. That really frosts my cookies, you know that? Nothing's in disarray. I don't even like that word now."

"Frosts my cookies?" he repeated, taking the least important part of my diatribe and focusing on it.

"Sorry. I'm hungry. My mind is on food at the moment."

Craig joined us just as I finished apologizing, and whatever Alex had been feeling faded away as a smile brightened his expression. "No time for food now. We need to go over everything Stephen did, including searching Amy's apartment for clues, and then talk to Tamara Ridgeway again and get some answers on how much a woman scorned she really was."

Turning toward Craig, Alex said, "You've taken a look at Stephen's notes about his interview with Amy's father. What do you think?"

Put on the spot, Craig looked frightened for a moment but then calmly said, "I don't think he had anything to do with his daughter's murder, but it might be good for one of us to speak to him again, just in case."

"I agree. That'll be our first stop, and then we'll head over to Amy's apartment to check there for any clues as to who would want her dead. If we're lucky, our killer sent her some threatening note or something," Alex said with a smile.

"Feeling particularly hopeful this morning?" I teased, knowing how unlikely it would be for us to find that kind of huge clue.

"I am. Let's get going so we can solve this case before the mayor and the council come down with a full case of witchcraft hysteria and send our chief around the bend."

THE INTERVIEW WITH Mr. Perkins gave us nothing more than what Stephen had reported in his notes from his talk with him, but it did provide Craig with the opportunity to see how a great cop did that part of the job. As we drove away from the Perkins house, I looked over at Alex with pride at how wonderful a mentor he was being to Craig.

"That was better than I imagined it would be, but I bet it's just that you make it look easy," Craig said from the backseat.

Looking up at the rearview mirror, Alex gave him a slight smile. "Just remember one thing and you'll always do fine with those kinds of interviews. Whether the person is a suspect or not, they're mourning the loss of someone they loved. Never forget that part of it."

I knew Alex spoke from experience not only as a police officer but as someone who had to endure losing his wife and being a suspect in her murder. Although he rarely talked about it, he'd told me a few times that he'd never forget how it felt to be grieving her death and have everyone suspicious of his every move.

"It doesn't take anything away from your performance on a case to act with some sympathy for what people are going through," he said as he pulled up in front of Amy Perkins' apartment and parked the police cruiser.

Looking back at Craig, I saw him nod in agreement. "Thanks, Alex. I won't forget that."

The three of us walked up to apartment 4B at 530 Sanderson Street to see a planter outside the door with bunny figurines just like at Kellen Martin's house welcoming us to her home. Pointing at it, I said, "Those look familiar?"

Alex and Craig both turned their attention to the friendly-looking rabbits holding the Welcome sign, and Alex nodded. Craig's expression said he was confused, but he didn't ask why I'd pointed them out.

Taking a sheet of paper out, he read off it. "It says that her landlord lives in apartment 1A. Want me to get the key off her?"

"Sounds good. Poppy and I will hang out here with the woodland creatures," Alex said with a chuckle.

Craig trotted off to speak to Amy's landlord, and I pushed on Alex's shoulder for that remark about the bunnies. "I like this kind of stuff. I think I'm going to get a planter for my front porch and put some welcoming woodland creatures in it, as you call them."

He looked down at the rabbits and then back at me. "It's not really my style, but it is your house."

Just the way he said that made me want to say, "It's basically an our house thing since you're always there." But I didn't. That was a conversation for another time.

Craig reappeared holding the key in front of him like some kind of treasure he'd found and opened the door for us. We walked into Amy's apartment and saw a neat and tidy home. Like her friend Crystal, she too liked nature, although her preference for it seemed limited to some plants on her kitchen counter and a few knockoff watercolor paintings hanging on the living room walls.

"Our victim sure did keep her house clean," Craig said under his breath as we all slid on plastic gloves to begin searching for anything that might help us understand who would want her dead.

"That makes it easier," Alex said with a smile, showing his pleasure at not having to sift through piles of junk like we'd had to in a number of cases. "Nothing like wading waist-deep through someone's life. That makes it ten times harder to find anything."

"So what are we looking for?" Craig asked as we began to look through the front room of the apartment.

"Anything that could tell us why someone would murder her," Alex said flatly, not helping Craig in the least.

As he stuck his hand in between the cushions on the couch, I opened the single drawer in her coffee table and began looking through the notes and papers Amy had hidden away in it. "Basically, it's like looking for a needle in a haystack. While we look in here, you could check the kitchen."

Happy to have something to do, he headed into the room next to the one we were checking. Alex finished his inspection of the couch and shook his head, and it dawned on me that I wasn't exactly the person who should be giving Craig directions on what to do.

"Sorry about that. I just thought it would be good for him to do this too."

"It's okay, Poppy. I was lost in thought there for a minute or I would have told him to check that room too. You did nothing wrong. Find anything in that drawer?"

I thumbed through an old magazine and shook my head. "No. She wasn't exactly hiding stuff in here. I think she just liked the top of the coffee table to be clean, so she stuffed the magazines and things that other people would keep on top of it in the drawer."

He looked around the very tidy room and sighed. "I'm beginning to wonder if this murder was because of her being a Druid. This woman seems to have very few people who disliked her, and other than having bad taste in the people she dated, she's a model citizen who went to work every day, did her job, and kept her house neat as a pin. Who kills someone like that?"

Closing the drawer, I looked into the kitchen to see Craig running his hand along the back of the counter and finding nothing in there either. "I don't know. We're still stuck with just two suspects—Kellen and Tamara."

Alex nodded. "And if those phone records show what his mother said was true, that leaves Tamara. I think it's time we drive out to the Third Eye Center and talk to her again. I want to know more details about her alibi for the night of the murder. We'll go right after we check Amy's bedroom."

We walked into the final room of Amy's three-room apartment to find it as spotless as the other two. The bed with its teal and purple sheets and comforter had been made, and every item on her dresser, from her makeup to the three perfume bottles lined up by size from smallest to largest, looked perfectly placed by someone who prized neatness and order.

Alex and I stood in the middle of the room shaking our heads after looking in her nightstand and finding nothing but a book on meditation and in her closet and finding every piece of clothing hung up perfectly and four pairs of shoes lined up on the floor. "Nothing. Looking at this place would lead anyone to think she was the straightest arrow out there," I said.

"And yet, she practiced a pagan religion and dated both men and women. That's not exactly a straight arrow in most people's books," he said as he took another look around the room.

"Neither of those things are exactly wild and crazy these days, Alex. It is the twenty-first century, you know," I said with a chuckle, having a little fun tweaking the proper side of his personality.

Shrugging, he turned to head back out into the kitchen. "To each his own, I guess."

I followed him out to join Craig, who stood at the end of the Formica counter next to Amy's refrigerator. In his hand, he held something round and green. "This looks just like the green rock we found near the body at the scene. Malachite?"

Taking a plastic baggie out of his pocket, Alex held it open and Craig dropped the stone into it. "Maybe the gods are looking down on us and there's a fingerprint on it other than the victim's," Alex said, flashing me a smile.

"The gods?" I asked as he announced it was time to move on to the Third Eye Mind and Body Center. "Why, Officer Montero, how open-minded of you."

He rolled his eyes while I walked past him out into the heat of the day.

WE DROPPED CRAIG off at the station with the malachite so he could get it to the lab to hopefully find a fingerprint that would help us while we drove out to speak to Tamara Ridgeway again at the Third Eye Center. I wanted to do nothing less in the whole world than speak to her again, but since she'd continued to be one of our strongest suspects in the case, it was time to ask her a few more questions.

Alex parked the car in the empty parking lot in front of the building and joined me to walk into the center. "How does this place stay in business? It's the middle of the day and there's not a car in the lot," he asked.

"Maybe all the customers are the eco-friendly type

who take the shoe leather express," I joked. "Seriously, though, other than The Grounds, what store in town does much business on any day? Somehow they all stay open."

As he opened the door, he muttered, "Another mystery of the small town."

Tamara Ridgeway stood behind the counter in all her glory sorting through receipts as we walked in. The heady scent of patchouli hit me like a baseball bat to the head two steps into the building, and I waved my hand in front of me to dispel the odor.

"Again? Should I call a lawyer?" Tamara asked in all her rudeness.

"Miss Ridgeway, we're here to ask you about your relationship with Amy Perkins. When I asked you last time we spoke, you said you didn't have a relationship with her, but we've since learned that you indeed did have more than just a passing knowledge of each other. Why didn't you tell us you were dating her at one time?"

"Who said that? Tell me who said that. It's a lie!" she shrieked.

Before the interview went completely off the rails, I jumped in and said, "Miss Ridgeway, we're not here to judge you. Love is love. We don't have any issue with you and Amy dating, but you did lie. We just want to know why."

Tamara stood there staring at us and saying nothing for a long moment. Alex gave me a tiny smile to let me know he appreciated my diffusing the situation, but I hoped I'd done more than that. I wanted her to give us the truth about her relationship with Amy so we could make some headway on this case.

She finally spoke, and I was struck by how

uncharacteristically gentle her voice sounded. Knitting her brows, she said quietly, "Because I didn't want to be judged yet again for loving her."

Before our eyes, Tamara Ridgeway morphed into a softer version of herself. Gone was the harshness in her expression, and her tone became far less shrill. "I didn't kill Amy. I would never hurt her."

Alex took out his pen and notebook and asked, "Why did the two of you break up?"

Tamara frowned and lowered her head. "I wanted something more serious, and she didn't."

"How did that make you feel?" he asked.

"It broke my heart. That's how it made me feel. Then she started dating that man and my heart broke all over again."

In a low voice, I said, "Stephen."

"Stephen," she repeated in a tone full of sadness. "He never cared about her. Not like I did. But she wanted something more traditional."

"Do you have anyone who can prove where you were Thursday night between eight and ten?"

She shook her head sadly. "No. All I can say to you is that I would never hurt Amy. We may have fought at times, but that wasn't because I hated her enough to kill her. It was because I loved her so much and couldn't stop her from turning away from what we had."

"That's why you called your fellow witches when you found out what had happened, isn't it? Because you loved her," I said.

Tamara nodded sadly but said nothing.

Alex flipped the cover over on his notepad and slipped it into his pocket. "Thank you, Miss Ridgeway."

I watched him turn and walk out of the Third Eye

Mind and Body Center, so after giving Tamara a smile, I followed him out to the car, surprised he had stopped the interview when he did. I caught up with him just as he opened his door.

"Is she still a suspect?"

He nodded and simply said, "Yes."

"I thought you'd have more to ask her."

Leaning against the car, he sighed like talking to her had exhausted him. "I didn't see any point in continuing. She lost someone she loved, and like I told Craig before, it doesn't take away from what we do to have sympathy for people."

"So you believe her when she says she loved Amy and would never hurt her?"

"I don't know if she would hurt her, but I do believe her when she says she loved Amy. For now, she stays on the list of suspects. Let's get back to the station and see what Craig has for us."

Chapter Twenty

"SINCE WE DON'T have time for a real lunch, why don't you grab us some coffee and a few danishes while I bring Craig up to speed on what's going on? Cheese for me, please."

He turned to ask Craig if he wanted one, and unlike earlier, our new partner jumped at the chance for a snack. "Thanks, I'd love one!"

"Cherry or cheese? I know you don't want a coffee, heaven forbid," I teased him.

"Cherry, please."

"Give me five minutes and I'll be back with the goodies."

I headed across Main Street and grabbed the two coffees and three danishes, cheese for Alex and two cherry for Craig and me. As I reached the front doors to the station, Alex came charging out, nearly knocking me over. Since I knew he couldn't have been that eager to get his black coffee and cheese danish, I wondered what had happened to make him like this as I quickly juggled the cardboard cup holder in my left hand and the paper bag in my right hand so nothing spilled out of its container.

"What is going on with you?" I exclaimed as he

grabbed the coffees from me and practically yanked me into the building.

"Come with me. I want you to see something Craig just pointed out to me," Alex said excitedly.

It wasn't like him to become agitated like this over any small thing, so his behavior piqued my interest and I hurried with him into his office. Craig sat in one of the chairs in the front of his desk waiting for us, and as we practically ran in to join him, he stared at us with a wide-eyed look of anticipation I imagined resembled what I looked like at that moment.

"What happened?" he asked in a nearly frantic voice. "What did I say to make you run out like that?"

Alex deposited the tray with our coffees on his desk, spilling some of mine as he set it in front of him, and sat down hard in his chair. Pointing at a sheet of paper in Craig's hand, he said, "I want you to tell Poppy what you just told me."

Craig drew his eyebrows in, clearly confused by the way Alex was acting, and looked down at the sheet of paper in his hand. "I spoke to the person who worked the ticket booth at the movie theater, Dick Montanga. He said he recognized one of the witches from the tarot readers convention from her handout Poppy gave me. Said she came to The Colonnade the night of the murder and saw the nine o'clock showing of *An Affair to Remember*. Also said she bought a big bucket of buttered popcorn and a box of those chocolate covered raisin candies."

He turned to look at me like I had the answer as to what Alex found so interesting in that report, but I had nothing. Had he been upset because Craig hadn't mentioned everything she ate when he first told us the details?

"Okay. So she eats a lot for a two hour movie." I looked over at Alex and asked, "Are you angry because he didn't tell us about the raisin candies the other day?"

"No. I'm not interested at all in what Melody Chamberlain ate at the movies that night. I'm more interested in the person who provided her with an alibi. Recognize the name?" he asked.

I racked my brain to think of how I would know this Dick Montanga person, but as far as I knew, I'd never met him. "I don't. Should I?"

"Remember Richard, the unhappy ticket person at the movies last night?"

Since Kellen Martin had outnastied him by a mile, I'd all but forgotten about that cranky guy. "Oh, yeah. He was pretty miserable. Okay, so why does that matter?"

"So you remember what he was doing when we got there?" Alex asked, clearly more interested in Mr. Montanga than I understood, but why?

I shook my head as I tried to figure out where he was going with all of this. "No. Reading a magazine? I remember he got startled when you tapped on the glass in front of him."

Alex nodded. "Close. He was looking at a greeting card he'd gotten from someone. A female someone. You didn't see it?"

"No, but good for him. He's got a girl."

I didn't give one fig about this guy or his girl, but at the moment, my partner looked like I'd succeeded in completely frustrating him the way he stared across the desk at me like I should be saying something different than the words that were coming out of my mouth. I had a feeling if I said one more flippant thing, Alex might throw his hands up and declare I was the world's worst partner.

"I'm sorry, but I didn't see who the card was from, and I'm clearly not getting where you're taking me. Instead of slow walking this whole thing, what if you just told me what you obviously saw so we all can figure out what you mean?"

"M. The card was from someone named M."

The way he said that sentence made me feel like he thought all the pieces of this puzzle of his would fall into place for me immediately, but unfortunately for all of us, they didn't. I still had no idea what was going on.

Craig stared at me almost helplessly while I tried to understand the importance of our interaction with the ticket guy at the movies. Finally, I threw my hands up in frustration.

"I don't know what that means. So this person who gave him a card is called M. Maybe he's dating Judi Dench?"

Clearly disgusted with my lack of help, Alex narrowed his eyes to angry slits and glared at me. "What? Who's that?"

That question I knew the answer to. "She plays M in the Bond movies."

Alex leaned back in his chair and stared up at the ceiling, pinching the bridge of his nose. "I usually love your cute comments, Poppy, but I have to admit I'm not crazy about them today."

I looked over at Craig and saw worry settle into his eyes. I wasn't worried about Alex being upset, but I did feel bad that his day was turning out to be pretty rocky. To reassure our new partner, I patted him on the forearm.

"It's okay. We do this kind of thing all the time. Some days we aren't on the same page, but we get there eventually."

Mumbling, Alex said, "This is one of those different pages days."

Craig cleared his throat and tentatively said, "Are you trying to say that Dick Montanga is dating one of the suspects?"

My eyes flew open as the realization of what my partner had been alluding to finally became clear. Snatching the paper out of Craig's hand, I scanned it in a hurry to find the three tarot readers' names and there on the very top they were listed.

Jerilyn
Susie
Melody

Alex lurched forward and leaned across his desk, pointing at the paper I held in my hand. "Not a suspect until you started to read me what you'd found out again this morning. If Melody Chamberlain's alibi is actually her boyfriend, which he might be if she's the person who gave him a card signed Love M, she might have just jumped to the number one spot on our suspect list. I think this is a lead we need to check out immediately."

Finally understanding, I became as excited as Alex and jumped to my feet. "So what do we do now? It's Saturday, so the movies opens early, but Richard or Dick might not be working today since he was working last night."

Alex stood too and came around his desk. "Craig, I

want you to go to that tarot readers convention in Caston and keep an eye on Melody Chamberlain. Today's the last day it's being held, so I'm betting she'll be there. Poppy and I are going to The Colonnade to find out more about Mr. Montanga. Call me if Melody isn't there or leaves at any time during the day."

Craig nodded and hurried out the door to leave, but I called after him, "Do you still have that pamphlet of hers I gave you? I think her picture is on the back."

He spun around and waved the pamphlet in front of him. "I got it! I'll let you know if she doesn't show or tries to get away!" he said excitedly as he ran out of the building.

Alex smiled at his enthusiasm, but I felt bad that I'd let my partner down. "I'm sorry I didn't get what you were trying to say before. I should have picked up on that so much earlier."

"I thought you had seen what I saw on that card last night. I didn't mean to make you look like you didn't know what was going on in front of Craig. I'm sorry about that."

Tapping him on the arm, I brushed off any idea that I had been bothered by Craig seeing me in the dark. "It's fine. You don't have to apologize, Alex. As long as we're on the same page now is all that's important."

He smiled in that sexy way he usually reserved for when we were in private. "Time to go check out Richard the cranky ticket taker. I hope the theater is open."

WE PARKED IN front of The Colonnade and saw two female workers going through the front doors, so Alex and I headed inside to look for the manager who might be able to help us find out more about Melody Chamberlain's alibi. The lobby of the theater looked different during the day than it did at night. The dark blue carpeting beneath our feet appeared far more worn than it had when I glanced at it not twenty-four hours earlier, and the walls covered with framed old movie posters looked quite bland without the lights beneath and above showcasing them. In the light of day, the lobby reminded me more of some hobbyist's collection kept in their attic than the grand entrance to the old theater.

Behind the concessions counter stood the two young women we'd seen come through the door a minute ago. We approached them, and the one cleaning the glass on the inside of the candy case looked up as we stopped in front of her.

"We're not open yet. Sorry."

Pressing his badge to the glass, Alex said, "We need to speak to someone in charge. Is there a manager around?"

The woman stared up at his badge for a moment and then quickly stood up to point toward a door at the far end of the lobby. "That's his office. He just got in."

Alex and I hurried over to the manager's door and before he could even lift his hand to knock on it, the door flew open and there stood Richard Montanga, the unhappy ticket man from the night before.

"You're quite the jack-of-all-trades, aren't you?" Alex said as he showed the man his badge.

One look at it and all the blood drained out of his face until he looked pale like he'd just seen a ghost. He opened his mouth to say something and then shook his head.

"I don't know what this is about, but I've done nothing wrong."

"Mr. Montanga, I'm Officer Alex Montero and this is my partner Poppy McGuire. We need to ask you some questions regarding someone you said you saw in the theater on Thursday night. Her name is Melody Chamberlain, and you told another officer that you saw her that night at the nine o'clock showing of *An Affair to Remember*."

I watched the man as Alex spoke. Even before he mentioned Melody's name, Richard Montanga's face froze in an expression of complete and utter fear. I waited for him to claim he knew nothing about seeing her that night, but when Alex finished, he simply averted his gaze to the floor and kept it there.

"Do you remember this, sir?" Alex asked.

"I think so. I mean, I do remember a woman paying to see that movie," he mumbled.

"Mr. Montanga, do you know Melody Chamberlain on a personal level?" I asked, hoping to get a reaction from him with my blunt question.

He didn't give it to me, though, and continued to stare down toward his feet. "I'm not sure what you mean."

Alex took a step forward, crowding his space. "What she means is is Melody Chamberlain your girlfriend?"

Richard Montanga continued to focus on the floor, so Alex crowded him even more and barked, "I want an answer! Is she your girlfriend?"

The man's head snapped up, and he looked at Alex right in front of him with terror in his eyes. "I...I didn't mean any harm. She told me to say she was here seeing a movie if anyone came around asking. I didn't ask why.

It didn't seem like a big deal."

Glaring down at him, Alex said, "Well, sir, it is a big deal. What you're saying is Melody Chamberlain wasn't here Thursday night for the nine o'clock movie?"

The manager shook his head. "No. I didn't see her until close to midnight after the last movie let out and we met at my apartment."

"You'll be expected to testify to that. For now, do you have anything else you want to tell us about when you saw her that night? Was she nervous or upset about anything?"

I waited with bated breath to hear his answer to Alex's question, but Richard Montanga simply stammered out that he just remembered her being happy to see him. He didn't seem able to recall anything else, so we left him looking shattered outside his office and headed toward the car.

Alex called Craig on our way there. "Is she there?"

I heard Craig answer, "Yeah, she's reading someone's cards."

"Okay. Don't let her leave. We're on our way."

Alex's phone rang almost as soon as he finished speaking to Craig, but this time it was Derek calling. I watched confusion settle into his face for a moment before he said, "Okay, Chief. Thanks."

"What was that about?" I asked, curious as to what Derek could have said to him to make him look so nonplussed.

"The lab got a fingerprint that wasn't Amy's off that malachite stone found at the scene. It belongs to someone named Morgan Tillerson. Derek says this woman has a rap sheet from when she lived in Ohio. She got caught passing bad checks and stealing credit cards."

Now I was the one who was confused. "So? Do we know where this Morgan Tillerson was the night Amy was murdered? Is she another suspect?"

Alex stopped walking and shook his head. "Not another suspect. Morgan Tillerson goes by a different name. Melody Chamberlain."

I opened my mouth to speak, but the words didn't come out as I sorted through what he was telling me. Finally, I said, "So Melody is really Morgan, but we still have no reason to believe either one of them disliked Amy, so what reason would she have to kill her?"

Shrugging, Alex leaned against his side of the car. "I don't know, but without an alibi and her being Morgan, she's at least as good as Tamara, who has no alibi, and better than Kellen since the phone records showed his mother was right about her call to him. The fact that Melody lied to us and had Richard in there lie so she'd have an alibi makes her my number one suspect. I guess we'll see what she has to say."

So Melody had no alibi and could be our murderer, but the question remained. Why would she kill Amy Perkins?

Chapter Twenty-One

THE MIDDAY HEAT pressed down on me as we walked into the building where the tarot readers convention was still going on for another few hours. The weatherman had promised a break in the heat wave by today, but if he thought this was a reprieve, he and I had vastly different definitions of what cooler meant.

As usual, Alex looked fresh and crisply dressed, as if the scorching temperatures and humidity didn't even affect him. While I wiped the sweat from my brow that had formed there in the matter of less than a minute that it took to get from the car to the building, I looked at him with part admiration and part resentment, wishing I could look that cool in these temperatures and as I was about to solve a big case.

"You ready?" he asked with a wink as he held open the door to Jacob's Hall for me to walk in.

"I'm ready for air conditioning. As for this Melody and Morgan thing, I have to say I'm still a little confused and more than a little worried," I replied as we walked into the main hall where all the tarot readers' booths stood. "She's a witch, so who knows what kind of hocus pocus she could whip up. What if she turns one of us into a toad?"

He stopped and looked at me like I'd said something amusing. Laughing, he shook his head. "That's one of the many reasons I love you, Poppy. You make me see the lighter side of things. I wouldn't worry about her turning anyone into a toad. I don't believe in any of that anyway, so stick with me and you'll be fine."

Whether or not he believed in witchcraft didn't matter. If she was backed into a corner, who knew what Melody would do?

Craig met us halfway between the door and her booth, looking more bored than anything else. "She's just been reading cards and drinking diet soda like all the other tarot readers since I got here."

"Like any other tarot reader who murdered someone in cold blood," Alex said snidely.

I looked over toward her area and saw her most recent customer walk away after grabbing one of the pamphlets from her table. Gently elbowing Alex, I whispered, "I think that's our cue."

We began walking toward her booth, but I noticed that Craig hung back and didn't join us. Alex turned around and waved him to us. He hurried to catch up with us wearing a smile that told me that damn Stephen had sidelined him the whole time they'd been partners. Well, not anymore. We three partners were in this case together, and that's how it would be until it was solved.

Just before we reached her, Alex leaned in and said to Craig, "You're in charge of watching her. If she tries to get away, stop her."

I heard hesitation in Craig's voice as he answered, "Okay. I won't let her get away, Alex."

Melody running away and having to be caught didn't worry me as much as the possibility that she had some kind of magical ability to vanish or something like that. Alex may not have believed in witchcraft or the supernatural, but I did. While I'd never witnessed anything like someone vanishing into thin air firsthand, I didn't discount the idea that it could be possible.

"Miss Chamberlain, I'm back to ask you a few more questions. Your alibi now says that you weren't at The Colonnade seeing a movie during the time that Amy Perkins was murdered. Can you tell me where you were between the hours of eight and ten Thursday night?"

Alex stood in front of Melody's booth with his pen and notepad in his hands waiting for her to answer, his body language relaying his confidence that he would find out the truth as he stood tall and straight, his focus zeroed in on her. I paid attention to her reaction to his succinct statement and saw how shaken she became by what he'd said.

Wearing those same necklaces as she had the last time we'd spoken to her, she tugged hard on them once again before standing up to answer his question. "I don't know what you're talking about, officer. I'm just a simple tarot card reader here to entertain people. As for where I was on Thursday night, I've already told you. I went to see a showing of *An Affair to Remember* at the movies."

"The Colonnade?" I quickly asked, running through my knowledge of any other theaters in the area and coming up with none that showed older films like The Colonnade did.

She hesitated and pulled the necklaces tighter against her neck before saying, "Well, now that you ask, I'm not sure. I usually go there to see movies, but it might have been another theater."

"Which one? Was it the one in Frederick? Or was it

the one in Millville?" I asked, naming all the theaters in the area in rapid fire succession.

Melody attempted to stay calm, but by the way she was pulling on those necklaces, I knew not being able to come up with a solid lie was getting to her. I also worried that at any moment she'd decapitate herself.

"Now that you mention it, I think it was the one in Frederick. Yeah, that's it. I'm sorry I got confused and said The Colonnade. I didn't mean to mislead you."

Before Alex could follow up on her statement, I stepped forward and shook my head. "I'm sorry, Melody, but that's not possible. The theater in Frederick had been getting a complete refurbishment for the past two months, so it couldn't have been there where you saw *An Affair to Remember*."

She released the necklaces and threw her hands up in frustration. "Fine. Then it was the theater in Millville."

"No, it wasn't. The theater in Millville only shows first-run films during the week. On Saturday nights, as Officer Montero can attest to, they show a weekly monster movie, which I can promise you is nothing like *An Affair to Remember*. The only movie theater in the area that was showing that film on Thursday night was The Colonnade."

"What does it matter where I saw the movie? I saw it and that means I couldn't have killed Amy," she said, her voice growing shrill by the time she said our victim's name.

Now Alex spoke up to tighten the noose. "It matters because your alibi who works at The Colonnade, Richard Montanga, will testify that you were never there that night. You asked him to lie for you and say you were there, and he said yes because he's your boyfriend. But while *An Affair to Remember* was playing, you were in the woods outside of Sunset Ridge killing Amy Perkins."

"That's a lie!" Melody cried out.

"No, it's not, Morgan. That is your name, isn't it? Morgan Tillerson? The game is over. We know all about your crimes as Morgan, and now as Melody, you can add murder. We have your fingerprint on a malachite stone found near Amy's body and your alibi has fallen apart, so Morgan Tillerson/Melody Chamberlain, you have the right to remain silent."

I saw her look to her left at the space that allowed her to leave her booth and knew what she planned to do. "Craig, don't let her go!"

In a flash, she rushed out into the hall and ran toward the fire exit. Craig chased after her, but she reached the doors before he could grab her, and suddenly, the room filled with the piercing high-pitched sound of the fire alarm. Instinctively, I pressed my fingers into my ears, but Alex tugged on my arm.

"She can't get away!" he yelled. "Come on!"

People rushed toward the front door and the fire exit door, creating a crowd at each one, so that by the time we got outside, neither Craig nor Melody were anywhere to be found. Alex pointed toward the street, so we hurried across it to get away from the earsplitting alarm that hadn't been shut off yet.

Able to finally hear ourselves think, Alex pulled out his cell phone and called Craig. As he waited for him to answer, he scanned the area as I had a second earlier and found the same thing.

Nothing.

"Damnit! I told him not to let her escape. If he let

her get away—"

Alex abruptly stopped talking and pointed down the street. I turned to see Craig holding Melody by the arm escorting her back to us. When they finally reached where we stood, I saw she had her hands behind her back because he had already placed the handcuffs on her wrists.

"Should I put her in the back of the cruiser?" Craig asked before letting out a huge sigh.

More than a little surprised, Alex nodded and handed him the keys. "Did you read her her rights?"

"Yep."

"Okay, then. Yeah. Put her in and we'll head back to the station. Good job, partner."

Craig beamed a smile I was sure I'd never forget. No one in the history of law enforcement had ever been so happy to put someone in the back of a police car before. I looked at Alex and saw he was pretty happy too. Craig had been important to this case, and when the time came for him to spring into action, he did just that and caught our suspect before she got away and managed to change her name to yet something else.

"I guess all's well that ends well?"

He smiled and shook his head. "Now comes the part that I have a feeling is going to be more than a little bizarre. Something tells me Melody or Morgan or whatever we're supposed to call her isn't going to be very helpful in helping us understand why she killed our victim."

I looked into the back seat and wished she would just spill the beans. What made her commit that awful and final act of murder?

THROUGH THE WINDOW into the interrogation room, Derek and I watched Alex ask Melody that very question I'd wondered about as I got into the car in front of Jacob's Hall. She insisted she had nothing to do with Amy's death, despite the fact that her fingerprint was found on the malachite stone near the body and her alibi had fallen apart once her boyfriend told us the truth.

"There's no point avoiding the reality that we know what happened. Fingerprints don't lie. You were out in those woods, and I say it was the night that you killed Amy Perkins. What I want to know is why. Why kill Amy Perkins? Was it because she refused to call herself a witch? Was that what it was? She belittled your beliefs and you lashed out?"

Melody looked across the table at him, grimacing as she shook her head. "I'm not this Morgan person you claim I am, and I was at the movies that night. That's all you're going to get from me."

Alex pushed a piece of paper across the table at her and tapped his finger on the top. "You and Morgan Tillerson have the same fingerprints. Interesting thing about fingerprints. They're unique to each person. So there is no chance you and this person have identical fingerprints. Now that we've settled that, if you tell me what happened, maybe there were extenuating circumstances. Were you defending yourself?" he asked in a low voice, attempting to lead her to a confession.

Derek nudged my left arm and chuckled. "I never fail to enjoy watching him do this with suspects. Your boyfriend has the golden touch. He says things so directly, but the sound of his voice lulls them into wanting to tell him all their secrets."

I smiled at his compliment on Alex's interrogation

style. He really did have a way of getting people to divulge what he wanted to know.

Melody pressed her lips together for a moment before she sighed and her entire body sagged in the chair. "Would it matter if I was defending myself?"

"It could. It would depend on the circumstances."

I held my breath as I watched the scene unfolding in front of us. I could almost see the wheels begin to spin in her mind while she struggled to figure out how to explain how she'd been defending herself against Amy, a woman who was considerably smaller than she was in height and stature.

And the biggest problem with any self-defense claim would be the fact that Amy wasn't killed by the dagger being buried in her chest. Alex hadn't mentioned the real cause of death—smothering. The inescapable reality was smothering didn't happen by accident and couldn't truthfully be a method anyone could use to defend themselves. Smothering was a purely aggressive movement.

"He's got her now. See how she's thinking about what he just said about it being better for her if she was defending herself? Watch. She's going to start talking now."

As if right on cue, Melody began explaining that she and Amy had gone up into the woods to perform a cleansing ritual, but just after they started, Amy accused her of sleeping with her boyfriend. Melody played it up well and actually mustered up some tears to compliment her story.

"She was crazy. I was just standing there chanting and she began ranting and raving about that Kellen person. I didn't know what to do. She lunged at me, and

I guess I just grabbed the dagger we'd used in raising energy," she sobbed.

I excitedly turned to my left and grabbed Derek's arm as the lies poured out of Melody's mouth. "That's a complete fabrication! Amy was a Druid. What she believed never involved raising energy. Her friend told us all about it when we spoke to her. Amy just wouldn't ever be a part of anything like this. She's so lying!"

"Shhh. Just watch. Alex is letting her talk her way into a corner. She's boxed herself in now."

Alex wrote a few notes, carefully using his silence to control the pace of the interrogation. Melody fidgeted in her seat as the seconds ticked by and he still hadn't looked up from his notepad. I loved watching him do this. There was something so skillful about it.

Finally, he lifted his head and looked across the table at her. "So you just grabbed the nearest thing to defend yourself, right? She was coming at you, not the other way around?"

She nodded her head up and down and pulled on those necklaces for the first time during their interview. "Yes. I was just defending myself. I swear."

Very slowly, Alex put his pen down in the center of his notepad and leaned back in his chair. Folding his arms across his chest, he said, "See, here's the problem with that story. Amy Perkins wasn't murdered by a knife jammed into her chest. The cause of her death was smothering. You pushed something against her mouth and nose and tried to suffocate her. But you panicked when it didn't happen fast enough and turned to a method you knew would work. You stabbed her in the chest. That's how it happened, Melody. We know it, and you know it too."

Stunned by Alex's accurate description of what she'd really done that night out in the woods, Melody opened her mouth to speak, but no words came out. She simply stared at him in disbelief before hanging her head.

"I didn't have a choice. I couldn't let her go after she told me she found out about who I really was. I don't know how she found out, but she did, and I knew she was the type of person who wouldn't keep my secret. I wasn't going to let her ruin everything. I'd started a new life, and I couldn't let her take that away from me."

Alex put his notepad and pen into his pocket and walked around the table to stand behind her. "Morgan Tillerson, you're going away for a long time for the murder of Amy Perkins."

After putting the handcuffs back on her wrists, he led her out of the interrogation room to start the process that I hoped would eventually lead to her spending the rest of her life behind bars. Turning to face Derek, I saw a smile on his face.

"How are you doing?"

His smile faded a little, and he shrugged. "I'm okay. The issue with Stephen worked itself out pretty well. I can't say I'll miss him much. I'm glad Alex decided to stay. You too."

"Thanks. Craig is turning out to be a pretty good cop too, so don't forget that," I said, happy to build him up with his chief.

Derek leaned away from me like he couldn't believe what I'd just said. "Really? I was going to ask Alex about how he did, but I'm glad to hear that you think he's shaping up. I like him, you know? He's a nice guy."

"He is. I think with a decent partner he will end up being a good cop."

Left unsaid was my concern that Derek would assign him permanently as Alex's partner. While I genuinely liked Craig, I also liked being able to work with Alex one-on-one. But like always, the truth was I wasn't a police officer. Craig was. So Derek had every right as the chief to place him with Alex, and I'd have no right to say a word about it.

"I think you're right. Any suggestions on who would be a good partner for him?" Derek asked, smirking the entire time.

Looking back into the empty interrogation room, I shrugged. "Why ask me? I'm not on the force."

We stood in silence until he said, "I've been meaning to talk to you about that. I've looked into it, and I can deputize anyone I want on any case. It's basically what I've been doing the whole time you've been working with Alex, but from now on, I'm going to make it official. It's only for the duration of each case, but it's something I think I should do."

My mouth dropped open at Derek's news. Deputized? A real member of the police force?

"Oh my God! That's so great! I don't know what to say."

Derek let out a hearty laugh at my surprise. "That's a first. Poppy McGuire not knowing what to say."

Actually, I did have one question.

"Do I get a badge?" I asked, hoping the answer would be yes.

He rolled his eyes and turned around to walk out. "I'll think about it. In the meantime, it's good to have you on the team, Poppy."

Poppy McGuire, deputy of the Sunset Ridge police department. I loved that!

As I headed out of the viewing room to find Alex, I couldn't wait to tell him. Tonight, we'd celebrate.

ALEX SAT BEHIND his desk filling out forms on the Amy Perkins case when I walked in and sat down in my usual seat. I didn't say anything until he looked over at me, but I was dying to share my news.

"You look like you're going to explode, Poppy. What's going on?"

"Derek just gave me the best news. He's going to make me a deputy for each case we work on. I might even be getting a badge! How cool is that? Deputized!"

A smile slowly lifted the corners of his mouth. "I was wondering when he would give you the news. I knew you'd be happy, though. I'm glad he did it after all this time."

"You knew? How long did you know he was planning to do this?"

"We talked about it a few times, but he told me this morning after talking to the town council about it."

I thought back to when he and Derek were meeting with the door closed. So that's what they were discussing. I'd assumed it had been about the Amy Perkins case.

"Why were you guys talking about this behind closed doors for so long? Was there a problem?" I asked, suddenly unsure Alex really wanted me to be deputized on each of our cases.

"No. We talked about a few other things too. We weren't just talking about you being deputized."

Now I was intrigued. Why wasn't he telling me what they talked about?

"Is there something going on that I should know about, Alex? Is something wrong?"

He shook his head and smiled. "I'll tell you what we talked about over dinner. How does pizza sound? We can sit outside in the backyard since the heatwave is supposed to break tonight."

"Pizza sounds great, but only if it cools down. If not, we're going to have to take our dinner inside."

"It's a deal. I can't have you melting on me now. That won't do."

Thrilled with how everything had turned out, I sat relaxed in my chair, happy to say we'd solved another case. "So in the end, Amy was killed because she was going to be an honest person and Melody couldn't stand that."

"Pretty much. It was never about witchcraft or her being a Druid. It wasn't Amy's secrets that did her in but Melody's."

It wouldn't be any consolation to her family, but they could be proud that she was a good person who believed in the truth above everything else.

Chapter Twenty-Two

I CAME DOWN the stairs to the delicious aroma of pizza with sausage and peppers, my favorite kind of fast food. Taking a deep breath in, I stopped next to the kitchen table and lifted the pizza box to see our dinner. It wasn't fancy or elegant, but I had a feeling it would hit the spot.

Alex peeked his head in the back door and smiled. "How was your shower? Feeling better now?"

"Human is how I'd describe it. How's the weather out there? Did that cold front actually come through and cool things down?"

"Yep. I think it's down to around just below eighty now," he said like that was anywhere close to the definition of cool.

"Eighty? Are you sure you don't want to eat in here? I just got cleaned up. Ten minutes out there and I'll be as melted as the cheese on the pizza, Alex."

He said nothing, but the resolute look in his eyes said he had his heart set on a nighttime picnic out at that old wooden picnic table in my backyard. If he wanted it that badly, how could I say no to such a simple desire?

Even though it would mean I'd probably be a sweaty mess in just a few minutes.

Love was all about compromise, so out I'd go into the warm night and eat pizza at that rickety old table.

"Do you have plates and silverware out there already?" I yelled out through the screen door.

"I've got it all taken care of. All that's missing is you," he yelled in to me.

How could I decline an offer like that?

Alex waited for me in the backyard, and as I made my way to the table, I saw he'd brought out my mother's silver candlesticks and had found the candles from the other night to illuminate our meal. Chuckling, I sat down and swung my legs over the bench.

"A candlelight dinner of pizza and root beer? You really pulled out all the stops tonight," I joked.

He handed me a paper plate with a slice of pizza on it and placed a glass of root beer on the table in front of me. Lifting his glass in the air, he said, "To another case solved."

I raised mine in front of me and tapped it against his. "You did a great job interrogating her, Alex. Derek and I watched in awe. You're a great cop, so I'm glad after everything that happened with Stephen that this case turned out like it did."

As I took my first sip of root beer and the sweet taste hit my tongue, he stood up and lifted his leg over the bench to walk around the table. I took a bite of pizza, relishing the delicious mix of green peppers, spicy sausage, warm cheese, and tangy sauce on the lightest crust I'd ever enjoyed.

Lost in the sensory delights of my dinner, I didn't notice Alex moving next to me until he was kneeling down on the ground looking up at me. Had he fallen?

Suddenly, he got up on one knee. "Poppy, I love

you. You brought me back into the land of the living after I'd convinced myself that I'd be alone for the rest of my life. You showed me I needed to follow the path I believed in before Helena's death. I'm only a police officer again because of you. I can't imagine my life without you."

He lifted his hand and held out a small black velvet box. Tilting the lid back, he revealed a diamond ring sitting in the middle of it. "Elizabeth McGuire, will you marry me?"

Even though I was surrounded by fresh air, my lungs felt like I couldn't get enough into them to breathe. The facets of the diamond glistened in the candlelight, and all I could think of was how foolish I'd been in the past few weeks. I'd been worried that he didn't want to take our relationship to the next level and move in together, and here he had been planning this.

"Oh my…" I couldn't get the words out. Clearing my throat, I tried again to tell him how happy he'd made me.

"Of course I'll marry you, Alex. I love you."

I swung my legs over the bench, dropped to my knees, and wrapped my arms around him. "I love you so much! I had no idea you were planning to do this tonight."

He took my left hand in his and slipped the beautiful oval-shaped diamond on my ring finger. Smiling, he said, "Now it's official."

I stared at the symbol of our love and commitment to each other and kissed him on the lips. He looked down at me with those brown eyes that hid so much of what he felt, but at that moment, I knew exactly the emotions he was experiencing because I was feeling them too.

"I can't wait to show everyone! I think they're going to be surprised."

A sheepish look came over his face, and he quietly said, "Your father and Derek already know, so you won't be able to surprise them."

"You told the two of them before asking me?" I asked with surprise.

"Well, I had to ask your father for his blessing, so that's why he knew before you. And Derek is the closest friend I have in town next to you, so I wanted to tell him."

Leave it to Alex to be so sweet even as he was telling me I was the third person to find out he wanted to marry me. Cradling his face, I kissed him on the lips and smiled.

"You are such an old-fashioned guy. You actually asked my father for his blessing? That's so wonderful!"

"I wanted to do it the right way. You deserve that. This time, you're going to get all the way to the church because your fiancé knows how to do things right."

He hugged me to him, and as we sat there in the cool grass in my backyard, I couldn't have been happier.

Poppy Montero.

I liked the sound of that.

Poppy and Alex return in
The Finest Hour:
A Poppy McGuire Mystery
(Poppy McGuire Mysteries Book #7)

About The Author

Anina Collins has always loved a good mystery. From Agatha Christie's Hercule Poirot to Sir Arthur Conan Doyle's famous detective Sherlock Holmes to Dan Brown's intrepid Professor Robert Langdon, she's spent some of her favorite reading times with mystery novels. When she's not writing her favorite mystery couple, she can be found watching entirely too much Supernatural and dreaming about the beach.

Visit Anina's Facebook page for news about her books, along with giveaways and other fun stuff!

And sign up for her newsletter today for exclusive news first! Visit her website at aninacollins.com for more details.

Books by Anina Collins:
The Eleventh Hour (Poppy McGuire Mysteries #1)
After Hours (Poppy McGuire Mysteries #2)
Top of the Hour (Poppy McGuire Mysteries #3)
The Darkest Hour (Poppy McGuire Mysteries #4)
Happy Hour (Poppy McGuire Mysteries #5)
The Witching Hour (Poppy McGuire Mysteries #6)
The Finest Hour (Poppy McGuire Mysteries #7)
COMING FEBRUARY 1, 2018!

www.ingramcontent.com/pod-product-compliance
Lightning Source LLC
Chambersburg PA
CBHW031123210626
46816CB00016B/1946